The
Tattered
Blue
Line

Short Stories of Contemporary Policing

Edited by Frank Zafiro

The Tattered Blue Line: Short Stories of Contemporary Policing

Cover Design by Zach McCain

ISBN: 9798435998733

Code 4 Press, an imprint of Frank Zafiro, LLC
Redmond, Oregon USA

Table of Contents

As a rule, strong feelings about issues do not emerge from deep understanding.

Steven Sloman and Philip Fernbach,
The Knowledge Illusion

Introduction

In 2017, scientists conducted a poll among Americans, asking whether or not the United States should intervene in events occurring in Crimea. As part of the poll, the respondents were asked to point out the Ukraine on a world map.

The median response was off by 1800 miles. That's more than the distance from Las Vegas to Chicago. Keep in mind, this was the *median* distance off from the actual country location. That means half of the responses were further away yet. For instance, some respondents positioned the Ukraine where Greenland is, others in South America.

Here's the interesting part. There was a direct correlation between how far off the respondent was in placing the Ukraine and how much s/he favored intervention. In other words, the less the respondent knew about the subject, the more s/he wanted to intervene.

In another experiment, subjects were shown two similar photographs and asked to choose which one was the more beautiful. A short time later, the participants were grouped together and shown the photographs they "chose" again. I say "chose" because some of the choices made by the participants were reversed. They may have chosen Photo A as more beautiful but when the group discussion began, their choice was represented to them as Photo B.

Some noticed the switch, of course, and spoke up. But most didn't.

And those that didn't notice proceeded to argue vehemently about the qualities that made that photo—one that they didn't actually choose—the most beautiful one. In effect, they argued with passion for a choice they didn't make.

People like to be right.

The Problem

Not only do people like to be right but once they've adopted a position, many (perhaps most) take a dissenting opinion personally. They react as if it were an attack on them.

That isn't good.

Our physiology is virtually unchanged since we roamed the wilds as hunter-gatherers. For the needs we had at the time—survival!—the system in place worked well. The bodily reaction and chemical releases when faced with a threat allowed us a better chance of staying alive. So it was a good response when a mastodon came stomping across the forest toward one of our ancestors. Or even when an armored warrior under a different flag was tramping across a battlefield toward another of our ancestors. But for that same reaction to affect us when someone is merely offering a different opinion?

Not so good.

This results in entrenched positions, polarity within our society, and not a lot of thoughtful discourse. In short, no one listens. But they'll argue with passion for their position.

The Purpose

That's where the germ of the idea for this anthology began. I was already working on a novel (*The Ride-Along*) that examined the many issues surrounding contemporary policing, and most especially, the many different viewpoints on the topic. As a retired law enforcement officer, watching all of the controversial events and the myriad of reactions caused me a great deal of angst.

I was torn.

Having worn the badge, I had an understanding of the profession and the realities of the work that most civilians did not. It hurt me to see my former colleagues being raked over the coals, especially when some of the accusations were predicated on a lack of understanding or the complete facts. It frustrated me how many people didn't understand the true nature of the job, the actual responsibilities and limitations.

At the same time, having been retired since 2013, I had acquired some clinical distance from the profession. I saw where we didn't do ourselves any favors or outright shot ourselves in the foot in terms of how we handled both situations and conversations about those situations. I saw how some of the law enforcement attitudes I had taken for granted while working in the field were flawed and needed to be re-examined. Or how, on a grand strategy level, the profession had suffered from mission drift, and had become focused on doing things in a way that wasn't conducive to good community relations. And, of course, I saw how the police had become a stop-gap for every social need that wasn't being fulfilled elsewhere, some of which officers are ill- or under-equipped to fulfill.

In short, I saw both "sides" of the discussion… at least the sides I had the experience to understand.

What frustrated me the most was that it seemed like no one was listening to each other. People on every side of the debate were chanting slogans, firing accusations, and shooting out sound bites. But there wasn't much listening happening on any side of the discussion. And I've always felt like listening to the other person is the best place to start solving a problem.

That's what motivated me to write *The Ride-Along*, a novel I'm proud of. But it is only one voice (two, technically—I co-wrote it with Colin Conway). The idea of this anthology was to bring together a lot of different voices, all of whom had one thing in common—law enforcement service.

The Roster

In assembling these stories, I sought to not only include good writers who penned stories worth your time as a crime fiction tale, but also to achieve significant diversity in the group. When I say diversity, I mean it in the broadest sense of the term. This roster of authors includes authors representing both men and women of several different races. They come from all over the United States, as well as Canada, Europe, and Australia. They vary in age and generation. I don't know the politics of most of them but even with the few of whose politics I'm aware, they are positioned all across the spectrum.

In terms of law enforcement experience, most were commissioned officers but some were civilians as well. They hail from agencies of all different sizes, from tiny operations to massive departments. Some have worked for local municipalities or counties, while others have worked for state or federal agencies. At least one served on an international peace-keeping force.

The roles these authors have held in their various careers run the gamut as well. From patrol officer to every kind of detective, from dispatch to internal affairs, from specialty units like SWAT or Hostage Negotiations to task forces, and including various leadership positions from sergeant to agency head... this group has either "done it all" or come close enough for it not to matter.

They are also diverse in terms of experience as a crime fiction writer. Some of these stories are among the first few published by an author. Other authors have published dozens of stories. Many have written novels as well.

What they all have, in all this diversity, is their own unique take on contemporary policing. And what I asked them to do was to show us all one sliver, one snapshot, of that view.

So we could listen to it.

The Result

The stories you're going to read are as varied as the authors I described above. In some, the reader is likely to feel some respect or understanding for the police officer in the story. In others, frustration. One of the points of this anthology was to show the humanity and the reality of the police experience in today's world, but also the humanity of those people the police interact with every day. In that sense, I made it clear that I was not looking for clear-cut cops-as-heroes stories. Instead, I wanted stories that, when read, gave the reader some measure of understanding into that small slice of life that the author chose to explore and share. Stories that helped move the conversation forward in a positive direction, even just a little.

To that end, there are other anthologies that are written by authors with other perspectives and experiences. You should read those, too. The world is a gray and nuanced place, and the more you listen, as they say, the more you know.

Thanks for listening.

Frank Zafiro
April 2022
Redmond, Oregon

The Tattered Blue Line

Short Stories of Contemporary Policing

ROUTINE TRAFFIC STOP
Pearson O'Meara

SUNDAY
2257 HOURS

"WE'RE OUTSIDE THE STATE CAPITOL WHERE PRO- AND ANTI-POLICE PROTESTORS HAVE GATHERED. IT'S BEEN TEN DAYS, BUT TENSIONS STILL RUN HIGH."

Three minutes before the start of the Sunday evening shift meeting, Officer Lanny Davis circled the precinct and found a safe spot to park his freshly washed, fully-marked unit. The sole working security light cast a sickly monochromatic yellow glow on the rows of soon-to-be-phased-out Crown Victoria Police Interceptors. Officially, the department insisted the vehicles' dark blue color represented trust and loyalty. Unofficially, blue was hard to see at night, and there were crumpled Crown Vics in the boneyard as proof.

Sunday evening shift meetings were mandatory and punctual. Lanny watched the smokers at the side door check their watches, take one last drag, then flick their cigarette butts in tumbling arcs into the grass. By the time he jogged into the building from the parking lot, the squad room's main door was closed, a sign the meeting had started. Lanny knew he'd pay for being late when he looked through the tall rectangular glass window at Lieutenant John Walters dwarfing the podium. Walter's convenience store black-framed reading glasses clung to the end of his sharp nose.

The squad room was a menagerie of government-issue dilapidated chairs, wobbly wooden desks sans drawer pulls, and retirement-ready officers. Sometimes Lanny's old college buddies asked if he was afraid while "on the job." He would relay a story of the interstate pursuit of the man who'd kidnapped the little girl from outside the elementary school, or tell about the time he dove into Martin Lake, in full uniform, to save an elderly man from drowning. Then he'd grin under the ensuing claps on his back.

Attitudes were changing, though, and it seemed to Lanny that fewer and fewer people respected police officers. He feared for what this meant for the country and the profession.

More than that, though, Lanny was truly fearful of ending up cynical, distrusting, apathetic, so psychologically damaged that the only place he'd fit in would be this godforsaken precinct, known around the department as Fort SNAFU. Situation Now All Fucked Up. Fort FU. Or, for brevity—The Foo.

Lt. Walters turned his back and aimed the remote control at a small television bearing a red and white evidence sticker. He had a DVR recording queued up to the state capital's "Defund the Police" rally. Lanny slipped through the door and stood with his back pressed to the wall.

"C'mon you motherffff …" Walters jabbed at the play button.

The precinct's midnight to eight D Shift roared to life when they saw images of the crowds pelting police officers with rocks and urine-filled plastic bottles.

"FUCK THE PO-LICE! FUCK THE PO-LICE!" came the chants from the TV's speakers.

Walters' face reddened, and he shook his head. "*This*, children! *This* is what your fellow citizens think of us."

A smooth narrator's voice broke in over the top of the chanting crowd. "A SPOKESPERSON FOR THE DEFUND THE

POLICE NOW ORGANIZATION TOLD NEWSTEAM10 THAT THE
CHANTS 'A-C-A-B' AND 'FUCK THE POLICE' ARE A GENERAL
CRITIQUE AGAINST POLICE BRUTALITY AND EXCESSIVE
FORCE BY POLICE OFFICERS."

Walters let the video play for a few minutes, got the shift
riled up good, then punched the remote's off button. The
screen went black.

Lanny abhorred the "us versus them" mentality and
refused to play the zero-sum game. Not with his cop friends.
Not with his parents. Not with his wife. He was proud of being
a cop and serving his community. It hurt him deeply that the
number of kids he coached on the PAL basketball team was
dwindling. The parents said having police officers with guns
at the games made them uncomfortable.

"Quiet down!" Walters slammed his palm on the podium.
"Quiet! Listen for your assignments!"

He read the instructions and shift assignments, stopping at
Lanny's name.

"Officer Davis." Walters looked over his glasses,
searching the room. "Have you graced us with your
presence?"

"Yes, sir."

"You have The Badlands."

Lanny suppressed a groan, but no one else did. "Martin
Lake Road. Yes, sir."

"You know The Foo's rules. You show up late, you get
the shaft. Besides, there's been complaints about speeding,
and you're the only one in this room with an ounce of initiative
and a working radar. So, make the mayor happy and bring me
some tickets." He turned his attention to the rest of the shift.
"Now, with the understanding that I either don't care or can't
do anything about it, does anyone besides Davis have any
problems?"

D Shift fell silent.

"Dismissed," Walters said with a hand flip. "Go be good
apples."

"You forgettin' somethin', Lieu?" an officer asked, violating the rule about asking questions at the end of a meeting.

"Ah, yes." Walters paused for effect. "Let's be careful out there."

Hill Street Blues was part of Walters' shift meeting shtick, so with Sgt. Phil Esterhaus' famous words, The Foo's night shift filed out of the squad room like a football team, each officer passing under the doorframe inscribed with Matthew 5:9: "Blessed are the peacemakers: for they shall be called the children of God."

Michael Anderson slowly twisted the brass doorknob until he heard a *click*. He pushed the door open six inches, stopping just before he knew the hinges would start to squeak. Andrew was a light sleeper, and Michael was careful not to wake him.

Sunday evening was laundry night, and Michael could smell the Downy fabric softener on the uniform shirt he'd pulled fresh from the dryer. He dressed by the glow of the nightlight in the laundry room, then picked up his boots and walked in his socks to the family room.

The Anderson's home was nearly one hundred years old and was raised on piers. Family photos hung from Victorian hooks attached to the Craftsman-style crown molding, and most of the historic wavy glass windows were still intact. The original longleaf pine floors creaked under Michael's weight.

After lacing and tying his boots, he sat hunched forward in his La-Z-Boy recliner, forearms on his thighs, hands hanging heavily between his knees. The house that their realtor had described as "cozy" and a "good starter home" was dark and quiet except for the television—its blue light cast everything but Michael in shadow.

"I wish you didn't have to work nights." Anna came out of the kitchen and handed him his travel coffee mug. She sat on the recliner's armrest, her arm draped over his shoulders.

"You just want me to stay home and make babies with you," Michael said.

"We make beautiful babies, you have to admit."

"I just looked in on him, love. Seems like last week he was wearing a onesie and sleeping in a crib. Now he's in Batman pajamas and a twin bed."

"He loves his superheroes."

"I know. That Spider-Man nightlight of his comes in handy when I'm getting dressed in the pitch black."

"He misses his Daddy-Man in the evenings." Anna toyed with a loose thread on her nightgown.

"I do my time on nights, do a good job, they'll move me up to days. Promise."

"If you're late again, you won't have a job!" She planted a teasing kiss on the back of Michael's neck, then hopped off the recliner and pulled him up into an embrace.

Michael watched the news over her shoulder.

"OFFICERS APPEAR TO USE A STUN GUN ON TALBOT AS HE TRIES TO RAISE HIS HANDS WHILE INSIDE HIS VEHICLE."

"Have you seen the video of that traffic stop up north?" Michael asked.

"I have."

"The cops murdered this guy. Over a speeding ticket!"

"That's not here, Mike."

"They killed him!"

"There's no "they," Mike. We have friends who are cops. We go to church with cops. They're just like us."

"Look at that video and see if they're just like us."

"AS THEY WRESTLE HIM TO THE GROUND, ONE OFFICER IS HEARD ON VIDEO SAYING, "LOOK, YOU'RE GONNA GET IT AGAIN IF YOU DON'T PUT YOUR [*BLEEEEEP*] HANDS BEHIND YOUR BACK." FROM THIS ANGLE, WE CAN SEE ANOTHER OFFICER THEN DRAGS MR. TALBOT—"

"This is horrible. Turn it off." Anna grabbed the remote and punched the power button.

"I'm sorry." Michael reached for Anna. "It just makes my

stomach burn."

"Be careful, baby," she whispered.

Michael waited until he heard Anna lock the door behind him, then went into the garage through the side door. He unlocked his toolbox, took out his Springfield 1911 pistol, and checked that it was loaded. He tucked it behind his back, in his waistband. Not tonight, but soon, he'd have to tell Anna about his night shift co-worker being robbed.

2346 HOURS

Michael felt the blue lights before he saw them in his rearview mirror.

"Shit. Anna's gonna kill me."

He braked hard—too hard—and jerked the steering wheel to the right, nearly skidding to a stop on the shoulder. He threw his SUV in park, frustrated with himself for not slowing when the oncoming car had flicked its bright lights. He read the dash's digital clock with his hands at ten and two on the wheel. 11:46. Fourteen minutes to get to work. The carotid artery throbbed in his neck.

Why's this guy gotta be the one citizen who pulls over as soon as I light him up? On a curve. No streetlights. Rookie move, Davis. Shit.

Lanny listened for a break in the precinct's radio traffic, then keyed up his mic. "D-Seventy-six, Precinct Nine."

"Precinct Nine," the dispatcher answered.

"D-Seventy-six, Precinct Nine, I'll be out on Martin Lake Road, northbound, just north of Wiley's Bar. Bravo-golf-November-six-two-six on a dark Ford Explorer."

"Ten-four, D-Seventy-six. Time of stop is 2346 hours."

He'd done hundreds of traffic stops with no problem, but Lanny couldn't get the gut-punching chant he'd heard at the shift meeting out of his head.

A! C! A! B! All cops are bastards! A! C! A! B! All cops are bastards!

Michael knew the instant he saw the tall cop approaching that a speeding ticket was imminent. Fit, flat belly, maybe ex-military like himself; flashlight in his left hand, right palm resting on the butt of his weapon. The cop's black tactical boots crunched on the shoulder. Slick sleeves, so not a supervisor on his way to riding the desk for the evening.

Blinded by the blue lights in his rearview mirror, Michael turned to the right in his seat and craned his neck to look out the back window. The cop's footsteps stopped.

As he approached, Lanny heard the mechanical whir of a window lowering and saw the driver shift in his seat.

"What's he doing?" Lanny wondered. The driver's movement niggled at the back of Lanny's brain, so he stopped momentarily, then continued to the driver's side door

The FBI has just released its year-end Law Enforcement Officers Killed and Assaulted report. The agency says last year saw the highest number of law enforcement officers intentionally killed in the line of duty since the 9/11 terrorist attacks.

"My name's Officer Davis, and the reason why I stopped you is you were speeding," Lanny said. "The speed limit on this road is fifty-five miles an hour. I clocked you doing eighty."

"Yes, sir—I'm really sorry. I'm late for work."

"Where do you work?"

The driver raised his right arm and patted the oval company patch above his shirt's chest pocket. "At Amazon…"

Lanny stepped back with his right foot, blading his body.

"I'm sorry. I was just showing you where I worked."

"Keep both hands on the steering wheel," the cop said.

THE HANDCUFFED MAN TRIED TO ROLL OVER, BUT OFFICERS ORDERED HIM TO STAY ON HIS STOMACH AND DRUG HIM BY HIS FEET.

"Yeah, sure. I'm not giving you any trouble."

"There's no trouble."

"I work the night shift at the Amazon warehouse. Running a little late." Michael's stomach clenched. He forced a smile.

2350 HOURS

"May I see your driver's license and registration, please?"

"Sure," the driver said. "My registration's in the glovebox."

"Go ahead and get it."

Lanny kept his eyes on the driver as the dispatcher's voice came over his portable radio.

"Precinct Nine, D Shift. All units stand by for wanted subject." She paused.

Lanny turned the volume up and cocked his head towards the mic clipped to his shoulder epaulet to hear better.

"Precinct Nine, all units, be advised Johnson County Sheriff's Office is seeking a black or dark-colored Ford SUV, possibly Explorer, wanted in connection with an aggravated assault with a firearm that occurred at approximately 2330 hours. Vehicle last seen in the area of Martin Lake Road and Highway 182. No further information or license plate at this time. Be on the lookout."

A spike of cold electricity shot up from the base of Lanny's spine.

"Precinct Nine, D-Seventy-six, you copy?"

"D-Seventy-six, Nine, Ten-four."

The driver's eyes widened. "That's not me!"

"Driver, step out of the vehicle."

"Officer, please …. I just left my house, my family."
"Step out of the vehicle."

2353 HOURS

"Sir, I'm not going to ask you again. Step out of the vehicle."

I'm … I'm afraid, Michael thought, but his lips didn't form the words. He didn't say them out loud. He'd heard them, or something similar, earlier. On television.

"'I'M SCARED! I'M SCARED! I'M YOUR BROTHER,' TALBOT TOLD OFFICERS."

"If you haven't done anything, there's nothing for you to be afraid of." The cop seemed to read Michael's mind.

"I haven't done anything." Michael sat, frozen, for about five seconds. "This is wrong," he heard himself say, cotton-mouthed.

Lanny yanked on the SUV's door handle, but it was locked.

He reached for his mic. "D-Seventy-six, Precinct Nine, send me some backup."

"Ten-four, Seventy-six."

Bursting with fear, Michael lunged across the Explorer's center console, unlocked the doors, and scrambled out the passenger door head first.

"You'd better fucking stop!"

Michael heard the cop's commands, and he looked back and hesitated. A split second, but then adrenaline drove his legs forward.

"D-Seventy-six, Precinct Nine. I'm in foot pursuit," Lanny called the chase in; his legs and brain fully accelerated. "Subject is running … southeast. Towards Wiley's. In the field."

"Ten-four, D-Seventy-six. All units, the net is Ten-thirty-three."

"Gray uniform shirt and pants. Dark shoes," Lanny puffed.

"Ten-four, Seventy-six."

"Subject is armed." Lanny had seen the pistol's grip in the driver's waistband when he'd crawled out of the SUV.

"PIGS IN A BLANKET. FRY 'EM LIKE BACON."

If he had been asked, Michael wouldn't have been able to explain why he'd run. He wasn't in charge of his actions. Fleeing was instinctual, as was the direction. Home. He ran towards home. To Anna, to Andrew.

The cop felt close. The commands to "fucking stop!" got louder and louder until each word felt like a punch to the back of his head. He could hear equipment jangling—keys, handcuffs. Boots pounding the dirt, then scraping the pavement.

Losing a suspect was never an option. It simply wasn't done, or admitted to, and the officer never lived it down when it was. It was taboo, fodder for cruel-edged squad room jokes.

Lanny closed in on the driver, then took aim with his body, tackling the man, driving him into the pavement, forcing all of the air out of his lungs.

"I didn't do …," the driver gasped for breath. "… nothing!"

"Get your fucking hands behind your back. Now!" Lanny grabbed the man's right wrist and struggled for control.

"I didn't … do … nothing. Please …."

The cop's weight compressed Michael's diaphragm, and he contorted his body, twisting, turning over on his back, straining for oxygen. The cop drove a knee into his rib cage and pinned his right hand to the ground.

"NEWSTEAM3 HAS OBTAINED VIDEO OF THE MAN BEING TASED BY OFFICERS, THEN DRAGGED FACE-FIRST, CHOKED, AND LEFT FOR ALMOST NINE MINUTES WITHOUT MEDICAL ASSISTANCE."

Michael tried to push the cop's hips off his stomach with his free hand.

Lanny felt the driver's hand on his right hip.

"You're not gettin' my gun, motherfucker!"

In one smooth movement, he planted his left hand on the driver's chest and used the leverage to drive himself up and back, creating distance. Then, he drew his Glock 22 from its holster and aimed.

"WHAT DO WE WANT? DEAD COPS. WHEN DO WE WANT IT? NOW."

"My gun."

Michael heard the words, and his adrenaline-fueled mind misfired. Then, he remembered his gun.

He wants me to give him my gun!

He held his left hand up to the cop, pleading. "Please, please … please."

Frantic, he searched for his pistol on the pavement, sweeping his right arm in a snow angel arc.

His fear was a wheel rolling forward, gaining momentum. There was only one off-ramp.

He felt hard metal, wrapped his fingers around the barrel, and raised the pistol. A peace offering.

Lanny saw the gun raising toward him.

A lethal threat.

He reacted.

"Precinct Nine, D-Seventy-six?"
  "D-Seventy-six?"
  "D-Seventy-six? Are you code four?"

MONDAY
1157 HOURS

COMING UP AT NOON .... OVERNIGHT, ANOTHER MOTORIST WAS KILLED IN A POLICE SHOOTING. TV7 IS AT POLICE HEADQUARTERS AWAITING THE OFFICIAL PRESS CONFERENCE, SEEKING ANSWERS TO WHY ANOTHER SEEMINGLY ROUTINE TRAFFIC STOP HAS TURNED DEADLY.

PERCEPTION

Mark Bergin

"Chief, let me explain," I said, rubbing my sore jaw.

He waved me on.

"Officer Reilly was enroute to a larceny report when he passed two men arguing on the corner, just standing there but they looked wrong. He decided to loop back to take another look and while he was turning around he heard the shots.

"He found the vic down and called it in. We all got there and I canvassed the crowd for witnesses. Like, 'Anybody see that man get shot?' Little girl, fifteen maybe with purple hair, looks right at me and says, 'Thass' your job.' You know how it is, they never tell us nothing in Housing."

The Chief of Police just stared at me.

"I looked over and saw Reilly running. He'd seen the shooter hiding in a crowd. I never saw him, he'd got around the corner out of sight. I caught Reilly and grabbed him by the arm." I shook my head and looked back at the Chief through steam rising from our coffee cups on the interview room table.

"You're pretty fast for an old lieutenant, huh, John?"

I sipped my coffee and shrugged. "Fast enough, Boss. Didn't want Reilly to get to the suspect or get close at all. Suspect'd just shot someone at the bus stop so he's not going to come in easy. Reilly shouldn'a chased him unarmed but habits die hard." I yawned and swollen tightness made me wonder if I was getting a black eye.

"You grabbed Reilly…?" Chief David Edwards stopped and waited as the steam rose. He knew how to use silence to pry information out of an interviewee. I was new to being on the other side of this table but was very used to interrogation techniques. I thought about just staring back, but this was taking time from the jobs we should be doing.

"Yeah, skidded him against the wall to stop him. He was mad. Hyped up from the foot pursuit. I mean, a murder suspect, right? But I'd got his attention. I pointed at his belt where his holster should have been and…"

"And?"

"And he decked me." I shook my head and rubbed my jaw more. "I caught his shirt as I fell and took him down with me. We rolled around and I got over him and was going to punch him."

"But you didn't," the Chief said. I just sighed and made wide eyes.

"Yessir. No, I didn't. I'm not going to hit another cop."

"And you don't think we should charge him? Internally or criminally." A statement but also a clear question.

"Hell, no. I get it. I get how frustrated he was, how tough it is to just watch and let the bad guy go." I took a deep breath, like I had done an hour ago after wrestling Reilly.

"I pushed off him and stood up and I said, 'What were you gonna do if you caught him, Mike? You don't have a gun.' "

I looked hard across the table. "None of us does, anymore, Boss."

It was six months since the Chief took our guns away. Well, not all the guns. Patrol units still carried shotguns in the cruiser trunks. And a special car of two armed officers was staffed every shift. But no uniformed patrolman or detective carried a sidearm. Maybe the ultimate police reform, dropped like a brick on the heads of angered and frustrated cops by a chief who expected me, as commander of the patrol division, to ram a cataclysmic change through a resistant and dispirited police force.

"How we gonna be cops without guns?"

I heard it over and over, starting with shouts at the first roll call where I brought it up. Two of my officers walked out, the remainder fumed, standing up and sitting down like fidgety school kids, trying to envision patrolling our diverse and angry city without means to defend themselves. Like no American modern police ever had.

"Lieutenant Dessiter, how can we go on calls? How can we stop people? How do we make arrests?"

My answer floored them. "You don't."

The Chief and I came to that same conclusion six months ago, after the surprise vote by City Council. Mayor Davis Goode projected a map onto a screen in Council chambers with red dots showing locations of officer-involved shootings over the past ten years. Not many, but they were clumped in three areas, our public housing projects, all with heavily or exclusively Black populations. The largest was in the southern part of our Virginia city, the other two to its northeast and northwest sectors, the three clumps combining as the familiar cartoon face of Mickey Mouse. But not funny.

"This must end, Chief," Mayor Goode pronounced to a surprised crowd at the meeting. A larger crowd than usual. *Tipped off?* "No longer will our young Black men fear the gunfire that has cost them so many brothers and sisters. No longer will our police be an armed occupying force, oppressing people who look like me."

And at the end of an all-night meeting/argument/sound-bite-generator/campaign rally for the politicians, Council voted and the Chief accepted the order to disarm the police. And we began to work out what that would look like. What we could still do. Can we still safely make arrests?

"We can't, John," the Chief repeated. "We don't do the same job from now on. We don't respond Code Three to crimes in progress, we don't chase bad guys, we don't confront suspicious persons, at least not in the same old way."

"That's crazy!" I said.

He nodded. "That's what the politicians want, and what they say the people want. They know your concerns. I told them all the same things, all the impacts this will have on policing, on crime, on arrests. They didn't listen. They don't care about reductions in performance, they care about one thing only – our image with the community. And their image with the voters, so maybe two things." He stared at me, knowing what was coming.

I said it anyway. "Image. Image? Our *image* will be totally trashed. Folks will make fun of us, laugh at us, ignore us…"

"But John, they won't fear us. *Fear us*." The Chief waved his hand over piles of newspapers, printed studies, books on enforcement techniques that covered his desk.

"They fear us now, John. They think we kill them. Murder them. Every time they turn on the news and cops shot somebody, there's a lawyer or pundit crying mom, saying he was unarmed, doing nothing wrong, making him a victim. I know the numbers don't bear it out but when Lebron James, a major sports figure, revered in the minority community and respected across all lines says he feels hunted by police, we have to take that into account. He says that cops hunt Black men."

"You know that's a myth, right, Chief?"

"Of course I do, but myths have power. It's perception, it's what people believe in their hearts. Their brains don't even try to compute the numbers. They perceive it to be true."

"But the numbers don't show that, Chief." I called up stats on my laptop and swung it around to face him. "You know how many unarmed Black men are shot each year by police nationwide? On average? Fifteen. And that includes ones who were trying to run over cops or were reaching for guns but didn't have them yet. Or for our guns. All these names, all the cases that Black Lives Matter or the ACLU or the lawyers and press and pundits recite, they've taken place over years." I poked at the laptop again.

"Look at this headline, Chief. 'Epidemic of Police

Violence.' But there were ten million public contacts with police in 2018 nationwide, according to the newest info we got. Ten *million*. And only fifteen of those were questionable."

"They're all questionable, John. People are asking questions. And that's the point. If a major part of the population perceives we're racially focused on them and questions everything we do, how do we get anything done?"

"Major part? If you're talking about the Black population of the United States, that's thirteen percent. Criminals and arrestees are primarily male, so cut that population number in half. Now we're gonna pander..."

The Chief's glare stopped me at *pander*, but we'd known each other a long time. We'd both started together on a small department elsewhere in the state. He rose in rank and ambition and eventually got the chief's job here, where he went on to hire me as his second in command two years ago. All of that gave me some latitude with him.

I went on. "Yes, *pander* to this tiny group and put the rest of the population at risk, good people who are Black, good and bad Whites and Hispanics and whatever, just so a few can feel better?"

"Feel *safer*, John. What do you think our job really is out there?" He stood up and rummaged through the piles on his desk until he found an FBI crime report and waved it at me. "Do we catch everybody? Guns or not, do we stop every crime now?"

He waited for my reply.

"No," I admitted.

"No," he repeated. "Of course not. Most crimes are closed by arrest after investigation. Running prints, checking videos, knocking on doors, tracking down leads, talking to people. And you know why people in the neighborhoods don't talk to us, John? Because we walk around with guns on, roughing people up. Shooting them..."

I stood suddenly.

The chief held out his hands "Wait. Sit down, John. I know

I'm not talking reality. I'm talking perception."

I hesitated, then lowered myself back into the seat, waiting for him to continue.

"So, what do we do? We change the perception. We change the officers' perception, too. That's where you come in, you Commander of Patrol you."

But I still pushed. "Officers will think they're gonna get killed, think they can't defend themselves." I knew he knew this but I had to lay out the arguments and get his reasoning, if only because it now had to become my own when I laid it out for the troops.

"Perception, John. We've seen a growth of the warrior mentality in law enforcement. The us versus them combative style of police work. It's why some departments have gone to the external vest carrier-type uniform. Ostensibly for comfort, but in reality it becomes a military-style weapon vest with all kinds of crap hanging off it – extra mags, utility knives. Seen one kid with a little hatchet-looking mini-fire axe. They look like they're on patrol in Afghanistan. And they're not, John. They're on patrol in a neighborhood that, yes, has crooks in it, but also has little kids and old ladies and working families. And we're occupying them. At least, that's how it looks. Why we gotta look so tough?"

"Because we're up against what is essentially a guerilla force against us," I argued. They blend into the neighborhoods. They don't wear uniforms that identify themselves as combatants. They pick and choose their time to emerge and shoot at us. We have to protect ourselves at all times from threats we can't anticipate. Militaristic? Yeah, because we're essentially at war."

"But we don't have to be, John. If we're not gonna pull on everyone, they won't have to pull on us. Look at the UK. Their regular front line cops aren't armed. And in Ireland, they call them the Guards. Isn't that a better model?"

"Guns are controlled in the UK, so it's rare that bad guys have them."

"But they still do. Especially organized crime. They just don't use them on the guards because they know the guards won't shoot them, either."

I didn't have an immediate answer to that.

He switched my laptop screen to another site. "Here, look. Line of Duty deaths. Three hundred and forty-nine this year, so far. Forty-eight of them were by gunfire, and three were stabbings. Fifty-one murders of police this year that a cop's gun might have stopped. *Might*. And according to that newspaper that started compiling stats nationwide after Michael Brown was killed..."

I started to rise from my seat again.

"Stop," said the chief. "I know he was attacking the Ferguson cop but that's when the movement started... anyway, look: the paper reports more than six hundred people were shot by police this year."

The Chief leaned in.

"I'm not saying they didn't deserve it. But what if we didn't shoot them at all? What if at the end of the year there were six hundred young men who weren't dead? It's not pandering, John. It's service. Isn't that a good thing? Isn't that why we're here?"

"Isn't that why we're here?" I said at the first roll call after the Council vote, announcing that, after some rapid retraining, Patrol would no longer carry sidearms. And repeated again a week later after a third of the force resigned. And repeated over and over again in the next few weeks to each of the new hires coming over from other departments, trained cops who wanted to try our new way. In the end, we were down twenty percent of our patrol force. But we were also responding to fewer calls, much to the disappointment of the citizens, and in a less effective way, if you counted as effective the old style of speeding around with blue lights and sirens even when it didn't end with handcuffs on somebody.

Mrs. Zabriskie sure wanted it the old way. I met Mrs. Zabriskie a few months into our experiment with disarming, out on the street in front of her row house, bleeding from her forehead, angrier at my officer than at the thug who pistol-whipped her and stole her purse, almost spitting over the shoulder of the EMT treating her. "This happened to me before one time and you all did your job. Now you gonna just stand there, you ain't gonna tell nobody to go find that man?" I stood behind Officer Tommy Jones on the dark sidewalk. In the past, a robbery call would bring as many as ten radio cars, all driving in circles around the blocks and stopping everybody who even remotely matched the thin suspect descriptions we usually got. Tonight, Mrs. Zabriskie just got Jones and me.

Before I took command of the Patrol Division a broadcast description of "Black male, dark hoodie," -- so common it would be laughable if it were not such a serious event -- made every cop within five blocks stop any "suspects" who happened to match that thin description merely by being in style. Walking while Black. I'd ended that, modifying procedures to force officers to hold out for greater detail. For example; metal-frame eyeglasses, high-top white Nikes, scars on a forehead, a Nats ballcap – at least three individual identifiers. The number of suspect stops went down, but those fewer stops resulted in more apprehensions percentage-wise. We didn't catch more, but we stopped the right guys more.

"Nothing worse for perception," I told Roll Call, "*lasting* perceptions, than if you're a kid just walking home from practice or the store or whatnot and a bunch of cops swoop in and draw down on you for no reason other than you are dark skinned and in a hoodie. That makes *you* perceived as the bastard, and that's how ACAB - All Cops Are Bastards - gets started." The troops finally got it and made the change.

But this no-gun thing was different. This was a much bigger step. Now, we chose not to stop suspects at all out of, let's say, *concern* that the suspect might be armed and could shoot. We didn't use the word *fear*. We don't admit that.

"You mean you ain't gonna even look for him?" Mrs. Zabriskie yelled at Officer Jones from inside the ambulance, eyes angry under the growing lump on her forehead.

"No, ma'am. There's not enough description to tell which of all the kids out there is him. And besides, we couldn't stop him even if we found him." Jones turned his holsterless hip toward her. "We got no guns. You just ride up with these guys, and I'll come talk with you at the hospital. Should I call anyone now?"

"Yeah, you call my daughter and you tell her you're all no-good cowards who can't do nothin' to stop these criminals beatin' us all down. You just..." and the EMTs closed the bus door and took off. Officer Jones turned to me with eyes down.

"You know, Lieutenant, this just sucks."

"I know it's hard, Jonesy. But what do you think usually happens here? We go and gunface fifteen kids and none of them's the right one, and even if he is, Mrs. Zabriskie's in the wagon on the way to the ER by then and we can't drive her by to make a show-up ID. This way, we don't roust innocent kids, we don't confront a gunman and shoot him, or worse, get shot ourselves. You know our detectives do pretty well following up. We got cameras in the Metro underpass between here and the projects, he's probably on video. We'll get him, maybe not tomorrow, maybe next week."

"Still sucks."

"Sucks, but doesn't kill, Tom."

Sucks, for sure. Sucks, and embarrasses.

One night I was called to speak in front of City Council. As second-in-command of the Department, I attended most monthly public meetings and many of the closed sessions. After seventeen different citizens got up to speak on the failures of the Police Department to stop crime, to chase robbers, to safeguard the city, one angry man turned to point at me as the lone uniform in the audience and say, "What you got to say for yourself, Mr. Policeman? How come you all letting them thieves and robbers just run away now? Used to be we had decent police here. We were safe. Why y'all so worthless now?"

I stood up and began to walk toward the podium but was waved to a stop by the Mayor. "I don't think Lieutenant Dessiter has prepared information on current crime trends to present tonight. Lieutenant, thank you."

Oh, but I had.

Angry Man kept yelling. "You won't let him talk to us? He the one that ain't doing the job, ain't protecting us. He can tell us why." Half the audience stood as I kept walking up, standing in front of the room until the Mayor could not ignore me or the clamoring crowd.

"Lieutenant Dessiter, now that you're up here," the Mayor began, "you're in command of our uniformed officers. Can you address the concerns we are hearing here?"

Oh, I can. You may not want me to. But here I go.

I looked at Angry Man then raised my arms to address the crowd. "Police work is fundamentally unchanged since the turn of the last century. We keep the peace, patrol for disorder, investigate crimes. And sometimes prevent them, but that's usually only when a cop happens to be somewhere a bad guy wants to do a bad thing, and we'll never know he did it because until a crook strikes he's not a crook, he's just someone walking around.

"But recently, there has been a lot of attention focused on how police treat people. Minorities. People of color. Some—many, in fact—say that police are harsh against Blacks and Hispanics, that cops are quick to kill them."

The noise level rose, but I pushed on.

"This is not true. The numbers do not bear this out or indicate a systemic brutality or murderous nature among cops."

The audience got louder still.

I raised my voice. "We are trained to use the least amount of force possible to make an arrest. We almost always start calmly and are pushed to react to bad actions by the suspect. Then, when things go badly, the suspect is made a hero by the press and social media. Some pundit gets in front of a news camera and says, in one recent example, how his client was shot in the back just getting into a car." My voice rose to clear the clamor. "Sounds terrible, right? That's the version that comes out immediately, before anybody knows anything, before police can investigate and reveal the full truth. So you won't immediately hear it this way. 'A suspect wanted for felony sexual assault and car theft fought police, pulled a knife and got into a car full of children not his own, and an officer shot him to stop what appeared to be a kidnapping.'"

Half the crowd shut up, thinking this one through.

"In almost all police shootings, the person who was shot was the one who initiated the violence by fighting, by running, by attacking officers or the public. The numbers prove this."

There were outright shouts now in the council chamber.

"BUT THE NUMBERS DON'T MATTER!" I finally shouted back, and the room went silent. "The numbers don't matter to you all. And we work for you. We do what you want. You have told your leaders," I pointed at the bank of council members and the Mayor at the front of the room, "the kind of police force you want. And they have told us, ordered us, to give you that. You do not want these confrontations to continue. You do not want young men to die at the hands of police in what you are told are large numbers. They're not, they never have been, according to the actual numbers. But. Numbers. Don't. Matter."

I looked around at the eyes of the crowd, some of whom were actually listening now.

Some.

"Perceptions matter," I continued, my voice falling back to a more reasonable level. "Beliefs matter. And the beliefs of the Mayor matter most. And he is the one who told the police department to put down our guns. So, we did. For you. This was not our idea, and the certain effects of this disarming were made clear to these fine folks up front before they gave us the order."

Mayor Goode tried to wave me quiet, failed, and leaned over to speak with an aide while I loaded a file into the projector at the front of Council chambers.

"Add this to your perceptions. Remember the Mayor's map he showed you six months ago, with locations of officer-involved shootings over the past ten years? The map dots mirrored our housing projects and, in his perception, the concentrations of our Black and other minority populations." I clicked up the Mayor's Mickey Mouse map. "There are three concentrations, and they all correspond fairly well to our three Housing Authority neighborhoods."

Click. Black dots appeared on the map. "And here are calls for police service, citywide. They are everywhere, but the densest concentrations are in the three Housing Authority communities. These are calls from people who need help from police."

Click. Green dots. "Here are gun seizures."

Click. Orange dots. "Here are armed robberies."

Click. Blue dots. "Here are assaults on police officers."

By now the projected dots of rainbow data completely covered the three neighborhoods.

"We shoot people because they are armed, because they are committing crimes, because they attack us and you." I had no pointer, so I pulled my side handle baton and tapped directly on the high projector screen. "We shoot them here, and here, and here. Yes, these are Black communities, but we don't shoot people because they are Black. We shoot people because they are dangerous criminals, and we shoot them here because these are poor areas, underprivileged areas, high crime areas, densely populated areas where cops tend to end up on calls or on routine patrol. We don't go here" (tap) "and here" (tap) "and here" (tap) "because that's where *Blacks* are, but because that's where *crooks* are."

Low muttering from the crowd. A few profane shouts of

disagreement.

I continued, undeterred. "Yes, these are numbers. And today, numbers don't matter. But our safety does. If any of you believes my officers will be effective in capturing violent offenders without the means to defend themselves, well, beliefs don't matter either. Beliefs aren't facts. And the fact is, I will not order my men and women to take dangerous police action without sidearms. If you want us to, you all need to tell *them*," and I pointed at the Mayor and Council with my baton, "that's what you want. Because they have given you what they *think* you want. You can tell them—"

My mic went silent, cut off by the Mayor's aide.

The next day, I was demoted to sergeant and assigned to the Midnight shift.

The Chief made me wear my old Sergeant's badge, "just till the smoke clears. You're still in charge of Patrol. Your pay won't get cut, that would take HR longer than I'm gonna let this crap run. But I want City Hall to stay out of it and let us put this no-gun program in gear."

I nodded, listening.

"And keep your little overlays up to date, for when we need them again. Maybe around election time."

"All right."

Finished, the chief flashed me a grin. "Hey, when are we having you and Randi and the kids over? What?"

Chief Edwards, one of my oldest friends, saw my face before I shielded my expression.

I shrugged. "Randi is… the kids are… away… right now. We, she needed some time to work on some things."

Like fear.

Two weeks ago, it'd all blown up.

"Dammit, John. We left Alexandria and came here because this was a *desk* job, not a street job. You were supposed to be in charge, not in danger." Randi almost sputtered, stomping back and forth in the living room, voice low, trying not to wake the kids.

But I could hear her.

"Now you're out working the streets and you say it's to guide your officers through the no-gun change. But its not just that, you're, running calls like you did when you started and you were all bulletproof and stuff., Yeah, you like showing the young guys what to do, but they're adults. They don't need you to do this, they have sergeants."

She sniffed back her anger.

"Well, I'm a sergeant now so…"

I thought she might throw her glass.

"You were supposed to be in charge, not in danger. And you never stopped running calls ever, and I didn't say a word. And you never got it. Ever. You never got what I go through." Her tears finally broke through but she pushed my hug away.

"You never got it, how we felt when you went to work and we'd never know whether you'd come home."

We?

"We worry about you every minute. We hear sirens and think it's you. Your home radio repeater? When you go out the door, I turn it off, I can't stand to think the kids will hear you on it when something bad happens."

Randi and I had met after I became a cop in Alexandria and I always thought she understood what my job was like, what our lives would be like. But I never talked about it with her, much less with the kids. I didn't want to be the one to bring up things to worry about. I didn't know they worried anyway. They never said.

"Hon, nothing has ever happened to make…"

"NOTHING? You got shot at and missed two years ago, back in Alexandria before we moved. You broke your arm in a foot pursuit and your nose in a fight. That's not nothing! You come home with blood on you and go to the basement to change clothes, as if we won't see. Yeah, tough guy, you just wall it off and it doesn't bother you. It bothers me. And now you can't carry a gun to protect yourself? Because of your chief's cockamamie ideas."

"The Mayor's co… ideas are worth trying."

"I don't give a goddamn, John. No way. Not acceptable."

I stood mute as she walked to the hall closet and pulled a suitcase off the shelf.

"You asked too much, John. You and David Edwards, your precious chief. I know he's your friend but no friend would ask you, ask *anyone* to do this. I can't stand it and I won't put the kids through it. I don't know if I'm divorcing you but I, *we*, aren't staying here. We had a good marriage. You were a good husband. But you never got it."

The worst was how she spoke in past tense.

I replayed that night in my head as I shook it at the Chief. "So dinner is kind of out right now. Thanks."

He opened his mouth to offer words of condolences, but I spoke first. "No, I'm okay." I got up and moved toward the door. "We'll be all right, whatever that is. The kids are cool. They think they're just visiting the grandparents. School's not in session, so we don't have to figure things out until Fall. It's fine."

Except she's not answering my calls.

Two nights later I stood on a downtown corner with another officer, Leslie Barrett, the patrol union president. We watched a crowd of young people, too many to fit on the sidewalk, flowing around parked cars and along the side of the street. A festival was ending and we hoped our presence would keep the boisterous ones settled. Hope against hope.

A kid on a moped was zipping up and down the block among the pedestrians. Dangerous but we weren't making traffic stops anymore, another safety setback since the change. Council was angry about it and the Mayor sound-bit me at a meeting one night.

"Police can't stop writing red light tickets, Lieutenant. It puts our citizens at risk and fails us all." This last delivered straight into the television cameras.

"We can and we have stopped, Mayor," I told him evenly. "Officers are killed approaching cars when they don't know who is inside or what they may have done. So I won't ask my troops to approach cars without the means to defend themselves."

Truth was, I had asked. And they had refused. Barrett and I were arguing about it now.

"C'mon, El Tee, you've seen the videos," she said. "Guys jumping out on cops when they get stopped. Hell, we train on them, show our guys how to handle themselves when it happens."

"*If. If* it happens."

Barrett represented our more than fifty patrol officers. Normally a voice of support in all but pay raise issues, she was now a bitter opponent of the disarmament. She and I squared off.

"We're not going to make traffic stops. Happens all the time, Lieutenant. We get new videos every year from all around the country. We see officers getting shot or shot at. Cops die over this. Happens all the time."

I understood her anger and was sorry it was aimed at me. "Not all the time. A big case every few months. Maybe one video a year gets circulated. DOJ figures are in for 2019. Know how many cops were murdered, total? Out of almost seven hundred thousand cops nationwide? Fifty-one. All year. Less than one a week."

"Still a lot. One a week is still a dead cop a week. Dead."

"Only six were killed on traffic stops. Tens of millions of stops, and six led to cop killings. DOJ says your chance of being murdered writing traffic is one is one in three million." Over her shoulder I kept watching the kid on the moped.

"Don't care, Boss. Y'all took our guns and we stood by for that, because we have some control over what we do on calls, how we handle ourselves, how we tactically approach, what we do on a scene. But traffic stops? Nope." She mimicked the finger flick of activating emergency lights. "There's the car, you stopped it and now you gotta walk up to it. And you can't see what the guy inside is up to. Did he just pull a bank job? Is his dead wife in the trunk? Will he kill us?"

"Six a year."

"Perception. Let them give us our guns back, we'll make traffic stops, write tickets, do all that good *po-po* stuff. Like we always have, perception or not." She side-eyed me while we watched the crowd.

"If we don't use traffic stops to control bad drivers, somebody's going to die."

"Probably. But it won't be us, Boss."

Now the moped kid taunted us, stopping just up the street and revving his motor, waving and wiggling his handlebars at the nearby officers. Encouraged by the lack of enforcement, other kids on mopeds and cycles had gathered, a baby bike gang. In the end, I was the one who broke. I strode toward the kid when he stopped a moment, thinking I could just talk with him, get him to put on a helmet or at least get a good look at him and find him at the high school later. He took off away from me down the sidewalk, never stopping as he drove off the curb at the next intersection.

And ran under the heavy wheels of a passing truck.

Randi didn't pick up when I called her from home. I was in the basement, taking off a uniform sodden with the moped kid's blood. I had crawled under the stopped truck to try to help before medics arrived, but he was almost gone. He bled out as I lay with my arm across him, face to silent face, holding him until medics arrived and pulled me out by my boots. Comforting him? Who knows. It was the only thing I could do.

I set my phone on speaker and put it on the dryer as I picked the badge, collar flashes and name tag off the shirt, dropping them into a bowl of soapy water to remove the blood. She didn't answer so I wiped my hands and texted: *I really need to talk with you. Please call me.*

His name had been William Farmer. I washed my hands. He had been seventeen. I texted again.

I need you.

Again and again.

The next day, the Chief slid a newspaper across his desk at me and banged the side of his fist on the headline: POLICE FAIL CITY, MAYOR SAYS.

"Did you read this? *'Children are dying and Chief Edwards is doing nothing to enforce the law or keep the peace,'* Mayor Goode told The Gazette.'" He threw the paper in the trashcan. "That useless prick. He made us change everything, and we told him and Council what was going to happen. This is on them. They say this is what the people want, but where are they now? Are they telling anybody they want this?"

He kicked the trashcan across the room and waited until it stopped bouncing before continuing.

"I know you feel like shit, John. No, don't wave me off, you're a human, you're allowed to have feelings, at least hidden inside the office here. I know the kid was reckless and might've got killed no matter what we did. I know traffic violations are through the roof, at least by observation if not by stats. We're not writing any tickets unless they're stationary, like at a crash. And those are way up too."

I looked for spin. "Drug arrests are down. We can tell Council that. That looks good."

The Chief raised a skeptical eyebrow and I looked away. "You know, and I know, even if they don't know, that drugs are up or down solely based on what we do. If we make a dozen crack arrests, it's not a surge in use, it's just that we showed up at the right corner and did something. Right now, there's a couple dozen folks smoking dope all across the city but if we don't arrest them, they don't exist, statistically. Robberies went up, car break-ins are up because we're not jacking up suspicious persons in the neighborhoods."

"Complaints on officers are down."

"Because they're not doing crap."

"They *are* doing cra…, er, stuff. They're walking around. With no traffic enforcement, and no traffic quota, they're out on foot patrol. Sure, a lot of them never learned how but the older ones are teaching them. They're proud of that. They're talking to people, even people in neighborhoods where they hate us. Or hated us. Isn't that a good thing Chief?"

"Talk is cheap."

"Talk is breaking cases for us. Look at arrest stats. Robbery arrests are way up, almost full clearance. And robberies went up but are down now because we keep busting the doers. Larceny-from-auto arrests are up, but stolen property recovery is higher than it's ever been. Why? We're getting tips. Folks know stuff and now they're finding ways to tell us. Arrests on warrants are up. The officers like warrant arrests, they can plan and be tactical and careful and can bring out the long guns so they are more confident. So they want to make more arrests. So they can, like," I used air quotes, "be all real cops and stuff."

He looked at me like I was an idiot.

"It's the way they all talk now," I said. "Like little kids. With feelings."

"Feelings." Chief Edwards shook his old hard-guy head.

"Perceptions. They want to be perceived as effective, and that dipped but it's coming back. Officer injuries are down because we're not fighting so many bad guys. Even sick leave usage is down. Coincidence? Feelings? I'll take it."

I set the trashcan upright and picked the newspaper out of it. "You asked who's talking about this now? Yeah, the Mayor's on the front page, but look at the editorial page." I smoothed it out on the desk between us. I'd read my copy earlier and knew where to open it to. "Here's a letter from a lady, writes she is a life-long resident, writes she is happy the police aren't, quote, *beating down the boys in her neighborhood.* Her words, boss, not mine. That's good because she doesn't hate us. And all those unbeaten kids don't hate us. I mean, we don't *beat* them, but when they run and we tackle them, that's what it looks like. And gets filmed like. And, of course, we haven't killed anybody since this started."

The chief opened his mouth but I held up my hand.

"I know, we don't kill all that often here in first place. Our last was, what, seven years ago, and that was a clean shoot. Here's another letter. Businessman thanks us for parking a cruiser by his store. I checked into it. That was Officer Orantes on foot patrol in the 600 block of King Street. He does that every day for an hour, and an hour on Royal, and an hour on Duke. That's visibility, and it's turning things around for us. We got a new crew of good, young officers who, you know what they do? They *smile* at people on the street. Know why? Because people smile back now."

The chief wasn't smiling but his frown had faded.

I put the paper back in front of the Chief and went on. "The Mayor does what a mayor does. Parades and pivots and pinwheels to get attention and appear to be serving his people, who are his voters. It's perception for him too. Yeah, the newspaper prodded him into that story. But has he called you about it? No. That's an equally good thing, right? That's…"

We both paused when our belt-borne radios carried word of a shooting just occurred in a convenience store in the West End. A single unit was dispatched to run full code, lights and sirens in hopes it would beat the ambulance and protect the EMTs.

We both reached for our microphones but I was first. "Unit Two to Dispatch, confirm Tiger One enroute to the shooting?" Tiger units were our compromise to reality, a single car with two fully-armed officers used for known or anticipated violent calls.

"Negative, Two. Tiger is already out at the hospital on a fight in the ER. They can't break. I'll advise."

"Copy, Dispatch. Have the responding unit back down to Code Two, send a second unit and have Fire stage until the scene is secured. I'm responding from the station." I looked at the Chief. "Hope the guy shot wasn't a voter."

"Don't say that anywhere but here, John. Keep me advised."

I ran Code Three because I could. I'm in charge of Patrol. The victim was a store clerk, wounded in the lower abdomen, not dead yet but in serious condition. After he was ambulanced out and the scene secured by patrol officers and a sergeant, I looked at the sparse crowd of onlookers held across the street by yellow tape. The usual crowd of potential witnesses was quieter than usual, not cursing us or throwing bottles like they used to. And I recognized one young girl looking at me with an unusual expression, purple hair under a white knit cap, her hand hidden from the crowd by her open jacket, her fingers hooking in a come-here wave.

I turned my back on the crowd as if looking into the store from the street and slowly began walking backward until I was a few feet from the tape, and the girl. There were no others within earshot when she whispered, "Tony Davis. An' he drop the gun in that sewer right down there."

I looked one way.

She whispered, "No, fool. Thuther way."

I looked and saw a sewer drain halfway down the block. I also saw Tony Davis, a frequent flyer, standing near the drain by the mouth of an alley. He stared at me and stood still. So did I, for a moment, then slowly walked over to a group of officers and their sergeant checking paperwork. I quietly gave them orders and left to walk down the block away from the suspect.

Around the corner, I broke into a run, turning the next corner and coming to the other alley opening behind Davis where I slowed, peeped around the edge of a house and saw him outlined against the streetlights. I sneaked halfway up the alley and stepped sideways into a dark patch. After a moment, right when I knew the sergeant would be walking toward him, I heard Davis begin running down the alley toward me. I stepped out when he was a few feet away and bellowed, "POLICE, DON'T MOVE!"

He reached into his pockets as if he had still had a gun and faltered a moment when he remembered he did not.

But he did have a knife.

And I had a side-handle baton.

"Already got a print match off the revolver from the sewer, Boss," the Sergeant reported an hour later. "Good thing we got Davis' prints on file. We can't really print him now, his hand all broken like that."

I looked up at the Sergeant from my cruiser's front seat while typing my supplements on the shooting, the arrest and my use of force. "They find the knife yet?"

"Just now, on the roof of the garage where you batted it to. Prints on that as well." He grinned a second, then continued to mentally process the scene and the investigation and its requirements. He looked around and said quietly, "Do we need purple-hair girl for this?"

"It would help, but no. She's not gonna come forward, be *eye-dee'ed* as a snitch. Things have changed around here but not that much. Yet. Her saying anything at all is miraculous. We can make the case without her. The gun's abandoned property and we can legally get that in. Prints are evidence. Vic's not dead and he should be able to testify, but we have someone with him in case we need to take a dying declaration."

"Why'd she talk to you then?"

"Don't know. My guess? All this no-gun stuff may be making a difference. Letting folks see we're on their side, not an occupying force. Not out to kill them."

"Spoken like a boss, Boss."

"No. A believer. We gotta do it, it's my orders to you all. But maybe there really is a benefit to it. And we haven't seen officer assaults go up like we thought."

"That's because we're not proactive anymore. I'm not gonna have my squaddies jumping out on suspicious perps like we used to." The sergeant trying to sound grizzled, all twenty-seven-years-old of him.

"Yes. But all the times we did that, we ever really get a lot of arrests? Honestly? You were one of the ones most against it when I backed us down off robbery stops without better descriptions. No, this is our new way. Maybe *the* new way. And tonight, it worked."

"And Davis assaulted you."

"And so we got another felony charge out of that, too."

"He almost got *you*."

"I had it under control. And better me than you or one of your baby cops over there."

"Bullshit, Lieutenant. That's what patrol officers are for, not commanders. You coulda' got yourself stabbed. He did get your jacket sleeve."

He pointed. I touched the slash.

Maybe it was a good thing Randi was away right now.

No. It was not.

I checked my phone and saw a missed call from her. Came in right when I was stopping Davis. I stared at the screen to make it tell me what she wanted to say, but that didn't work.

"Yeah, that's true enough. But you can use tonight's little grand slam to make the kids pay attention during Defensive Tactics retraining this Fall. We got no guns, so we gotta be good with sticks…, errr, batons."

The sergeant frowned. "Yeah, great. The return of stick-time. That'll make us popular with the populace."

"One paradigm at a time, Sarge." I started to dial.

9 MINUTES

Elizabeth Nguyen

You can do a lot of things in nine minutes.

You can hard boil an egg.

Duck into a Starbucks and grab a coffee.

Take a fairly leisurely smoke break.

You can probably watch half a dozen mindless Tik Tok videos.

Your whole world can fall apart in nine minutes.

Nine minutes at work can be interminably long or inexplicably fast, depending on the day. Break down a twelve-hour shift into nine minute intervals, you get eighty intervals. In ten years as a 911 police dispatcher, I have experienced over a hundred fifty thousand such intervals. I've forgotten more nine-minute intervals than I remember.

I have taken and transferred a dozen calls in nine minutes.

I have saved someone's life in nine minutes.

I have put my phone on "Not Ready" to go and reheat my coffee.

No nine minutes are the same.

1546 hours

"Hey Lori, do you mind if I have a quick smoke before I relieve you?"

I look down at the time on the bottom right of my computer screen. 3:46PM. I guess I could wait a few more minutes before I take my lunch break. The kids would be home from

school then and I could FaceTime them at the babysitter's.
"Sure, Chrissy. Take your time."

I glance at the three screens in front of me. No calls requiring immediate dispatch. I scan the screen, seeking out Unit 23. There he is, parked in the back parking lot of the police station. I'm glad one of us is getting a break. I tamp down my annoyance along with my yawn. I lean back in my chair and savour the "Q" moment without a word. Saying the "Q" word out loud—or even thinking it—is an unpardonable sin in the Communications Centre. Everyone knows that as soon as you do, you've jinxed it.

1547 hours

A new item pops up on the pending calls screen, indicating that there is a Priority 1 call waiting to be dispatched. I sit up straight. Priority 1 means an immediate threat to life or risk of serious injury exists, so it gets my attention.

I quickly scan the details of the call for service, then frown. Puh-leaze.

This is a Priority 2 call, at best.

I check out who the call-taker is. Michelle. Okay, fine. She's relatively new. I'll let this one slide, but I'll still need to ask the supervisor to talk to her about it later. Over-prioritizing a call can be just as dangerous as under-prioritizing a call. I scan my screen for available units. Unit 23 is still parked in the back parking lot. My fingers hover over the keyboard for a moment while I decide. It only takes a moment. If I'm going to have to work on no sleep, then I'm going to make sure he does too.

"Charlie 1 to 23 and 35".

"23." I swear I could hear his irritation through my headset.

"35."

"We have a domestic conflict at eight-oh-four Whitmore Road. Domestic conflict at 804 Whitmore Road. Complainant states that her neighbours are fighting again. She heard the male yelling and the female crying about ten minutes ago. Now the argument seems more heated than usual and she can hear glass breaking. There have been six calls to this address over the past month, mostly domestics and noise complaints.

"10-4."

"10-4."

1548 hours

I track the two units on my CAD map as they make their way to 804 Whitmore Road. There are no other calls pending dispatch and no call-takers are on the phone. I lean back in my chair again. While my eyes continue to scan the screens for new calls, updates, and messages, my mind wanders to our argument last night...

Last night

I slammed the kitchen cabinet shut. That felt good. I aggressively set the dining room table for dinner, each clank and bang punctuating my irritable thoughts. I walked over to the utensils drawer, grabbed some forks, and slammed it shut even harder. That felt even better. I glanced into the living room and looked at him and the kids on the couch, all fixated like zombies on their tablets and phones. My chest tightened with anger and annoyance.

"Can you come help me set the table? Babe. BABE. BABE!"

He tapped his right AirPod. "What?"

"Can you come help with supper?"

"You don't have to yell." He heaved himself reluctantly off the couch, eyes still locked onto some dumb TikTok video on his phone.

I walked over, grabbed his phone, throwing it on the floor. "Maybe if you didn't have those damn AirPods in your ears all the time, I wouldn't have to yell."

He stared at me, equal parts annoyance and confusion. "What's your problem?"

"My *problem?* We work the same damn shift and get home at the same time. Yet I'm the one scrambling to get supper ready while you're on your phone."

"I'm just trying to wind down."

"Fine, but you're not engaged with the kids, and you don't talk to me. You're just watching stupid fucking TikTok videos."

"Can I just come home and relax for a little bit before you start nagging at me?"

"I'd like to come home and relax for a bit too, but supper doesn't make itself."

He ignored me and continued. "I just spent 12 hours out in the cold, being yelled at, being called racist just because I'm white, literally getting into fights with people who called us for help. I just want to come home and have some peace and quiet, and not get nagged at."

"I'm not nagging."

"What do you call this?"

I took a deep breath and tried to control my anger, which threatened to explode all over his TikTok-watching face. "My job isn't easy either and I just need some fucking help when we get home!"

"You have a desk job."

I glared at him, unbelieving. He knew how I hated when cops act like all dispatchers are basically just administrative assistants. That was a low blow.

"Fuck you." I slowly spit out the words, knowing that it would be the turning point in the argument. We both swore a lot, but we had an unwritten rule that we would never swear *at* each other.

"I'm done. I don't need this." He bent to pick up his phone. "I just wanted to come home and relax." He turned and headed to the basement.

"Great," I called after him. "Just walk away like you always do. Don't worry, I'll just take care of supper and the kids. AS ALWAYS!"

My voice escalated to a shriek as he slammed the basement door. I looked at my kids who were staring at me with wide, terrified eyes. My expression softened. "Kids, go wash your hands," I said more quietly. "It's time for supper."

Later that night after the kids were fed, bathed and in bed, I laid by myself in bed and slowly talked myself into reconciling. I hated going to bed angry. I grabbed my phone from the nightstand and texted him.

THERE'S SUPPER IN THE FRIDGE IF YOU'RE HUNGRY. I'M SORRY IF I WAS NAGGING.

I waited for a few seconds.

Nothing.

BABE, I DON'T WANT TO GO TO BED ANGRY. ARE WE 10-4?

I stared at my phone.

Still nothing.

I debated going down to the basement for a face-to-face talk, then decided against it. If he was going to be petty and not answer my text, I wasn't going to pursue a truce. I plugged in my phone, turned off the lamp, and rolled over to sleep.

Angry.

1549 hours

…My eyes refocus on the monitors before me as I push the events of last night out of my head. We will have to talk about it after work. Going to bed angry two nights in a row is not an option.

I double-check the status of all the patrol units on my screen. All good.

I stand up to stretch and grab some hand lotion on the filing cabinet beside me. I tune in half-heartedly to a conversation that two of my co-workers are having about the overtime sign-up sheet that is going around.

An emergency alarm sounds from my monitor and the words a dispatcher never wants to hear comes through the radio.

"Shots fired! Shots fired!" Even elevated, I recognize his voice almost immediately. *"804 Whitmore Road, shots fired from inside the house."*

The bottle of hand lotion slips from my hands, hits the filing cabinet and rolls to the floor. I drop into my seat, my heart in my throat. The 10-10 emergency signal is glaring at me and I can see confirmation that the radio transmission came from unit 23. My heart seizes for a millisecond before my experience kicks in. I transmit on all channels simultaneously. "Charlie 1 to all units. Be advised unit 23 states shots fired at 804 Whitmore Road. Shots fired."

A chorus of responses come through the radio.

"10-4!"

"On my way!"

"Put me on the call!"

"Charlie 1 to all units, keep the air *CLEAR*!" I snap.

The patrol Sergeant comes on the air. *"23, 35, what do you got?"*

35 comes on the air. *"Shots fired from inside the house. I can't get to – shit! We're pinned down and taking fire!"*

My breath hitches as I key my mic on all-channels again. "All units, 35 advises that they're pinned down and taking fire at 804 Whitmore."

I release my mic and yell to the call-takers in the room. "Someone get EMS to 804 Whitmore!"

"I've got it!" The call-taker in front of me spins her chair around and starts dialing. The other call-takers all have their eyes on me, waiting to hear if there's anything else that I need.

I key my mic again. "Car 1, we have EMS en route staging." A garbled transmission comes through as another patrol officer tries to talk. "Stay off the air. Everybody stay *off* the air. Keep the air clear for 23, 35, and Car 1." I swallow before continuing. "23, what's your status?"

No response.

"35, what's your status?"

"We need more units here now!" I can hear the sound of gunfire in the background of unit 35's transmission.

"35, do you have eyes on 23?"

"No!"

A tiny hitch in my voice is the only indicator of my skyrocketing adrenaline. "23, what's your location?" There is no response.

1551 hours

The patrol Sergeant comes on the air. "Charlie 1, I need more units here."

I scan my screen, looking for available units. I pick the four closest. "37, 45, 47, 49, make your way to 804 Whitmore Road. Car 1 requires more units." I assign the four units to the call.

"Car 1, where do you want them?"

No response.

I scan the map on screen, looking to see if a perimeter or command post has been set. "37, 45, 47, 49, head to where EMS is staging, one block east of 804 Whitmore Road."

On my map, I see units from all corners of the city converge upon the central location of 804 Whitmore Road. I turn to tell my supervisor that I can't get a hold of Car 1 to determine a perimeter. Her phone is to her ear and she nods at me. She is already on it, trying to get a hold of him on his cell phone. Outside of my headset, I can hear the other call-takers notifying police superiors and calling neighbouring houses and schools to lock down and stay in place.

As soon as units arrive on scene, the radio falls silent. I sit with my fingers poised over the keyboard, my heart pounding and blood rushing in my ears, waiting for the next radio transmission to come in.

Please let him be okay.

Silence on the air. Outside of my headset, I can hear the second hand on the clock behind my workstation ticking slowly. My heart is beating in double time to the ticking of the clock, creating a percussive background to my rising anxiety.

Was he distracted because of our fight last night?

1553 hours

Silence on the air.

I should have gone down to the basement to talk to him last night.

The radio chirps, startling me. *"Subject in custody."* It is the sergeant. *"Car 1 to Charlie 1, get EMS to come to the front of the house hot."*

My voice is steady and calm as I direct the ambulance to move up to the front 804 Whitmore Road, but inside I am screaming, "Who is the ambulance for?"

1554 hours

Silence on the air.

I constantly check both the CAD and radio screens.

I monitor the CAD screen in case there is a message from one of the officers on scene who might not want to say anything on the radio to tie up air time.

I am also desperately hoping that I'll see a message from him telling me that he's okay.

My ears are tuned into the radio. I don't want to miss even the slightest mic click. If someone, anyone—please let it be him—transmits, I want to be all over that.

I'm sure he's fine, I tell myself.

Seconds pass.

I hope he's fine.

A few more seconds.

Please God, let him be fine.

I double check and see that EMS is at the front of the house. All other patrol units are still showing on my screen layered on top of each other at the address. I swallow hard, but it does nothing to ease the lump now in my throat. I swallow again – still unsuccessfully.

Very purposefully, I take a deep breath through my nose, and exhale through my mouth. I need that oxygen to stay focused and clear. I wiggle my lower jaw to try and unclench it. The corners of my jaw ache with tension. I take another deep breath.

Please, let him be—

I hear a click.

1555 hours

"23 to Charlie 1. I'm 10-4."

The air leaves my lungs when I hear his voice. I bend over my keyboard, allowing myself to lose my composure for just a second.

He's okay.

The radio clicks in my headset. *"I'm 10-4,"* he says again. *"We're 10-4."*

ALL THE LESSONS
J.J. Hensley

The motorcade pulled to a stop along the curb on Massachusetts Avenue. The mid-morning traffic flowed as well as could be expected for a weekday on the spoke of pavement that fired northwest off DuPont Circle and was commonly known as Embassy Row. Sunlight blazed off the front door of the Egyptian ambassador's residence. The house was situated in extreme close proximity to the street and driveway led up to the front door. The Protective Intelligence (PI) agent thought the undersized horseshoe driveway somewhat comical in appearance, at least by D.C. standards.

A drive-thru assassination venue. How convenient, Lora Bledsoe thought to herself from behind the wheel. *Oklahoma City happened in what… 1995, yet anyone could pull up there.*

"Jesus, that's close to the street."

The utterance came from the passenger side of the car where her Washington Field Office colleague sat perched turned toward the beige building.

"That's exactly what I was thinking," Lora said. "That's why we're blocking it with this motorcade. Still, I'm glad the ambassador's not our concern on a daily basis."

"I'm just glad we're out here and not digging through psych records or some nonsense."

Josh DeMarco stepped out of the vehicle and took a look at the sidewalk and the street, as did multiple other agents who had exited other vehicles in the motorcade. Lora stayed behind the wheel of the unmarked black sedan that screamed *police car* in case there was an attack and the motorcade had to move suddenly. From the limo parked several vehicles ahead, the President of Egypt moved with his detail of agents to the front of the house and through the door that had been opened by the site agent who had been waiting for our arrival. Eyes scanned every building and each passing car, the memories of the September 11th attacks which had occurred a few months prior still fresh in everyone's minds. In the aftermath of the attacks, the government of Egypt had aligned itself with the United States, making its leaders targets for jihadists worldwide.

Jihadists. The word had been on the tip of everyone's tongue since *that* day just a few months ago. Lora remembered her mother talking about the JFK assassination and how everyone in that generation remembered exactly where they were when they heard the news. The generation before that had Pearl Harbor. Lora had thought the faux-wood-paneled televisions being rolled into elementary school classrooms when the Challenger space shuttle exploded had been that moment for her generation, but the Gen Xers got a sickening double dose fifteen years later when the planes hit the towers. Now, agents like her were getting specialized training on how to deal with suicide bombers.

Jesus, she thought. *That training.* Everything she'd been taught in law enforcement had changed overnight and now there were people teaching her—

The car door opened and Josh leaned in to speak.

"He's secure inside the residence. I'm going to walk up to the lead car and talk to Billy."

"Sure," Lora said. "Just keep your radio turned up in case we need someone to interview."

"Yeah. That would be lovely,"

Lora sighed, but was doing her best to sympathize with Josh. He was new to the PI squad and she knew he was hating every single minute of it. While her initial instinct was to dismiss his negativity for typical cop jadedness, she realized she shouldn't fault him for his lack of enthusiasm. The truth of the matter was working protective intelligence was pretty much the opposite of what most agents imagined doing when they joined the Secret Service. New recruits are sold on dreams of protecting the President, traveling the world, and making major arrests in multimillion dollar criminal cases. Lora knew she had the benefit of having started her career outside of D.C. and had only asked to transfer inside the beltway after the 9/11 attacks. In a normal field office, she'd actually had time to work criminal investigations while occasionally bouncing around the country for various protection assignments. Josh had come out of the academy and been thrown straight into WFO where he spent most of his time standing post in doorways at events, rarely traveling, since there was always enough protection to do in D.C., and just when he thought he was going to get more responsibility on protection assignments he got bounced to the PI squad to interview and assess threat cases, most of whom are mentally ill.

Lora had thrived working PI. Sometimes, in the momentary quiet of the car, she allowed herself a moment to wonder why that was. Perhaps she was attracted to the analytical aspects of dissecting a person's motivations and triggers. Or maybe it was simply because with PI work she felt she was being proactive and maybe, just maybe she had identified a potential assassin before he or she acted out. Or perhaps it was the hope that, with some of the more troubled subjects, she even helped them a little by getting them into a psychiatric facility or calling a family member who could get them on the right meds.

When she thought about that last possibility, a memory flashed through her mind. Lora and her sister. Running through a small, nondescript office building. Bland paint all around – state government issue. Their father's office off to the side of a cubicle farm. A weekend visit to the office with her father who had to pick up one last file or check on one last case. Her dad. The Marine-turned-social worker who returned to the heart of Appalachia and dared to navigate chaotic and corrupt state and local bureaucracies.

Lora remembered back to a time when her mother had taken her by that office, and it wasn't a weekend. They were stopping by on the way to some dentist or pediatrician appointment and Lora's mother had needed to grab the checkbook from her father. Lora must have been six or seven at the time and her mother had said they would run inside to get the checkbook, but they had to be quick because they were running late. Lora wasn't to run around like she did on the weekend visits because people would be working, and the office wasn't a playground. But they never made it inside. When they pulled up in their old rust-colored Chevy Nova, Lora's father was standing outside in the parking lot talking to a man wearing a ripped flannel shirt and jeans that were caked with mud and cement.

"Don't open the door. You stay right there," her mother had commanded from the front seat. Lora craned her neck to see out her window and thought about grabbing the window handle to roll it down but knew her mother would tell her to stop. The man in the shabby clothing was screaming and gesturing wildly at Lora's father. He stomped around, circled back, and put a finger in her father's face. Her dad, who always had the remarkable ability to get more calm as others became more aggravated, simply stood there and nodded, listening to the man. The scene continued for what Lora thought was an eternity, but what she now knew was probably no more than two minutes before the inexplicable happened. The man seemed to run out of steam and then Lora could see that her father was speaking. He wasn't angry. Not like that time she'd broken the kitchen window with the tennis racket. No, he was talking to the man like he'd talked to her after Leo died. He and mom owned Leo before Lora was born, raised him from a puppy, but he felt like Lora's dog. Lora remembered her father's expression as he broke the news about Leo. It was like the water on lake they would visit on long weekends, when there was no wind. It was so still and peaceful. That's what Lora saw in her father's expression while he was talking to this man who seemed so upset a few moments earlier.

She looked on as her father appeared to end a sentence and gave a subtle nod. Then the man…he reached out and shook her father's hand. In a heartbeat, it was over. The ruffled man walked away, got into a black van, and pulled out onto the West Virginia highway. Lora's father, unaware he was being watched by his wife and daughter, stared expressionless into the wooded hills surrounding the lot of cracked and cratered pavement. The moment of contemplation was broken when Lora's mom honked the horn of the Nova. Lora jolted at the noise and watched as her father strode over to the driver's side of the car. Her mother rolled down the car window.

"You okay?" her mother asked as he leaned down.

"Another day in paradise," he responded with a hint of a smile. "How are you doing back there, pumpkin?"

Lora leaned forward. "Why was that man mad at you?"

"He wasn't mad at me, honey. He knows this is the place people come to get help when they don't have a job and don't have any money. So, he thought he could just show up here and get money, but it's not that simple. He was angry because someone inside told him he'd have to fill out some paperwork and that the process would take some time. He didn't like that answer, so I came down to explain things to him."

"He was yelling," Lora said. "I thought he was going to hit you. He's a bad man."

"No, he's not," Lora's father said, keeping his coolness while conveying a sense of certainty. "He's desperate. He's in a bad situation. Sometimes life has a way of punching people in the face and all we see is the blood and the bruises. We don't like seeing blood and bruises, do we? We tend to look away."

Lora shook her head.

"He may have wanted to use his fists today, but it was only

because he didn't have anything to hold onto."

Her dad always knew how to explain things.

Lora looked down at the controls for the automatic car windows in the Secret Service issued sedan she had been assigned. It was quite a contrast to the Nova with the windows that took a Herculean effort to roll up and down as child. God, that car got so hot in the summer. She didn't remember if the seats were made of real leather, but they cooked anything they touched. Lora let her mind drift though the contours of that vehicle. A tap at the passenger window jarred her back to the present.

She used one of the modern window controls to lower the window where a local patrol officer who was assisting with the motorcade was standing. The MPD officer removed his sunglasses and smiled as he spoke.

"Hey, just wanted to let you know that I think your rear tire over here is getting a little low," he said. "You'll probably want to get that filled up whenever you can."

"Thanks, I'll take care of it," Lora replied.

The officer seemed to hover, maybe wanting to kill time during a boring period of an assignment; perhaps wanting to flirt. Either way, Lora killed the moment by raising the window. She waited for him to walk away and then decided to check the tire for herself. The Egyptian President had a full schedule for the day, so getting a flat tire in the middle of a protective movement wasn't an option. The PI car wasn't the most critical part of the 'secure package', but Lora wanted to make sure she didn't have to pull out of traffic while in motion.

Lora waited for a moment when the Mass Ave. traffic seemed less likely to kill her and then squeezed out the door, quickly skirting around the back of the car. She peered down at the tire. It looked a little low on air, but certainly it wasn't on the verge of spinning off the rim. She shook her head, deciding the helpful MPD officer had been angling for a phone number as much as helping out a fellow law enforcement officer. It was tiresome. Five years on the job, and still the feeling of being on the outside in a male-dominated profession. Some days it wasn't bad at all, but other days it was intolerable. The snarky comments; the long stares in the office gym; last year when they went on a raid and a supervisor started to hand her a shotgun but then decided to give it to a male agent who "might be able to handle it better." For the love of God, it was 2002 and women still had to deal with this shit.

She looked up from the tire and scanned the sidewalk. To her left, cops and agents were killing time by bitching about the job and rehashing the Redskins' most recent mediocre season. Nora turned her head to the right and had expected to see fewer badges on the curb, but hadn't expected to see none. Apparently, only the drivers had remained in the vehicles and everyone else had migrated toward the front of the motorcade to congregate. She glanced at her watch. Well, why shouldn't they? They were scheduled to be there at least another twenty minutes, which, in politician speak, could mean an hour and a half.

The sole individual on the sidewalk in that direction was little more than a silhouette to her. He – she thought it was a he, anyway – was drifting back and forth on the concrete and appeared to have something draped around, or maybe over him. It was difficult to tell from that distance. He probably lived at one of the houses down the street or was going to try to take his chances at crossing the Ave through Sheridan Circle.

Lora twisted back and forth, stretching her back. She looked down at her shoes. What was it that the instructor had said about shoes in that training session last month? That's right. He had been talking about an incident in Israel where a suicide bomber had disguised himself as an orthodox Jew and was attempting to get on a crowded bus in order to detonate the explosives. But a soldier had noticed the shoes were wrong and shot the bomber without hesitation. The shoes had been an indicator that something was amiss.

Indicators. The training had been all about indicators and what to look for with suicide bombers. The instructors weren't Secret Service agents but had been some private outfit that consisted of a combination of military contractors and defense attorneys. The military contractors were there to teach agents how to identify the indicators that a subject was a suicide bomber and then act accordingly—which meant, shoot the individual in the head. It had to be a head shot, because you didn't want to accidently trigger a suicide vest. The defense lawyers were there to assure the agents that any such shooting was legally justified, if the indicators were present and the agent could articulate the threat.

Simple.

Except it hadn't been to Lora. It hadn't been simple to many agents in the class, who had given sideways glances to each other as the lawyers kept insisting the agents would be just fine, even if they guessed wrong and the suicide bomber was anything but. The attorneys even handed out their cards and guaranteed they would defend the agents in court for free, should it ever become necessary.

Lora remembered sitting there in that darkened classroom wondering what she would do in a situation where a potential suicide bomber was present. Do you risk letting the person detonate, killing your protectee as well as your friends and coworkers? Do put a bullet in the head of someone because of *indicators*? Throughout all of her prior law enforcement training, she'd been taught to use deadly force only if there was an imminent, deadly threat to herself or others. But what if you couldn't be one hundred percent certain? What would she do?

A car horn sounded from the direction of Sheridan Circle. Lora looked that way and eyed the man who had apparently made an unsuccessful attempt to cross the street. Now he was wandering in the direction of the motorcade.

"Oh, don't come this way," Lora muttered to herself. Although the Egyptian president was in the residence, the agents weren't going to let anyone get near the vehicles or any closer to the house than necessary. Now another man—no, this was a woman—came into view. She was on a bike and was wearing expensive looking cycling gear and a helmet. The woman was hugging the curb while passing to the right of cars which were moving along at the D.C. assembly line pace. Alertly, the woman spotted the motorcade and realized her curb space was being occupied by a dozen cars and SUVs. Lora thought the lady must be a veteran of the city because she adeptly slowed, propped a foot up on the sidewalk, twirled the bike under her to make a turn in the opposite direction and then disappeared around a corner, having decided to find an alternate round.

Impressive agility, thought Lora, who had always been an avid cyclist. Still, the quick turnaround after seeing a gaggle of cops was a bit odd and cycling down Embassy Row wasn't extremely common. Lora decided to alert the countersurveillance units to let them know what she saw. The countersurveillance, or CS, units were nothing more than agents who were in plainclothes and driving inconspicuous cars. Lora knew that for this particular assignment, there were two agents circling the area in separate cars. She raised one of them on the radio.

"It's probably nothing, but a female cyclist was down here on Mass Ave. As soon as she saw us, she did a one-eighty down the R street sidewalk."

"Got a description?" asked Aimee Shore, an agent Lora had known for a couple of years.

"White female, wearing a red and yellow cycling outfit and a black helmet," said Lora. "I haven't seen any other cyclist around, so she'll be easy to spot. She's probably long gone, but I'd appreciate it if you see her come back this way."

"No problem. I'll pass the info on to Boone as well," said

Aimee.

Lora knew Jerrod Boone was the other CS agent assigned to the area. He was a veteran agent, with a likable personality. Both Aimee and Jerrod were extremely good at their jobs and it had been their responsibility to notice if anyone was watching either the Egyptian president or those who were protecting them. Lora had no doubt if there was any kind of problem outside of her view, the two of them would pick up on it and relay in information immediately.

"I'll never be in the Olympics," came the words from with a young girl's voice.

It was her voice. She was older now, not the six-year-old who witnessed her father weather the storm of another's desperation. Now she was nine. She wasn't upset, but matter of fact.

"Why would you say that?" her mother responded. "You don't know what you can accomplish."

It was 1984 and Lora had just discovered the Olympics in the weeks prior. For whatever reason, she had caught a glimpse of cyclists speeding around a track while watching the sporadic television coverage and, for a kid who was faster on her bike than *all* the neighborhood boys, that was an event that made sense. For days after the games had ended, Lora had taken a cheap plastic watch, marked off an indeterminate distance on the gravel road in front of their house, and timed herself on her Huffy Sweet Thunder. Then one day, her mother had made some innocuous statement, the way parents do, about how Lora was going to be an Olympian if she kept practicing like she was. That's when Lora announced that she was sure that wasn't in the cards for her.

"Why couldn't you be?" Lora's mother asked again after not getting a response.

Lora was young, but old enough to know her mom, who had been born in their small town and was never going to leave, might be offended by her answer.

"Well?" her mother prodded politely.

"Because..." Lora dropped her head. "I'm from here."

When Lora looked back up she saw her mother wasn't upset, but rather she was puzzled.

She asked, "What do you mean by that? What difference would that make?"

"We...," Lora hesitated. "Nobody from here *does* anything. There are no famous athletes, or painters, or scientists. And I watch TV. Everything happens in the big cities. Big city kids are the ones who end up going big things.

Lora waited for her mother's scolding, but none came. Instead, she smiled, nodded, and said, "Get your shoes on, honey."

Lora checked back in the direction of R street for the cyclist, but she was gone. However, the other figure had drifted a few steps closer, still unable to cross the street. The morning sun had relented slightly and now she could make out he was wearing a flannel shirt. She could see that this man was in his twenties and now he was coming her direction. His path on the sidewalk wasn't exactly straight, but it wasn't out of control. His stride wasn't hesitant, but neither was it purposeful. His movements were noncommittal at best.

What were those indicators from that training session? Lora tried to recall. *Sedation.* It was an old tactic learned from the Tamil Tigers. Some suicide bombers would sedate themselves prior to an attack in order to remain calm and to keep from chickening out. Well, this guy was unsteady on his feet and there was a reluctance in his advance. Was he middle eastern? Lora couldn't tell, but from his complexion he could be? Did it matter? The instructors said it did. It was another indicator.

The cyclist. The damn cyclist appeared again and zipped by in the background, but she sped down Mass Ave going the other direction. The woman was going with the flow of traffic now. Lora could handle a bike like that. She'd never gotten to the level of an Olympian, but she'd tried her best. Her mother had convinced her she should try. Her mother knew how to explain the similarities among people.

"The librarian says this is every book they have about recent Olympics. Now scoot over and make some room."

Lora's mother used her broad hips to give her daughter a nudge as she placed a stack of books down on the table. The tower spilled over and the resulting crash echoed off the walls of the county library. The only other noises one heard in the building was the sounds of the card catalog opening and closing and the occasional whispered warnings from a parent to a rambunctious child.

Lora's mother spread the books out on the cheap wooden table in no particular order and took a seat along side her child. "Let's take a look at this one first."

One by one, they went through the books which told the stories of many American Olympians. Lora remembered her mother placing her plump index finger on page after page and scrolling down the lines until she found biographical information that included where that athlete was from.

"Uh-huh," she'd utter. "This swimmer is from Hood River, Oregon. She won the gold medal. Here's a silver medalist from Whittier, California. Here's a cyclist from Joplin, Missouri. This guy here is a pole vaulter who was born in Slippery Rock, Pennsylvania."

Lora's mother turned toward her and looked down over the top of her glasses. "Do you know where Slippery Rock is?"

Lora shook her head.

"Me neither."

After her mother had found the biographical information for several American athletes, she started in on those from other nations. Time and time again, she mentioned the names of places that were completely unfamiliar to Lora. This had gone on for more than thirty minutes by the time Lora had gotten up the nerve to speak.

"Okay, I get it."

"You get what?" asked her mother, not really asking. "I want to hear you say it."

"It doesn't matter where I'm from."

Now her mom placed a book down on the table, turned toward her daughter and held her hands. "Listen, girl. I'm not going to say where you're from and what you start with doesn't matter. That's not always the case. The fact of the matter is, not everyone is born into this world with the same advantages, and you have to remember that for sure. But there are going to be plenty of others in this life who try to set limitations for you, and *you* can't be one of those people. Not everyone has the exact same chances, but when it comes down to it, people are pretty much the same underneath. They want the same things and have the same dreams. Where they're from is just one piece of the puzzle. Do you understand?"

Lora did. Or she thought she did at the time. But life wasn't that simple, was it? People weren't the same. How many times had she been cursed at, spat at, and attacked, simply for doing her job? And how many times had she understood, even empathized with those she'd arrested? Those who had made bad, desperate decisions, or who had been failed by the system. Life was complex and messy. Her mother didn't grasp those complexities because she'd never seen the things Lora had seen.

The man was now within thirty yards of her position. Lora took a quick glance over her shoulder, noticed the other agents talking to each other on the sidewalk. Nobody seemed to be paying any mind to the newcomer. Maybe she shouldn't either. Pedestrian traffic in Washington, D.C. is anything but unusual. However, she was focusing on him. Why?

Now he glanced up, made the briefest moment of eye contact with her. She looked him up and down, assessing the possible threat. The shirt. The flannel shirt wasn't really *on* his body. At least not his entire body. It was on one arm and the rest was dangling behind him, but not freely—like it was stuck to his back.

Disheveled clothing. That had been another *indicator* they had pointed out in that training class. Look for disheveled clothing, because a suicide vest might be concealed under those garments. *Well*, Lora had thought when she'd heard the instructor pass on that gem, *I hope they don't see me on one my days off.*

Damn this morning sun, Lora thought. Even with her sunglasses on, the glare from the surrounding concrete, steel, and glass made it difficult to see details. People thought Secret Service agents wore shades as a fashion statement. No. It was because it kills your eyes to stand post in the daylight for eight to twelve hours at a time, afraid to blink or you'll miss something.

Lora stepped forward, decided to close the distance between her and the figure. Better to approach him now and engage him in polite discussion while getting a better read on him. She took several strides forward—not too fast, not tentative. The man's eyes met hers and his steps ground to a halt. His eyes. Red. Bloodshot. The word came back into Lora's mind. *Sedated.*

She'd seen eyes like that so many times. How many DUI's had she arrested back in the days when she'd been a uniformed officer? How many drug addicts and psych patients did she deal with now when she worked threat cases? But she'd seen eyes like those long before she'd started carrying a badge. She remembered those eyes. She'd seen them when she was eighteen, home one summer from college, and heard a sound in her parent's basement.

People left their doors unlocked in the neighborhood where Lora grew up. Not only did they not bother locking the doors to their houses, but they also didn't trouble themselves to lock the doors of their pickup trucks or American-made sedans. There was simply no need. So when Lora had been awakened at two in the morning by a sound in her parent's basement, it hadn't occurred to her that it was anything else than one of the cats knocking over plant or possibly a mouse knocking over a yardstick her mother had haphazardly left leaning up in a corner. But it wasn't a cat or a mouse. It was Lora's twenty-five-year-old cousin, Eric.

Lora had stifled a scream and Eric, dressed in a black Mötley Crüe t-shirt had barely reacted. He'd been digging through a set of cabinets and seemed annoyed to have to acknowledge anyone had entered the room. When he did turn toward Lora enough for him to see his face, his eyes—those blood shot eyes with pupils the size of coasters—seemed to stare through her.

"Don't tell them, okay?" was all he said.

And then he walked out the same unlocked door he'd entered, without bothering to close it.

Of course, Lora, still innocent and naïve, did tell her parents the next morning and to her surprise their reaction was subdued.

"I don't understand," Lora had said. "Why did Eric come in here? Has he been staying here? I didn't hear him knock or anything."

"He doesn't stay here," her father had explained. "But we've tried to help him out from time to time. He's been having a rough time of it as of late."

Lora looked at her father, not a man accustomed to sharing, and eventually gave up and turned her attention to her mother.

"What kind of rough time?" asked Lora. "He acted drunk."

Her mother explained, "Eric got himself hooked on drugs. Cocaine, I think. I'm sure he was here looking for something to take and sell. He's having money problems and his parents have kicked him out."

Eric? Her older cousin who she'd looked up to all those years? The one who was always the trusted member of the extended family? How could this have happened?

It was too much for Lora's mind to grasp at the time. How a trusted member of the family could break that trust by stealing from those who wanted to help. It was unconscionable. This was a breach of trust. Lora decided right then and there that Eric was a lost cause. She was writing him off. He was done. Excluded. She was finished with him forever.

Thinking back, Lora cringed at having those thoughts. She had been so young, stubborn and self-righteous. Years later, Eric had bounced back. He'd gotten clean. After hitting rock bottom, he married a wonderful woman and was now an addiction counselor helping others put their lives together. He'd circled the drain, gotten sucked down, and pulled himself back out. It happened. Lora had learned a lesson from watching his recovery. Sometimes the image of bloodshot, non-seeing eyes were just a snapshot of person's existence, not the total sum.

Now the man, seeing Lora's approach pivoted to his left, as if he wanted nothing more than to cross the street. However, the flow of traffic was unrelenting. Lora took another step and began to speak and that's when the man turned to his right and she saw why his shirt—the shirt hanging off one arm—wasn't swinging behind him in a natural way. A *backpack*. It was another indicator. Lora's muscles tightened and she moved toward the man. She made a conscious effort to let her non-weapon hand move her jacket aside to reveal the badge on her belt.

She spoke. "Sir, can I help you with something?"

He didn't speak. His head moved on a swivel. Left. Right. Left. Right. Straight at Lora.

Lora quickened her pace and closed the distance. "Sir—"

The man turned his entire body to the right toward the ambassador's residence and Lora could get a full glimpse of the backpack. It was unzipped and there were wires sticking out of the top. *Wires*. Another indicator.

Lora's heart pounded as she put her hand on her gun. "Police. I need you to stop right there."

Lora thought he might stop. Lora thought he might back up slowly. Lora thought he might run away. The man did none of those things. Suddenly, the man who had shown nothing but reluctance and hesitation in every movement while coming down the street broke into a full sprint toward the ambassador's residence.

Without thinking, Lora reacted by running in a direct line to intercept the man. She drew her pistol while managing to get in between the bomber and the front door of the residence. She remembered more of the training.

The instructor had said, "If the bomber is stopped by law enforcement, he or she will detonate in order to inflict as many casualties as possible."

Well, this is it, thought Lora, knowing she had no time to waste. She raised her weapon at the man's head. He stopped, frozen in his tracks. The indicators flashed through her mind: sedation, disheveled clothing, a backpack, wires, possibly middle eastern…it was all there.

It

was

all

there.

The pad of Lora's index finger was on the trigger and she felt the pressure building. If the man was going to detonate and Lora didn't pull the trigger she would certainly die and so might several other people. She heard the voices of the trainers in her head. *The indicators are there! Take the shot! Do your job. These can't be coincidences. We…are…at…war!"*

Lora had other memories too and now they filtered into her

consciousness. Her father deescalating a situation with another man in a tattered flannel shirt and disheveled clothing. Her mother, reminding her that people from all over the world have more in common than not. Her cousin, showing her that one page, or even several, in a person's life doesn't have to define the entire direction of the novel. She recalled those lessons as well.

"Keep your hands where I can see them and get down on the ground," she heard herself say.

She heard footsteps approaching and guns being drawn from behind her.

The man froze, but only momentarily before once again defying logic. With unexpected speed, he sprinted in the direction of the street, paying no mind to the river of traffic. Instinctively, Lora took up pursuit and found herself standing at the edge of Mass Ave watching the suspect dodge cars. Without reservation, the man had run full speed down into the middle of the road and was following the center line, in the hopes of not getting hit. Lora watched in disbelief as his flannel shirt dangled behind his body like a sheet on a clothing line on a windy day.

"Sure, this seems smart," she said to herself before taking a step off the curb and taking up the pursuit down the middle of the busy thoroughfare. Lora's earpiece, attached to the radio on her belt was exploding with radio traffic as news of the foot pursuit erupted over the channel. Some voices were familiar to her, others were not. Lora realized her friend Aimee Shore was in the area watching the action because as Lora sidestepped a honking Toyota, she heard Aimee call out to the other countersurveillance unit, who Lora realized must not have been able to see what was transpiring.

"Jerrod, get over here," Aimee said. "Lora's in pursuit."

"What?" Jerrod replied.

"Lora's in pursuit. She's… she's chasing some guy in a cape!"

The shirt, Lora thought as she had another close call with a motorist. *The damn shirt is flapping behind the guy.*

There was a pause on the radio and Lora watched as a woman slammed on her brakes to avoid hitting the suspect.

The radio silence was broken when Jerrod came back on the radio. "Why is Lora wearing a cape?"

Great. Now I may have to shoot two people today, Lora thought.

If Jerrod's question was ever answered, Lora didn't hear it. The next sound she heard was that of a man's body rolling over the hood of a silver Ford and then a cacophony of car horns. Lora watched as other agents and officers took started flashing badges and stepped into the street as her suspect staggered to the opposite curb. Lora managed to slip between cars, get across the street and then take a run at the man with the backpack. But now she saw he no longer had the backpack. In his collision with the car, the backpack had slid off his shoulder and was now laying several feet away. *Did he have a remote trigger?* Lora wondered as she approached the man. *A dead man switch?*

His hands were empty when she got to him and she decided to chance that he wasn't going to detonate simply because he hadn't done so earlier. In one swift move, she took him to the ground while doing her best to feel for a suicide vest in case the backpack wasn't the only threat. She got the cuffs on him and felt for weapons, none. Sweat rolled down Lora's forehead and she tried to control her breathing.

It's all adrenaline, she told herself. *Control it. Work the problem. What's next?*

The backpack. Explosive protocols.

Lora knew they had to treat the backpack as they would any suspicious package at a scene. Nobody would touch it until they could get an explosive detection dog to come and—

"Well, let's see what we've got here," she heard an officer say.

Jesus Christ, Lora cringed. *He's looking through the fucking backpack and grabbing the wires!*

As if showing off the kill from a hunt, the officer withdrew the contents of the backpack for everyone to see.

Josh DeMarco, her protective intelligence colleague, stepped forward to see what the officer was holding.

"It's a Nintendo," Josh announced. "A goddamned Nintendo."

Lora shook her head and then maneuvered the suspect into a sitting position. "What the hell are you doing? Why did you run?"

The kid—and that's why he looked like to Lora now—a kid, stared at her wide-eyed, the black discs of his eyes blotting out the white.

"I...I was partying all night with some friends. I've got some strong weed in that backpack. I'm sorry, lady. I could tell you guys were cops. Are you going to bust me?"

Lora stood up and looked over to Josh. "Get all of his information and run it. See if he's got any warrants."

"What are you going to be doing?" asked Josh.

"I need a minute."

She did need a minute. In fact, she needed a day, but she knew she wasn't going to get that. In a few moments they would cut the kid loose and the motorcade would move on to the next stop. The machinery would continue to move ahead and this day would be a footnote. It would be a non-incident. A hiccup. She didn't give a damn about marijuana. She'd cut this guy loose and there wouldn't even be a report. It would be like none of it ever happened.

"Bledsoe."

The calling of her name cut through the sound of the traffic that had resumed.

"It's Lora Bledsoe, right?"

"Yes, sir," she said to ASAIC Landon Mitchell. Lora didn't know the Assistant Special Agent in Charge well, but their first few encounters hadn't been pleasant. To Lora, he'd come across as an egotist, but that was something she could handle. Now that she thought about it, the first time she'd met him was in a training class. It was *that* training class.

"I was up at the front of the motorcade and saw what you did," he said.

Lora waited.

"From where I was standing, that was a suicide bomber. Weren't you in that same class with me not that long ago?"

"I was," Lora replied.

The ASAIC stared at her, but Lora didn't expound.

"Are you going to explain to me why you didn't react to your training?"

Lora gazed back down the street. She looked past her agents, the officers, the patrol cars, and the cars with government tags. She watched the people past Sheridan Circle; the ones walking to their jobs where they weren't appreciated; the ones sleeping on the street; the ones driving home to abusive spouses; the ones kicking a habit or possibly developing a new one. She looked on as people walked dogs and held their kids, not knowing what tomorrow would hold. She took in a deep breath and inhaled the same air that had been exhaled by people who were struggling or helping others through their struggles. Some of those people were bad, Lora knew. There was no question. Some would cut your throat without a second thought. And some would hit you in the face. But how many would clench that fist because they had nothing else to hold?

Lora allowed her vision to go back even further; to a father who helped others; to a mother who saw value in everyone; to a cousin who demonstrated redemption. Lora remembered.

Lora let her eyes come back to the man who was questioning her actions and told him the truth.

"I followed my training to the letter."

OFFICER SAFETY

Colin Conway

The yellow Toyota Tundra raced through the red light at Spokane Falls Boulevard and turned north onto Ruby Street. The pickup narrowly avoided hitting a newer Lexus as it careened through the last intersection on the edge of downtown. It fishtailed into the furthest of the three northbound lanes on Ruby. When the Toyota straightened its course, it sideswiped an early '70s Volkswagen Beetle. The little orange car lurched away from the middle lane.

Officer Lucas Jefferson sped through the corner in pursuit. His patrol car's engine revved in protest as he accelerated. Above him, emergency lights flicked between red and blue. A siren wailed its warning into the night.

"Out of the way!" Jefferson yelled as the Lexus drifted to the side of the road.

In the passenger seat of the patrol car, Officer Ron Rowe keyed his microphone. "David-435, northbound on Ruby."

The two men were using Jefferson's callsign that night since he'd logged them into the car.

"*Copy, four-thirty-five,*" the dispatcher said. "*Channel is still restricted. Lieutenant is now monitoring the call.*"

"Better hurry," Rowe said.

The engine revved louder and Jefferson pounded the steering wheel. "He's gonna terminate the pursuit!"

Rowe pointed at the Volkswagen. "Pay attention!"

"What do you think I'm doing?"

The orange Beetle overcorrected and shot into their lane.

Jefferson jerked the steering wheel to the left and immediately back to the right. The patrol car whipped around the little car.

Up head, the Toyota weaved in and out of the Friday night traffic. It was nearly midnight. The colleges hadn't yet let out for the summer so traffic this time of night was active. The downtown bars were still jammed, and it was too early for the high school kids to be home.

"Move!" shouted Jefferson. He angrily waved his free hand back and forth.

A minivan lurched to the side of the road and the patrol car zoomed by. The female driver scowled at them as they passed.

"David-four-thirty-five, advise of speed and conditions."

"He's gonna do it," Jefferson said with a shake of his head. "What did I tell you?"

Rowe leaned over and glanced at the speedometer. He activated the microphone. "Four-thirty-five, speed is seventy-four." He sat upright. "Road is dry. Traffic is moderate."

"Four-thirty-five, any other PC for pursuit?"

"Are you kidding?" Jefferson shouted. "It's fucking stolen and used in a robbery!"

Rowe waggled the microphone in the direction of his partner. "You done?"

Further up the road, the Toyota Tundra swerved widely onto a side street.

Jefferson zoomed around a slow-moving Buick that refused to move to the side of the road.

Rowe keyed the microphone. "Four-thirty-five. We've also got PC for hit and run, reckless driving, and—"

"Terminate pursuit," the dispatcher announced.

"But we can get Pierre!" Jefferson hollered.

"All units, slow down. Pursuit is terminated. Channel is unrestricted."

Rowe faced his partner. "Slow down." Into the microphone, he said, "David-435, copy. Terminating pursuit." Once again to Jefferson, Rowe dejectedly said, "Slow down."

The engine stopped whining and the car coasted to a slower

speed.

Rowe silenced the siren before clicking off the emergency flashers.

The dispatcher called out the particulars of Macon Pierre, the suspect behind the wheel of the truck. She also provided the plate number and another description of the pickup.

But Lucas Jefferson wasn't listening. Instead, he smacked the wheel with the palm of his hand. "That lieutenant."

"Next time."

Jefferson shook his head. "Dickless wonder."

"We knew the driver. What'd you expect?"

They turned onto Desmet Avenue. It was a natural desire to follow the path that the truck had taken. In the middle of the road was the Toyota Tundra. It had collided with an Audi and blocked the roadway. Parked cars lined both sides of the street. The driver's door of the pickup was open, and Macon Pierre was gone. The driver of the Audi was climbing out of his car.

"He's out," Jefferson said excitedly.

"Stop!" Rowe hollered as he jumped from the patrol car and jogged over to the Audi driver.

Jefferson snatched the microphone from its holder. "David-435."

"*Four-thirty-five?*"

The driver gesticulated wildly to Rowe and brought his hands together to simulate a crash.

"Four-thirty-five, our suspect has collided with a vehicle at Desmet and Ruby. Medics are not required. And?"

The driver pointed east then slapped his hands. Jefferson knew what the driver was telling his partner. Rowe faced Jefferson and thumbed over his shoulder.

"*Four-thirty-five, go ahead.*"

Officer Ron Rowe turned and ran eastbound.

"Four-thirty-five, Pierre's fled on foot. Eastbound on Desmet. David-436 is out of the car. We're gonna see if we can find him."

"*Four-thirty-five, copy.*"

The Mobile Data Computer next to Jefferson's elbow beeped multiple times. He didn't check what was occurring because he already knew. Other units joined his call, but they stayed off the air in case Rowe needed to jump back on with an update.

Jefferson activated the emergency flashers again, dropped his car into gear, and reversed onto Ruby Street. Once he was clear of the corner, he popped the gearshift into Drive, and raced ahead two blocks to Sharp Avenue. He figured that was far enough to—

"*Four-thirty-six,*" Rowe called. "*Foot pursuit!*"

Jefferson turned eastbound onto Sharp Avenue.

"*Northbound on Pearl, approaching Boone.*" Rowe's voice was strong, but the exertion of running was evident.

"*Channel is restricted for David-four-thirty-six,*" the dispatcher announced.

Jefferson's patrol car accelerated as it raced along Sharp. He tapped the brakes before spinning the wheel to right. The tires protested the physics of the turn, but the car eventually straightened and propelled him southbound.

Macon Pierre was a tall, thin white male with scraggly long hair. He wore jeans and Doc Martens, but no shirt. He sprinted northbound. Behind him but gaining ground was Ron Rowe.

Jefferson jammed the brakes and skidded the patrol car to a stop. He shoved the gearshift into Park, jumped out, and moved to the front of the car.

Pierre was trapped between two buildings. There was no escape route. He had to go through Jefferson or turn around and run back toward Rowe.

The tall white man lowered his head and kicked like a fullback sprinting for the endzone.

Lucas Jefferson hunched, took a couple of gauging steps, then hit Macon Pierre in the midsection just like his college football coach had taught him—head to the side, shoulder tucked in, arms wrapped around the midsection. It was designed to keep both players safe.

Unfortunately, it had been years since Jefferson tackled anyone like that.

Macon Pierre stood in front of the patrol car with his hands cuffed. His long hair hung in front of his face. Some of it was matted to his forehead due to sweat. Tattoos covered his bare chest. Over his left breast was a swastika. On the other breast, a circle and a cross were in the middle of flames. Across his flat stomach were the words *White Devil*.

Lucas Jefferson and Ron Rowe stood nearby. Jefferson rubbed his aching shoulder while his partner shook his head.

Corporal Tom Clary lowered his camera. "One of you guys, pull his hair back so I can see his face."

A single eye peered through Pierre's matted hair. "Not the boo."

Jefferson cocked his head.

Rowe touched his partner's arm. "I got it. Besides, I've got gloves on."

Macon Pierre lifted his chin toward the night sky as Rowe brushed the hair away from his face. When he lowered his head, an abrasion was seen on the arrested man's left cheek.

"How bad is it?" Pierre asked.

"Barely a scratch," Clary said.

"Hurts worse than that." Pierre clucked his tongue and glanced at Jefferson. "Lucky you had your backup."

"Yeah?" Jefferson asked.

"Look at the camera," the corporal said.

Pierre curled his lip and continued to glare at Jefferson.

"This is for you, Pierre," Corporal Clary said. "If you don't want me to document your injuries, I'm happy to go about my day."

The arrested man faced Clary. "Why didn't you say so? Want me to smile?"

Clary lifted the camera. "Do what you like."

Pierre grinned. Blood covered his teeth.

"Turn to the right," the corporal said.

Pierre faced Jefferson. "I owe you, bunny."

"Keep talking," Jefferson said.

"When you least expect it."

The camera flashed.

"Let me see the other side," the corporal said.

Pierre sneered at Jefferson. "Trust me. It's coming."

Rowe chuckled. "Big talk for a man in handcuffs."

Pierre eyed Rowe. "He your boyfriend? Is that why you defend him?"

"Shut up," the corporal ordered, "and let me see the other side."

"I'll fuck you up, too," Pierre said to Rowe.

"Last chance," the corporal said, "or I'm done."

The suspect slowly turned. "They were rough on me, Sarge. I want that in your report."

"He's a corporal," Rowe said, "And you shouldn't have resisted."

"I didn't resist."

Rowe tapped his chest. "Tell that to my body camera. You don't think I wear this because I want to."

Another flash of the camera.

"Now," Clary said. "Let me see your back."

Pierre shuffled around. On his right shoulder was a large rash.

Corporal Clary leaned in with the camera and snapped a picture. He examined the screen then shook his head in frustration. "Ron, put your finger next to abrasion."

Rowe eyed his partner.

"That's right," Pierre said. He spoke to Clary's reflection in the windshield. "Make sure you get a good picture for my lawsuit, Sarge. Ol' boo is gonna lose his badge. I think he broke my ribs, too."

"If he did," Rowe said, "you wouldn't be talking." He tapped his chest near the body camera. "You know I'm still recording this, right?" He jerked his head toward Jefferson.

"Him, too."

Neither officer was recording now.

"What do I care?" Pierre said. "Boo is a term of endearment."

"Sure, it is," Jefferson said. "I feel all warm and fuzzy every time you say it."

The corporal looked over the viewfinder at Rowe. "Ron, *please.*"

Reluctantly, Rowe stepped toward the long-haired man and pointed to the abrasion on his shoulder.

The camera flashed.

Pierre laughed. "Cha-ching, baby."

"White lives matter."

Lucas Jefferson glanced over his left his shoulder and winced from the pain. "Don't start."

"Hey, man." Macon Pierre scooted awkwardly across the plastic-covered backseat. It squeaked as he moved. Scooching anywhere in the tight confines of the rear seat was a difficult task as Pierre's hands remained cuffed behind his back. His face hovered near the Plexiglass shield that separated the passengers. Pierre's attention remained locked onto the passenger. "Fuck your black lives."

From behind the steering wheel, Ron Rowe glanced into the rearview mirror. Pierre's eyes were again hidden among a swath of long hair that had fallen in front of his face. "He said shut up."

Pierre continued. "Your lives aren't any more special than ours."

Jefferson didn't respond. Instead, he rubbed his shoulder.

"I hope you popped that out of its socket."

Rowe flicked on the radio and turned it up. Whoever was last in the car had it tuned to a country music channel. A song about calling the po-po filled the car.

"Oh yeah," Pierre exclaimed. "Five-one-five-oh," he sang

out.

Jefferson flicked it off and the car went silent.

"Turn it back. That was my jam."

Rowe's eyes went to the rearview mirror. "Five-oh is already here, dumbass."

"Oh, you want some of this, too?" Pierre jerked to his head to flick his hair from his face. He then looked in the rearview mirror to catch Rowe's attention. "You two a couple butt buddies or what? Always coming to his protection." He spat on the protective shield. "That's what I think of that."

"Sit back," Jefferson said.

Pierre dropped into his seat. That only lasted for a few seconds. He returned to his position next to the Plexiglass divider and craned his neck to look at Jefferson. "You think you can double dip? Blue lives matter, too? Fuck that. You're no better than us." Pierre hocked a loogie onto the Plexiglass this time. "There's more where that came from."

Rowe tapped the brakes and the car jerked as if stopping. Pierre's face slammed into the Plexiglass divider. The car accelerated quickly again, and Pierre was tossed backward into his seat.

Jefferson glanced over his shoulder which caused a twinge of pain in his shoulder. He winced.

"Jesus!" Pierre's face scrunched with obvious pain. "What was that?"

"A cat," Rowe muttered.

"Cat, my ass." Pierre looked up at the roof of the car and blinked several times. "You did that on purpose."

"It was a cat," Rowe insisted.

Pierre's face pinched and relaxed several times. "You guys need seatbelts back here. It's not safe."

Rowe glanced into the rearview mirror. "Next time, maybe listen. That's safe."

"There wasn't no cat."

"Sure, there was."

"Yeah?" Pierre stared at the ceiling. "Did you hit it?"

Jefferson eyed his partner then faced the man in the backseat. "No. He missed it."

"I wasn't talking to you, boo." Pierre awkwardly sat up and scooted forward again. He moved to within inches of the Plexiglass again. He tilted his head so he could see Jefferson. "Hey, tell me something. What's it like being a fly in a bowl full of rice?"

Rowe tapped the brakes again. Pierre's face slammed into the separation shield once more. When the car accelerated, the suspect flopped into his seat. "Jesus!"

Jefferson turned to see Pierre. His shoulder hurt doing so, but he fought back the grimace.

Pierre lay on the back seat. He looked up as his face repeatedly squeezed and relaxed. "What the fuck, man?"

"Dog," said Rowe.

"There wasn't no dog!" Pierre shouted.

"Sure, there was."

Jefferson settled into his seat.

"I know what you're doing!" Pierre hollered. "I'm gonna have your badge. Both of—"

Rowe tapped the brakes and the car lurched forward once more. There was a thud in the backseat. Jefferson turned to look.

Pierre had slid off the plastic covered seats and now lay on the floorboard. He cried out in discomfort.

"Sorry about that," Rowe said. "Cats and dogs are running wild tonight. It's pandemonium."

Pierre struggled to get himself back into the seat. After a moment, he gave up. "I think I'll stay here until we get to jail."

"Probably a good idea," Jefferson said. His attention returned to the road ahead. "Safety first."

In the sally port of the Spokane County Jail, Jefferson and Rowe exited the patrol car and moved to the gun-secure station. Jefferson put his Glock into a small locker and removed the key. Rowe did the same.

Jefferson held out his hand to stop his partner from returning to their car. Inside, Macon Pierre still lay on the floorboard.

"What was that about?" Jefferson whispered.

"What?"

"The brake checks."

Rowe flicked his hand toward the car. "He wouldn't shut up."

"But the corporal already checked him at the scene for the use of force. What if he's got a broken nose or a black eye?"

"He doesn't."

"But what if?"

"He *doesn't*."

The two men returned to the patrol car. They opened the back door and pulled Pierre from the floorboard. They were careful to make sure he didn't bump his head on the way out. When Pierre stood, he turned and angrily shouted, "I'm gonna have your badges!"

"We've heard it before," Rowe said.

"Then I'm gonna kill your wives!"

Rowe pointed to a camera in the lobby. "Say that again. They might not have heard you."

He tugged on Pierre's elbow and escorted him into the jail lobby. Jefferson remained behind and flipped up the backseat. This was always done to ensure that an arrestee hadn't dumped anything that might have missed during a search incident to arrest.

Jefferson didn't find anything. He slapped the seat into place and went into the lobby.

Inside the harsh lights of the booking lobby, Lucas Jefferson studied Macon Pierre. The man's nose twitched as blood trickled from it. Bruising appeared to be forming around his left eye. He worried that Rowe's brake checks were going to haunt them.

Deputy Sheriff Jerry Brasch read from his clipboard. Attached to it was the in-processing checklist. "Any allergies, diseases, or medical conditions?"

"They assaulted me."

Brasch looked up with a bored expression.

"With their car." Pierre glanced at the two officers then to the deputy. "Aren't you gonna do something about it?"

The deputy raised his eyebrows. "They hit you with their car?"

"No. I was inside, but they—"

Brasch cleared his throat. "Any allergies, diseases, or medical conditions?"

"You don't believe me?"

The deputy looked up. The bored expression had returned.

Pierre's eyes narrowed. "I see how it is. You fuckers are all the same."

"Do I need to repeat my question?"

"No."

"Well?"

Pierre leaned his shoulders against a nearby wall. "I got a peanut allergy."

Brasch made a note on the checklist. "Peanut."

"And I'm lactose intolerant."

The deputy looked up from his clipboard. "For real?"

"Like I would joke about that. So what if I can't drink milk?" Pierre lifted his chin in the direction of the deputy's clipboard. "Write it down. I need a special diet."

Rowe and Jefferson chuckled.

Pierre glared at them. "That shit ain't funny."

Brasch frowned as he jotted the note on the clipboard.

"And I got diverticulitis, too"

"How do you spell that?" the deputy asked.

"Do I look like a doctor? You need to know this shit. Not me."

Rowe moved toward the deputy. "It's probably better if

you ask what he doesn't have. For the master race, he seems pretty fragile."

Pierre rested the back of his head against the wall. "And I got a headache." Pierre looked down his nose at Brasch. "I think I got a concussion from the beating they gave me."

"We didn't give you a beating," Rowe said.

"Maybe it came from those cats and dogs running wild." Pierre looked to the deputy. "I wanna see the nurse. I know my rights."

Brasch cocked his head. "You're serious?"

"I think I might pass out from the pain."

Rowe stepped toward Pierre. "You stole a truck and robbed a family business." He pointed outside. "There are still cops out there investigating the collisions you caused, and you got the balls to cry about having a headache?"

"I think I got a busted rib, too."

Rowe lifted his hands in frustration. "Unbelievable."

Jefferson watched as a smile grew on Macon Pierre's face.

Sergeant Gene Summerhill crossed his arms and studied both Lucas Jefferson and Ron Rowe. He stood a few inches over six feet with thick arms and a bushy mustache.

They were in the parking lot of an office supply store on North Division. All three men stood in front of the sergeant's unmarked patrol car. It was almost three in the morning. Traffic had thinned noticeably on the arterial.

"So he fought with you?" Summerhill asked.

"He resisted," Rowe said, "but he didn't fight."

The sergeant eyed Jefferson. "You tackled him, though?"

"That's right. Like they taught in college." Jefferson patted his left shoulder. Doing so brought a twinge of pain, but he kept his face flat.

"Were your cameras activated?" Summerhill asked.

Both Rowe and Jefferson nodded.

"The camera in the car, too," Jefferson said. "The

takedown should be on there."

"It was beautiful," Rowe said. "Luke brought him down like Brian Urlacher in his prime."

"I'd have gone with Mike Singletary." Jefferson hunched in a pre-snap linebacker pose. "But thanks for the compliment."

Summerhill frowned. "This is serious, you two. Anything else I need to know?"

Rowe and Jefferson eyed each other before both shaking their heads.

"The jail nurse gave Pierre a onceover."

Rowe shrugged. "He was crying about that before we left. So what?"

"So what?" Summerhill said. "I got a heads up from the jail sergeant that he's pretty banged up."

"He got some road rash from the resisting," Jefferson said. "Hell, my shoulder is so screwed right now that I can't get my arm above my head." He lifted his arm to show the limited range of motion he had. "Nobody's crying for me."

Summerhill lifted his chin. "Want to go to the ER?"

Jefferson shook his head. "I'll sleep it off and see how it is later."

"If it's not better, go to the doctor. We'll fill out an on-the-job injury report. Probably should do it anyway."

Rowe pointed at the sergeant. "What he said."

Summerhill watched a tricked-out Honda race southbound. Its engine rattled into the night. When it was out of earshot, he continued. "The jail staff photographed Pierre's injuries and the nurse is completing her report now."

Jefferson shoved his hands into his pockets. "We had Corporal Clary document Pierre's scuffs at the scene. They weren't that bad, all things considered."

"I know. Clary told me."

"There you go," Rowe said.

"He also said there wasn't a black eye and bloody nose."

Both officers remained silent.

Summerhill took a deep breath and held it. "I don't know what happened in the car, but it's time for you to write a report like your jobs depend upon it."

"Pierre isn't going to do anything," Rowe said. "His type never do."

"Until they do," Summerhill said. "You know the drill. Paper beats everything. It's more important than anything you do out on the street. Find a quiet place now and write your report. Detail exactly why you had to stop suddenly."

Jefferson and Rowe stared at the sergeant.

He frowned. "You two geniuses didn't invent the brake checks. So, what was it? A squirrel?"

"Dog," Rowe said.

Jefferson nodded.

"Did you tell Pierre that?"

"We did."

Jefferson eyed his partner. "We also told him about the cat."

"You did two?" Summerhill asked excitedly. "Christ, what were you thinking?" The sergeant put his hands on his hips. "It's always fun and games until someone gets sued." He turned away for a moment then quickly faced them. Summerhill pointed at each officer. "I've told you both this more than once—report writing is an officer safety skill. Tonight, you better treat it as such."

Sergeant Summerhill climbed into his car and drove southbound on Division.

Ron Rowe eyed his partner. "Yeah. I probably went too far."

Lucas Jefferson shrugged. "Too late for that now. Let's write the reports. There'll be no reason to worry after that."

ZEBRAS
Stacy Woodson

Blue Ridge Elementary School Announcements:

Goooooood morning, Sea Lions! Principal Taylor, here. Happy morning to you. Ms. Libby wants me to remind you the book return is for library books ONLY. NOT food wrappers or bubble gum or your underwear. If she catches a student tossing trash into the return, she WILL revoke your library card. Lunch today will be chicken fingers, crispy tater tots, and mixed vegetables—no groaning, please. Finally, we are thrilled to welcome two new members to our Sea Lion family—coming to us from our very own Blue Ridge Police Department—School Resource Officer Bradley will be filling in for SRO Allison while she's on maternity leave, along with his canine partner. Boomer is a black lab who loves stories, belly rubs, and hugs. No this isn't Boomer's dating profile. During recess today, near the basketball courts, Boomer and SRO Bradley will hand out COP-sicles...get it? COP-sicles? Please be sure to stop and say hello before you load up on sugar and return to the classroom. Yes, I know how much you love me right now, teachers. Now, go attack the day, Sea Lions. Remember: Be Brave. Be Brilliant. Be Bold. Be you.

Police Contact Report

Subject: Canine on Campus Pilot Program

Location: Blue Ridge Elementary
Program objective: Create safe learning environment by building a strong bond between SRO and students.
Task: Meet staff, faculty, and students. Introduce program.
Summary of Actions & Observations: Met with guidance counselor and special education team. Discussed ways Boomer can complement teaching strategies with students who struggle with reading, anxiety, depression. Seeking opportunities to use Boomer as part of an academic incentive program. Distributed popsicles at recess. Made contact with approximately 300 students. Most excited to see Boomer. Two students were afraid. Both revealed negative past experiences with dogs.
Way Ahead: Be mindful of students afraid of dogs. Seek ways to include all students in Boomer-related activities.

Message
SRO Allison to Bradley
How was the first day?
Sticky.
Welcome to elementary school.
I miss the bomb squad.
I miss my waistline.

Blue Ridge Elementary School Announcements:

Goooooood morning, Sea Lions! Principal Taylor, here. Happy morning to you. SRO Bradley has a special treat.

Next to the library—by the book return that's still NOT a trash receptacle—you will find a doghouse. Yes, I said doghouse. This isn't an ordinary doghouse. It's a mailbox. Now you can write letters to Boomer. Not an email, not a tweet. An actual letter. If you don't know what those are, ask your teacher. Didn't have a chance to meet Boomer at recess yesterday? Boomer wants to connect with you! Drop him a line and introduce yourself. He LOVES mail and pictures. He will respond to each correspondence. So, put those keyboards away. Crack out some old-fashioned paper and a writing implement—pen, pencil, whatever. In Guidance Counselor Carpenter's case—a crayon. Lunch today will be spaghetti with meatballs. Sorry, Sea Lions—after the post a-popsicle-lyptic sugar rush surging through the classrooms yesterday, teachers have requested dessert not be served. Now, go attack the day—perhaps a little gentler than yesterday. And remember: Be Brave. Be Brilliant. Be Bold. Be you.

Dear Boomer,

My name is Lizzie Miller. I am 9 years old. I am in the third grade. I love popsicles but not school very much.

What do you like to eat?

I didn't say hi yesterday on account I don't like to talk in front of folks. I try to be brave like Principal Taylor says but it's hard. My insides swell up and words get stuck in my throat on little fish hooks. Especially S-words. I try really hard to push them out. But it doesn't usually work.

Granma says I'm this way on account mama saw a snake when she was pregnant, and a demon got ahold of my tongue.

Uncle Karl says I'm this way on account I'm stupid. I don't like my Uncle Karl very much.

I like writing though. Words don't get stuck on paper.

Your friend,
Lizzie Miller

Dear Lizzie,

It's paw-some to meet you! My favorite food is kibble. You probably don't think that's very yummy. I'm sorry you didn't get a popsicle yesterday. SRO Bradley says he has more in our hooch—that's what he likes to call our office. You know, the one by the gym where SRO Allison used to hang out. We will be there at recess today if you'd like to stop by and share a popsicle with me.

Fur-ever yours,
Boomer

Contact Report

Subject: Canine on Campus Pilot Program
Location: Blue Ridge Elementary
Program objective: No change.
Tasks: Participate and assess school Code Red drill. Continue Letters to Boomer (L2B) program.
Summary of Actions & Observations: Noted the following discrepancies during school drill: Two locks (school gym &

first grade classroom not secured). Five
students failed to follow lockdown
protocol and remained visible from the
hall. Passed noted discrepancies along
to Principal Taylor. Today marks day
three of L2B Program. Fifteen letters
received so far. Responded to all
through students' assigned teachers.
Flagged letter from third grader Lizzie
Miller (copy attached). Highlights
specific challenges she faces at school.
Reached out to school guidance
counselor, Barry Carpenter, seeking more
information on Miller. Carpenter reports
Lizzie is extremely bright, excels at
writing, and achieves above average
scores on exams. Despite her success,
she suffers from a stutter, struggles
with reading aloud and social
interactions. Lizzie's teacher, Ms.
Wyncoop, submitted request to have
Lizzie read to Boomer in lieu of P.E. in
order to improve her confidence.
Way Ahead: Meet Lizzie. Seek ways to
help her make a deeper connection with
Boomer while continuing to implement
other student outreach programs.

Dear Boomer,

Nice meeting you in person today. Thanks for the
popsicle! Grape is my favorite flavor. Sorry I didn't read
the story about a nite that slays dragons. I am not good at
reading out loud. Spencer makes fun of me and everyone
laughs. It makes me want to crawl under my desk and

hide. Uncle Karl says if you don't stand up for yourself folks will step all over you. Especially the government. They want to take our guns. Uncle Karl seems to have plenty though. My brother Billy is in fifth grade. He stands up for me. But it never works. Spencer puts the hurt on him pretty bad. I told Granma. She said me and Billy need to turn the other cheek. That's what Jesus would do. I'm not so sure about that. Jesus never met Spencer Blaylock.

　　Your friend,
　　Lizzie Miller

Dear Lizzie,

　　Kids can be mean sometimes, especially to people who are different. I'm sorry you are going through that. I've had my share of school struggles, too. I'll tell you a secret, but ONLY if you paw-promise not to tell anyone...I flunked bomb-sniffing school. Yup. Me. Boomer. I had problems sorting out all the smells and sometimes sat at the wrong time. (Kind of like you have problems sorting out your words.) It was awful. Especially with a name like mine. Life is tough sometimes. But good things happen too. Take my situation now. The Brass—that's what SRO Bradley calls the bosses—they made it so I can hang out with kids, and I love being here with you. I promise there are good things in your future, too. I hope you will come back and read your story. It sounds paw-some.

Fur-ever yours,
Boomer

Message
SRO Bradley to Allison
Spencer Blaylock kid—what's his deal?
Classic Scut Farkus.
Who?
Kid in the racoon cap.
...?
You know, from the movie Christmas Story.
Still, not following...
Never mind.
So, Blaylock?
He's a bully.
Ever talk to the school admin?
Yes & filed reports. They won't touch him.
Daddy is the school super.
I hate bullies.
Who is his latest target?
Miller kids.
That's been going on for a while.
Harasses them at the bus stop.
Boomer & I will start walking the bus line.
Let me know how it goes.

Message
SRO Bradley to Allison
Walked the bus line with Boomer this afternoon.

And?
No sign of Blaylock. Found Billy.
Torn clothes. Black eye. Wouldn't talk.
Not surprised. Uncle tells the kids not to trust cops.
Lizzie trusts me.
Lizzie trusts Boomer.
There's more...Boomer indicated.
Indicated what? A bomb?
He snuffled down the line of kids, stopped,
and laid at Lizzie's feet.
*Did you call the bomb squad? Put the school on
lockdown?*
This is sarcasm, right?
Boomer FAILED bomb school.
Still...
Did you check her?
Visually. Her hands were empty.
Billy had her backpack.
So, it's nothing.
What if it isn't?
Don't look for Zebras, Bradley.
Zebras?
*You know the old saying, when you hear hoof beats,
think horses, not zebras.*
Yeah. Meaning?
SRO duty isn't the bomb squad.
Don't look for something that isn't there.

Dear Boomer,

I can't read during P.E. today. Granma is making me
leave early for singing practice. She plays guitar at church
and wants me to sing with her on Sunday. She says if I try
real hard maybe this time I'll be touched by the holy

spirit and Pastor Jones will be able to exercise the demon holding my tongue. Don't know why Granma thinks it will work. Didn't work last time or the time before that. There were just a bunch of people screaming and moaning and grunting and such. Instead of exercising my demon, it was like they was exercising themselves.

Your Friend,
Lizzie Miller

Dear Lizzie,

Sometimes people make us do uncomfortable things even though they mean well. Take SRO Bradley. He makes me take a bath. I hate baths. I know it's not the same as singing in front of people. That takes a lot of courage. I'll let you in on another secret. As far as demons go—everyone has one. Some people just live with theirs better than others.

Fur-ever yours,
Boomer

Blue Ridge Elementary School Announcements:

Goooooood morning, Sea Lions! Principal Taylor, here. Happy morning to you. Lunch today will be hot dogs with tater tots and chocolate chip cookies. Books-are-a-Blast! Yes, Sea Lions, I said BOOKS. Ms. Libby is proud to announce she's partnering with SRO Bradley for a new reading incentive program. Astronaut bookmarks, moon pies, and rocket pops are just some of the fun prizes you can win when you read. Swing by the library to check out Boomer's reading picks for the week, and grab punch cards to track your progress. The class who turns in the most cards at the end of the month wins a pizza party donated by The-Zah. Now, go attack the day, Sea Lions. And remember: Be Brave. Be Brilliant. Be Bold. Be you.

Contact Report

Subject: Canine on Campus Pilot Program
Location: Blue Ridge Elementary
Program objective: No change.
Tasks: Partner with school librarian to create campus-wide reading incentive program. Respond to call about inappropriate material found in library book return.
Summary of Actions & Observations: Books-are-a-Blast kicked off this week. More than 100 punch cards distributed so far. Working with teachers to create diverse list of titles for Boomer's reading picks. Secured copy of ANARCHIST COOKBOOK found in book return. Markings revealed book originated at a defunct library in Junction City KS. Submitted incident report and book to Criminal Intelligence Division.
Way Ahead: Continue partnering with faculty on school initiatives. Follow up with the Criminal Intelligence Division on ANARCHIST COOKBOOK and be prepared to

field any requests from higher.

Message
SRO Bradley to Allison
Anarchist Cookbook dumped
in the school book return.
Funny.
Not funny.
Didn't Books-are-a-Blast start this week? It's a prank.
Elementary school kids
aren't that sophisticated.
*Sure, they are. They've been dumping weird things
in that return for months.*
What if it's something more...
If it were something more why turn in the book?
Maybe...
Zebras, Bradley.

Blue Ridge Elementary School Announcements:

*Goooooood morning, Sea Lions! Principal Taylor, here.
Happy morning to you. Lunch today will be cheese piz—
excuse me students—if he thinks I'm going to stop in the
middle of—what do you mean he's going to come down to
the school. I'll talk to him. Give me the phone...Mr.
Miller...No, we aren't directly targeting your niece... If she's
allergic, fine. I'll pass the information along to Nurse
Young... Ahem...Sorry about that, Sea Lions. Where were
we? Oh. That's right. Our school fundraiser begins next
week. Catalogs for cookie dough sales will be available in
the office starting tomorrow. Proceeds will be used to
purchase new playground equipment. Remind your parents
sweet treats are good for any occasion—birthdays,
Christmas, Cousin Caleb's Bar Mitzvah. Now, go attack the*

day, Sea Lions. And remember: Be Brave. Be Brilliant. Be Bold. Be you.

Dear Boomer,

Nurse Young said I can't see you anymore on account Uncle Karl told her I was lergic to dogs. Which isn't true. You see after school each day I stop at Ms. McLusky's and get her mail. On account of her bad hip she can't go down the driveway to her mailbox. Each Friday she pays me five dollars. I told her I don't need money. Granma says that Jesus wants folks to look out for one another. But Ms. McLusky says everyone needs a little pocket change. Anyway, Uncle Karl was short yesterday—that's what he says when he doesn't have money for smokes. He went through my backpack and found your letters. He got angry. Said cops are just an extension of the government, and he don't need that kind of trouble sniffing around his family. I tried to tell him he didn't need to worry about the sniffing on account you had a bad sniffer and all. But you know I'm bad with S-words. By the time I finally got the words out he'd already walked away. I'm sorry. I hope we can still be friends.

Your friend,
Lizzie Miller

Message
SRO Bradley to Allison
Ever run background check on the Millers?
Yes.
Reason?
Besides Karl & his mother both being wack-jobs...

That, too.
Billy showed up with burns on his arm.
Requested CPS run a health and welfare.
And?
No hazards. No neglect. No abuse noted.
Who has custody of the kids?
Ethel.
The bible-thumping grandma?
Yup. Karl lives with them, too.
Where's the mother?
Blue Ridge Cemetery.
Poor kids. & Karl? Any priors?
Dishonorable discharge from military.
Struck officer when stationed at Fort Riley.
Fort Riley. As in KS?
Yeah. Why?
More zebras.

Dear Boomer,

Uncle Karl would kill me if he knew I was writing you. It's just I don't know what to do. I try to stop the bad things from happening. But things are getting worse. Billy says he's trying to take back his power. Not sure what that means except that it involves hanging out with Uncle Karl, shooting guns with my Uncle's boys, and being proud. Nothing prideful in what they're doing if you ask me. Uncle Karl's got his anger. Granma's got Jesus. And I got Billy. I'm scared he's going to turn into Uncle Karl or end up like Mama. Not sure what's worse.

Your friend,
Lizzie Miller

Message
SRO Bradley to Allison
Did you know Karl Miller runs
with the Proud Boys?
He's not the job, Bradley.
What if he is?
Not while I'm on maternity leave.
What if Karl is planning something
& Lizzie is trying to stop it?
Little Lizzie Miller.
The latest letter I got from her.
Boomer indicating.
The book.
You don't know she put the book in the drop box.
It came from a Kansas library.
My bet is it belonged to Karl.
So, you think Lizzie took it because...
Maybe he/his boys were building something?
No book=No instructions=No boom
Zebras, Bradley. Stay focused on the kids.

Message
SRO Bradley to Allison
CSI lifted prints from the cookbook—Karl's.
Zebras my ass.

Message
SRO Allison to Bradley
*Heard intel put surveillance on Karl. They have enough
evidence now to execute a search warrant.*
When?
Not sure.
I need to know what's going on with these kids.
I'm going to talk to Billy & Lizzie.

You could tip off Karl, blow the case they're building.
I'm an SRO. This isn't the bomb squad.
The kids are my priority.
My work here is done.
Walking over to the bus line now.
Blaylock is already here.
I can't stand that kid.
Billy is carrying a guitar case. Is he in the band?
Blue Ridge Elementary doesn't have a band.
Jesus. This was never about Karl.
It was about Billy and Blaylock.

Blue Ridge Emergency Annoucement:

Blue Ridge Elementary—staff, students, teachers.
CODE RED.
I repeat CODE RED.
LOCKDOWN. LOCKS, LIGHTS. OUT OF SIGHT.
LOCKDOWN. LOCKS, LIGHTS. OUT OF SIGHT.
THIS IS NOT A DRILL.

SITUATION REPORT

Venue: Blue Ridge Elementary
Brief Description of Incident:
At 8:05 a.m. on February 1, I observed
fifth grade Billy Miller at the bus stop
brandishing a shotgun with the intent to
do harm to fellow student Spencer
Blaylock. I subdued Miller before he
could discharge his weapon. Miller
received only minor injuries when
disarmed and taken to the ground.
Detailed report to follow.

How's my favorite SRO holding up?
Just glad the kids are okay.
Wish I could have done something sooner.
Not you. Boomer. Heard he saved the day.
When Billy pulled the gun, I let Boomer off lead
& he indicated.
Is it true? Did Boomer sit right on Billy's feet?
Yeah. That split-second distracted Billy
& I was able to grab the gun.
*Maybe you should approach the Brass about
putting Boomer through bomb school again.*
No. I think he's found a new calling.
I think we both have.

Dear Boomer,

Thank you for saving my brother. I tried to talk him
out of bringing that gun to school. He was just so angry.
Uncle Karl and his boys stoked a fire in him something
fierce. Guess it's like you said, he's got one of those
demons, too. I saw it yesterday—the demon. Not live in
the flesh. It was in Billy's eyes. It scared the pants off me.
I tried telling him killing was a sin. At least that's what
Pastor Jones and Granma always say. Billy didn't care. He
was ready to kill that Spencer Blaylock. But my brother
he couldn't kill no dog. Billy is in Juvie now. That's the
place they call the jail for kids. I miss him. But I'm glad
he's away from Uncle Karl and not pushing up daisies
like Mama.

Your Friend,
Lizzie Miller

Dear Lizzie,

I'm sorry I couldn't do something to help you and Billy sooner. You should be able to go to school without being picked on. I've been talking to the higher-ups, people BIGGER than the Brass, and we've come up with a plan. Something I hope will fix things. Principal Taylor will share it with the school soon. I talked to Nurse Young, told her about your Uncle Karl and how you're not allergic to dogs. She said you can visit me if you want to chat about things or just share a popsicle. We have some rocket ones in our hooch.

Fur-ever yours,
Boomer

One Month Later…

Blue Ridge Elementary School Announcements:

Goooooood morning, Sea Lions! Principal Taylor, here. Happy morning to you. Ms. Libby wanted to let you know that the library book return has been removed. Books will now be returned to the circulation counter inside the library. Lunch today will be macaroni and cheese, steamed carrots, and devil's food cake for dessert. Finally, superintendent Blaylock approved Blue Ridge County School's first Bullying Awareness and Prevention Month. This will become an annual event. Staff and faculty in collaboration with SRO

Bradley and Boomer will be implementing training for our Sea Lion family throughout the upcoming weeks. Now, go attack the day Sea Lions. Remember: Be Brave. Be Brilliant. Be Bold. Be you.

CONVICT CODE

James L'Etoile

Convicts hustle and manipulate their way through prison life. It's part of the convict code—get what you can, while you can, and get over on the cops. That's why Officer Billy Hutton hated working on Fish Row. The thirty cells on the fifth tier of 2-Building were reserved for new arrivals coming into Folsom Prison. Each man was an unknown. It was called Fish Row because the prison was like a huge fish tank and the new arrivals were either sharks, or bait fish—predator or prey. Serving two years, or two hundred. A cop-killer, or dope dealer—held in quarantine until their records were screened and each man classified and rehoused safely in the general population. Until then, they resided on Fish Row and only leaving their cells for the hundred-yard slog to the dining room, which left the cons nothing but time to scheme and manipulate.

Fish Row wasn't like out on the yard where two hundred convicts mixed it up, with an occasional warning shot from a tower officer's rifle when one inmate stabbed another for breaking the convict code. "Don't snitch" being the First Convict Commandment.

On this graveyard shift, everything on the row was locked down. The cells were double locked, their tier gates closed, and twenty-eight new fish convicts from the reception center were tucked in their bunks for an unsettled first night's rest in the Big House. Fish didn't know how to be convicts yet. Despite no television, radios, or personal property, they were a loud, needy bunch. Exaggerated tales of street cred were swapped to puff up their gangster status, something which always struck Hutton as funny because these master criminals were entombed behind granite walls, defining them as felony failures. This busload from the Los Angeles County Jail was no different.

A folded paper message, or "kite," as it was called in prison lingo, skittered down the concrete tier and landed at the gate as Officer Hutton climbed to the landing.

The tightly folded paper triangle bore a penciled "C/O" on the front. Hutton unfold the kite and read the short, hand-printed message. An inmate who scrawled his name as "Johnson" in cell 5A-4, claimed the other man in the cell smuggled heroin in from the county jail. At the bottom of the note, Johnson added a PS: "I don't want no more time because I'm short to the house."

Hutton glanced at his watch. A half-an-hour until shift change. Of course, the snitch would wait until the end of shift to grow a conscience.

He took the message downstairs to the Sergeant's desk. "Hey Sarge, we got us a guy packing the rabbit up on five." Hutton handed the kite to Sergeant Terri Sanchez.

The sergeant grinned at the old school reference to a convict's rectal stash. "5A-4?" Let's see who we've got in there." Sergeant Sanchez tapped the computer keyboard to bring up the records of two men assigned to the cell. "I'm still getting used to having records online. A year ago, I'd have to send an escort officer from custody to go pull a key for the records office and bring the files down."

"Progress," Hutton muttered. He looked at the screen over her shoulder. "Lawrence Johnson, twenty-four years old, from L.A., doing two-years-eight months for a carjacking. Apparently, he pulled an Airsoft gun on a pregnant driver. Says he doesn't have any history of drugs, or connection with known gang factions."

"Here's his cellie," the sergeant said. "Tyson McCloud got

out less than a year ago from Corcoran. Got picked up on second degree murder and a fifteen-to-life sentence. Says he came out of L.A. County's High-Power when they shipped him to us."

"He was in their lockup unit? We should have put him in Ad Seg when he drove up yesterday," Hutton said.

"The Watch Commander must have missed it when they screened the bus. I'll get the Lieutenant to start a lock up order and investigate it. Meanwhile, you know what you have to do. Grab Smith and go shake that cell down."

"Aw, Sarge, can't you let second watch deal with this?" Officer Smith whined from a chair near the sergeant's desk.

"Get to it, Smitty," the sergeant said.

Hutton and Smith made it back to the fifth tier where an inmate worker waited for them at the grill gate. "Morning officers. Want me to sweep and mop the tier? Looks like it needs it."

"Start on B side," Hutton said. "We got to move some guys around."

"I can stay out of your way."

"B-side. You'll be out of the way over there."

The tier tender did as he was told, but he didn't look happy about it. Hutton knew the convict worker's eagerness meant he was supposed to pick up the drug stash and move it out to the yard.

Hutton and Smith rapped on the cell bars in front of the fourth cell. "You two. Back up to the bars and cuff up."

"What you want?" McCloud asked from his bunk.

"I want you over here at the bars, McCloud," Hutton said.

Johnson, the inmate who signed the note, got off his bunk and backed up to the cell bars with his hands behind his back. Officer Smith put the cuffs on Johnson and waited.

"Let's go McCloud."

McCloud, all six-foot-three of him, ambled from his bunk and glared down at Hutton. "What's this about?"

"It's about cuffing up."

McCloud's face tensed as he considered another response. He shook his head and backed up to the bars.

Hutton put him in cuffs and then keyed the cell lock. "Let's go, guys."

"Where to?" McCloud said.

"Sergeant wants to see you."

They went down the stairs to the holding cages in the rotunda and locked the two fish in separate cages apart from one another.

Hutton and Smith trudged back up to the fifth tier and began searching the cell, dividing it in half.

Ten minutes into the search, Hutton found a plastic wrapped bindle wedged behind the unflushed stainless-steel toilet. "Got it."

"Good, you get to write the report," Smith said.

Hutton took the contraband down to the Sergeant's desk, bagged it and began writing the report. He glanced over at McCloud who looked more worried than upset at being caught.

Hutton stood in front of the holding cages. "I found something that could buy you a whole lot of trouble."

McCloud chested up in the holding cage. "I don't know what you're talking about."

Hutton pointed to the bagged contraband on the desk. "Thing is, even though it wasn't found in your possession, we can tell where it was."

McCloud looked confused.

"Let me break it down for you. You pulled that turd-shaped gift basket out of your ass. Your DNA is all over it."

It was a bluff, but McCloud began to pull at the handcuffs. "I got nothing to do with whatever it was you found." He turned to Johnson in the next cage and spit at him. "You. You snitched me out? You're dead."

"Who were you supposed to get it to?" Hutton asked.

McCloud fell quiet.

Officers from the prison's investigative squad entered the

rotunda and checked in with the Sergeant. She pointed out the two men in the holding cages.

"What's going on?" Johnson asked from the far cage.

"The Squad is going to interview you both and take you to Ad Seg."

"They're taking us to the hole?" Johnson said. His eyes went wide, and he looked from the Squad officers to Hutton.

"Take McCloud first. I'll finish up the paperwork and escort Johnson over in a couple minutes," Hutton said.

A squad officer unlocked the holding cage and pulled McCloud from the cell by his elbow, and he pulled away from the officer's grip.

"He's gonna regret that move," Hutton said.

A second squad officer pulled a canister of OC Pepper spray from his belt and shot a thick stream of orange slime into the cage, striking McCloud in the chest.

McCloud instantly began coughing and snot ran down his chin. His eyes squinted against the powerful chemical agent.

Johnson got a whiff of the spray, and his eyes began to water.

The squad wrenched McCloud out of the holding cage and stood him under a nearby shower, rinsing the chemical agent from his body.

Once McCloud was out of earshot, Johnson whispered, "You found it, right? Why do I gotta go to the hole?"

"You'll have to unless you want everyone to think you're a rat. The write up for drug possession will be dismissed, and you'll be cut loose."

"You heard him. He knows I told."

"He doesn't know anything. I'll make sure he thinks the information came from someone else."

"You promise?"

"Dude, it happens all the time. I'll take you to Ad Seg and when they ask you what exercise yard you want, tell them you don't have troubles with anyone. Just don't go to the yard—stay in your house. Got that?"

"Yeah, you sure that will work?"

"I'll let the hearing officer know what you did—the note and all."

"Make sure you let him know. I don't need to catch more time."

Hutton unlocked the holding cage and escorted Johnson across the yard to Ad Seg. The gang shot callers eyed Johnson and if they knew he'd given up their smuggled dope, Johnson would be feeling the sharpened end of a toothbrush in his back. The tower officers tracked the escort across the yard, ready to fire on inmates who tried rushing Hutton or his prisoner. Once in the Ad Seg cellblock, Hutton checked in with the desk officer to make sure he knew to keep the new arrival away from the Aryan Brotherhood thugs who ran most of the drug traffic in the prison. If there was a white inmate with drugs, they had their hands in it.

Back in his unit, Hutton finished all the reports and wrote a confidential memorandum to the hearing officer detailing Johnson's actions which resulted in the discovery of an ounce of black tar heroin. He'd kept his promise to Johnson. Maybe the kid could put this behind him and get back out on the streets and make a life for himself.

With his report completed, Hutton ended his shift and hit the gate. He felt good about what he accomplished and maybe gave Johnson a chance to change his life.

Hutton remembered to roll down the top half of his jumpsuit so people couldn't tag him as a prison cop while he drove home. Even in his own neighborhood, it wasn't safe to make it known where he worked. Inmate families, gangs, and anti-incarceration protestors were known to harass officers at home. The hours and irregular days off made it hard to establish relationships outside of other cops who understood the grind. Usually, Hutton was good about compartmentalizing his life—keeping work and home separate. He'd seen too many of his friends' marriages and home lives ruined because they couldn't leave the trauma and violence behind the walls when they came home. More than a few officers he worked with quit after drunk driving arrests or being caught up in domestic violence. Prison has a way of seeping into your soul if you weren't careful. The lifestyle led to isolation and everything that went along with it, so much that Hutton looked forward to getting back on the job and the normality of the prison routine.

His first night back on Fish Row was quiet. Everyone on the tier was scheduled for classification in the morning. They'd all be rehoused in general population or transferred to another prison. Two busloads from reception centers were due tomorrow afternoon. More new fish in the tank.

Hutton walked down the tier, picking up outgoing mail resting on the cell bars. He passed the vacant cell where McCloud and Johnson had been housed. He paused and backed up a step. In the darkness of the empty cell, a glint of something white got his attention. It was under the left-hand bunk and Hutton lit it up with his flashlight.

A scrap of paper no larger than half of an index card lay on the concrete floor. Inmates tore up legal documents all the time—a convict paper shredder—to keep sensitive information out of the hands of snooping cellmates, or gang enforcers who would use it to extort rent.

This rolled and discolored paper scrap had a Los Angeles County Superior Court heading and a small piece of plastic wrap sticking to it. It was greasy from whatever lubricant McCloud had used in the county jail. It probably fell out of his boxer shorts when he came out of his cell.

Hutton donned a pair of protective gloves, got on one knee, and reached for the scrap. In the light he confirmed it was a scrap of court transcript, but it was too large.

"What the hell?"

Hutton took the piece of document downstairs and bagged it. In the light, he confirmed the torn court transcript page had wrapped a keister stash like the one he found behind the toilet, except it was at least double in size.

He grabbed the phone on the desk and called the Ad Seg Unit.

"ASU, Officer Benjamin."

"Hey Benny, it's Hutton."

"What's up man?"

"We brought two guys over there a couple days ago?"

"Oh yeah. You heard right?"

"Heard what?"

"One of them got stabbed up on the exercise yard over here. Didn't make it to the Med Center."

"What?"

"Yeah, dude stayed in his cell for the first day, then I guess he felt he'd be cool with the homies on the White yard and got hit as soon as he got out there."

"Damn. I told Johnson to stay off the yard until his hearing."

"It wasn't Johnson. McCloud's the one who got hit."

"McCloud?"

"Yeah, I guess the white boys blame him for losing the dope he was supposed to bring up from county."

"How did they pin losing the stash on him?" Hutton asked.

"You know how it is. Secrets and cell bars don't mix. It was the usual yard with ten guys out there and no one saw anything. They had to be pissed at him for losing the stuff, right?"

"Yeah. Hey thanks, Benny. Take care over there."

"Always."

Hutton hung up the phone while an unsettled feeling crept over him. McCloud getting taken out on the yard didn't make sense. Sure, he lost a dope shipment. It happens. It was a convict's "job" to try and find ways to beat the system. There was always risk smuggling drugs into a prison. Most of the illicit contraband was discovered before it landed into the network behind the walls. McCloud was only doing what convicts do and wasn't a snitch.

One of the Investigative Squad officers passed by the desk

and spotted the evidence bag on the surface. "You digging up more business for me, Hutton?"

"I dunno. Maybe? Hey, Collins, you processed that bindle of heroin I pulled out of McCloud's cell, right?"

"Yep. Good find on that one. An ounce of black tar."

"How much would something like that be worth in here?"

"Almost two-grand, double the street value."

"That would be enough to get killed over—McCloud, I mean."

"Apparently," Officer Collins said.

Hutton glanced at the scrap of paper in the evidence bag. When you processed that dope, did they happen to use a piece of court transcript to roll it up?"

"Yeah, he did. Guess he didn't have a balloon, or enough plastic wrap. I've seen it before. McCloud compressed the dope with the transcript paper, then lubed-up the plastic wrap before he hid it where the sun don't shine."

Hutton pushed the baggie toward Officer Collins. "Found more of it up in the cell."

The officer lifted the bag and held it to the light. "Huh."

"What?"

"The dope I processed was wrapped and compressed with legal paperwork like that. Except it seemed—I don't know—fresh. If you can call anything pulled from a convict's ass, fresh."

"Is rewrapping it common?"

"I don't know about common. But after a long bus ride from county jail, things get a little bent out of shape—so to speak. When they get here, they've been known to repackage it into smaller bindles to make it easier to move. The one I processed used court transcripts from McCloud's case."

"He admit the stuff was his?"

"Didn't have to. It literally had his name on it. Swore he didn't know anything about it—like they all do."

"You interview his cellie, Johnson?"

"He's the one who tipped you off to the stash. Yeah, said

he saw the guy hide the package and claimed it was supposed to go to the white boys on the yard. Why?"

"I dunno. Something doesn't feel right about this whole thing."

"Doesn't matter much now. McCloud's dead and gone and Johnson got kicked to the general pop this morning."

"That was quick. I thought he'd try to work a transfer to get away from the Aryan Brotherhood."

The Squad Officer shrugged. "I guess he figures his secret died with McCloud."

"Sorry to bust up your party, boys. We got work to do," Sergeant Sanchez said handing Hutton a copy of the daily movement sheet. The computer printout listed all intake, transfers, and cell moves inside the prison.

Hutton's eye caught Johnson's name and prison number being released from Ad Seg and his new general population housing in 3-Building. The movement sheet let prison staff keep track of inmate housing, but it also helped ensure an inmate's property ended up in the right place.

"Hey, Sarge. Did anyone pack up Johnson's property after he got locked up?"

"Second watch was supposed to take care of it. Look for a property receipt online."

Hutton scooted his chair to the computer terminal. He tapped in Johnson's name and prison number and clicked on the tab which listed approved property. Sure enough, second watch officers packed up all the property in the cell and shipped it to the property room. The receipt listed the usual personal hygiene items—deodorant, toothpaste, and soap. As a Fish Row inmate, he'd only have minimal personal property and Johnson's consisted of a pencil, envelopes, stamps, ten sheets of state-issued writing paper, and one large envelope of legal materials.

Hutton logged off even more confused. He didn't know what he expected to find, but there wasn't anything other than the prison-issued supplies and legal papers in Johnson's property.

Prison-issued. No, that couldn't be.

"Sarge, I'm gonna run down to property and get Johnson's stuff over to 3-Building."

"You adopt that kid or what? Yeah, go on."

The inmate property room was a cavernous space stacked high with television sets, musical instruments, handicraft projects, and cardboard boxes emblazoned with the inmate's name and prison number. The crusty old Sergeant who ran the place demanded every box be filed in order according to the last two digits of the prison number. Tedious work, but he could find any inmate's property in seconds.

"Hey Hutton, what brings out to our little boutique?" Sergeant Corin asked.

"Just a little window-shopping. Looking for Johnson's stuff, last two of 07."

Corin pointed down the shelving unit on the far left.

Hutton spotted the single brown cardboard box he was looking for. It was light, befitting a new arrival and not filled with the accumulated cellblock treasures collected by lifers.

He placed the box on a table and opened the lid. True to the property receipt online there was very little inside. The ten envelopes were all empty, the ten stamps were all accounted for, and the ten empty sheets of paper were still stuck together as they were when issued to Johnson.

All accounted for. Then what did Johnson use to write the note that he sent down the tier snitching about the dope in the cell?

Hutton pulled the sentencing transcript from a brown manila envelope. It wasn't much, maybe twenty pages or so. He thumbed through the document making sure there wasn't contraband hidden within the pages. Nothing dropped from the individual pages, but a single sheet in the middle of the document was torn in half.

Hutton placed the transcript face up with the torn page exposed. He snagged the evidence bag from his jumpsuit pocket and laid the scrap of paper next to the ripped page.

It lined up an exact match. The rows of text connected, and the case number matched the court docket.

"Son-of-a-bitch!"

Hutton asked Sergeant Corin where the property of deceased inmates was stored. McCloud's property box stood out in its pristine condition. A Fish Row inmate got caught up in the tank and learned who the sharks really were.

The box held a bit more than Johnson's. There were a handful of canteen items—top ramen, chips, and cookies. He wasn't in lockup long enough to get a regular canteen draw, but Hutton knew other inmates regularly kicked down some of their stash to new Ad Seg arrivals. Maybe. Or lure him out to the yard for the hit.

The sentencing transcript was on top, and the first page was torn in half. The dope was wrapped in the paper. Like the Squad Officer said, the drugs had McCloud's name on it.

Hutton grabbed the thin pad of state-issued paper and counted out nine sheets. One was missing.

He grabbed a pencil from the property table and ran it lightly back and forth on the topmost sheet. Hutton's gut clenched as the message appeared on the page. There was no signature. McCloud wrote the note. Johnson had taken it, signed it, added the "I'm short to the house" message, and claimed it as his own.

Hutton flashed to McCloud in the holding cell. He'd been scared.

A quick look through a small address book in the property box and Hutton knew. The handwriting matched McCloud. He wasn't a handwriting analyst, but the peculiar slant on the signature and post-script was different than the text of the note.

Why would McCloud rat on himself?

He wouldn't.

He placed the dead man's property back on the shelf. How could he have missed it?

Hutton had been played. He fumed as he crossed the yard back to the cellblock. Johnson's meager property was tucked in an envelope under his arm.

In 3-Building, Hutton found Johnson hanging out near the barber chair with a couple of Aryan Brotherhood shot callers.

"You get a job already, Johnson?"

"Hey, Officer Hutton. I'm on the waitlist, but told the Sergeant I don't mind pitching in."

Hutton tossed the property envelope to Hutton. "Here's your stuff. Thought you'd want it."

"Thanks, man. And thanks for keeping your word about getting the charges dropped." Johnson grinned.

"Shame about what happened to McCloud."

"Some folks don't like it when their stuff gets lost. Shoulda known better."

"How'd you keep the crew off your ass for losing their dope?"

"That was all McCloud—"

"I called L.A. County. I wanted to know how a guy in High Power could get that much heroin and wrap it in his court transcripts."

The two white convicts began paying attention to the discussion. One flexed his neck when Hutton mentioned the county lockup unit.

"Samuels, you were in High Power down south, weren't you?"

"Uh hum. Musta changed since I been there. We couldn't have no property. We never got legal papers back then."

"No, they still don't," Hutton said.

Johnson swallowed hard.

"How else would he pack his dope with his own transcripts?" Johnson said.

"He didn't. You did. L.A. County has an informant says you were supposed to take two ounces of dope to the Ad Seg unit here."

"That's all bullshit,"

"McCloud didn't want anything to do with it, did he? You even know where he was in county?"

Johnson shuffled and tried to draw his white buddies to his aide. "Who cares what he got locked up for. Don't much matter now. He played fast and loose with someone else's stuff—I had nothing to do with it."

"Well, someone sent me that kite saying there was dope in the cell, right? McCloud got killed behind it. If he was locked up in High Power, how would he have wrapped that bindle with *your* legal paperwork? It's a mystery, isn't it?" Hutton took a step away.

The two white boys put it together and closed on Johnson. One clamped a hand on Johnson's shoulder. "We need to go have a talk,"

The blood drained from Johnson's face.

"Hutton wait."

Hutton turned back. "Yeah?"

"I need to talk to you a sec."

"I gotta get back to 2-Building."

Johnson tried to step away from his white supremacist buddies and they held him back.

"Officer, you gotta help me. It was my stuff."

"You set up a solid white dude?" Samuels said, the veins in his neck bulging.

"I didn't have a choice. He was going to rat me out. I did my part. I came through…"

"So, you out-ratted him?" Hutton said.

"I go home in less than a year."

"You're not goin' home," Samuels said flatly.

The other white power shot caller slipped away from the tense conversation and headed to the main yard.

"Please Hutton, you gotta help me."

"Last time I helped you, it was all a lie."

"Listen. I did what I had to do. You'd have done the same."

"No, I don't think I would pack dope in my butt."

"Come on man. I need to lock up. I want protective

custody."

"You're saying you smuggled heroin into a state prison? Took half of it into Ad Seg when you got locked up? And to top it off, you conspired with the Aryan Brotherhood to have McCloud killed?"

"Yes, yes, I admit all of it. Now get me outta here."

"You get all that, Officer Collins?"

The Squad Officer waved from the second-tier landing. He held a directional microphone and digital recorder.

"Got it."

"Looks like you won't be going home next year after all. Bringing drugs into a prison and conspiracy to commit murder are felonies. You'll be old and grey before you hit the streets again."

"You can't do that. I was found not guilty in my hearing."

"This is for trafficking drugs into the prison—whole different crime. Not to mention setting up McCloud for murder."

"You'll be spending the rest of your life in protective custody," Officer Hutton said, cuffing Johnson for the walk across the yard to Ad Seg.

Hutton watched Officer Collins escort Johnson from the building. He turned to Samuels and said, "I'd hate to do as much time as he's looking at in protective custody."

Samuels grunted. "Thanks for taking out the trash. I have a feeling he won't spend too much time in the hole." He shrugged and dragged a thick thumb across his throat. "Thou shalt not snitch."

MYSTERIOUS WAYS

Quintin Peterson

The dreadful crime scene was on Half Street, SW. I was the first officer to arrive on the scene.

I was working the Chief's high visibility patrols crime fighting initiative dubbed All Hands on Deck (AHOD) – A-HOD we pronounce it. Consequently, I was temporarily reassigned from Narcotics Branch, where I'm assigned as a detective, and ordered back into uniform to push a scout car in the First District on July 6th and 7th, working 1800 – 0230 hours.

At about 2100 hours on the night of the 6th, the driver of a silver-colored Oldsmobile Aurora evaded the roadblock aka "Safety Compliance Checkpoint" that my AHOD team was operating on M Street at Delaware Avenue, SW. I lit up the marked Chase Car I was assigned to and followed the Aurora, siren off.

I keyed the mic of the Chase Car's radio and gave the dispatcher the vehicle's description, tag number, and direction of flight.

I had expected the driver to turn left off of Half Street SW onto N Street, then make a right onto South Capitol Street and flee across the Frederick Douglass Bridge into Anacostia, but instead he barreled on, eastbound on Half Street. In the 1400 block, the driver lost control of the careening automobile. The hurtling juggernaut jumped the curb and crushed a young girl and her mother against an old tree.

I skidded to a halt at the intersection of Half and O just as a gunman I learned later was the enraged husband and father of the victims strode from his town house toward the Aurora and opened fire on the driver with a revolver…like he was prepared for this calamity. The driver returned fire.

By the time I threw my police cruiser in Park and jumped out, the gunfight was over. I drew my Glock and took aim as I approached the car wreck with caution.

When I looked inside the Aurora, I instantly recognized the driver. He lived close to here on I Street, SW, in a public housing project near luxury apartment complexes and town houses, within walking distance of Arena Stage, the Wharf, and L'Enfant Plaza.

"Oh hell," I groaned.

Above the deployed airbag, I could tell by the suspect's blank stare that he was no longer a threat. He did not look as though he'd died in pain, despite the multiple gunshot wounds he'd sustained and the smoldering V8 engine resting in his lap. He simply looked surprised.

I holstered my service sidearm and sighed.

I removed my flashlight from my Sam Browne belt and shined it into the wreck. Finally, I spotted the suspect's gun on the passenger floor mat. It was safe where it was, so I left it for evidence technicians to collect.

I stepped toward the front of the car and caught a glimpse of the mother and daughter pinned between the auto and the tree. I winced and turned away. It was the stuff that nightmares are made of.

Quickly, I moved to the man lying in the street. I removed my smartphone from its carrying case attached to my Sam Browne belt and took a few photos of the man holding his gun. I then put away my cell phone, snapped on a pair of surgical gloves I had stored in a pouch attached to my Sam Browne, and took possession of the dead man's S&W .357 Magnum. I secured the weapon by tucking it into the front of my BDU pants.

The dispatcher came back with a hit on the Aurora's tag

number. The vehicle had been reported stolen.

I took my radio from my Sam Browne and called for assistance, including EMTs, not because anything could be done for the casualties, but because it was procedure.

Outraged and horrified neighbors crowded me. A tearful middle aged white woman identified the dead family as the Horwitzes: Stan, the Neighborhood Watch Block Captain, his wife Dawn, and their eight-year-old daughter Rose. Stan was some kind of medical doctor with a private practice.

I thanked her and asked her and everyone who had actually witnessed the tragedy to please stand back and stand by to give statements to detectives when they arrived.

I went to the trunk of the Chase Car, unlocked the lid, and flung it open. I grabbed a large roll of yellow police line tape and went to work securing the crime scene, tying tape off on a bus stop sign, a utility pole, fence posts…

The EMTs long gone, the disgruntled 1D Watch Commander now quarterbacking the game, I stood at one end of the block on the inside of the area cordoned off by yellow police line tape while another officer stood at the other end of the block, guarding the bloody crime scene. More mortified than appalled, I surveyed the catastrophe. As spectators gawked, evidence technicians and detectives processed the crime scene; detectives and uniformed officers took statements from witnesses; and the police tow truck driver prepared to pull the wrecked Aurora off of what remained of Rose and Dawn.

I wiped sweat from my brow. The heat was stifling. The city was in the grip of a heat wave with temperatures in the triple digits for days, the air so muggy it was like breathing through a wet army blanket: air you can wear. Still, I played it cool and effectively concealed my thousand-yard stare. I suppressed my emotions and acted natural. No one would suspect that I was responsible for this tragedy, and I wouldn't voluntarily disclose that information. I'd keep my shame to myself.

The weight of the world on my shoulders, I lit a Newport with my trusty Zippo *Anarchy* lighter and reflected on this career I have been pursuing for most of my adult life, dealing with life and death situations on a daily basis and coping with the consequences of things I have done in the line of duty. The choices you make can cost you. In police work, as in life, even when you do the right thing sometimes things turn out horribly wrong. Such dilemmas come with this job, which is filled with pitfalls one cannot anticipate.

The job cost me my first marriage and my family; my own children now strangers to me. Police work, with its constant shift changes, makes cultivating any meaningful relationship difficult. Few people can accept being married to a ghost. But that was one of the pitfalls I was aware of.

Tonight's catastrophe was not...

Reminiscing was a convenient defense mechanism to cope with my guilty conscience, so I retreated down memory lane. Looking back was easy; facing the present and looking toward the future was hard. Hell, the crime scene was where I lived when I was a kid, right in front of my old address, 1417 Half Street, SW; a six-unit, red brick apartment building built circa the early 1940's. Cozy units with screened balconies, all sharing a view of the spacious courtyard in back where children could play under the watchful eyes of their parents and the shade of grand old oak trees.

Way back then, children played with G.I. Joes and Barbie dolls, and played board games and sports and arguments were settled by way of fistfights instead of with guns and knives. Radio airwaves were filled with hits such as *Under the Boardwalk* by The Drifters, *Baby Love* and *Where Did I Love Go* by The Supremes, *Wishin' and Hopin'* by Dusty Springfield, and *Dancing in the Street* by Martha Reeves and the Vandellas, shared with all within earshot of the dozens of portable 9-volt battery transistor radios in any given block, all tuned to the same radio station dependent upon which station was jamming at the moment, either WOL or WOOK. When a particular favorite aired, everyone would tune in to that station. And we all sang along.

Back then the neighborhood did not look much different than it does now. The elementary school I attended down the street, William Syphax, closed its doors long ago, yet still stands, the historic landmark reincarnated as the Syphax Condominium Complex; the residences of the James Creek Dwelling public housing project across the street from Syphax is still occupied; the Friendly Food Market on the corner of Half and O, now owned and operated by Koreans, is the same building that once was known as Gold Star Market, which back in the day was owned and operated by the Goldsteins, who also lived above the store. When I returned an empty soda bottle for the two cents deposit I could buy a bag of Wise Potato Chips, a bottle of Pepsi, and a Hershey candy bar and get ten cents change back from a quarter.

The other public housing projects nearby are still there as well, but expensive townhomes have replaced the old row houses built in the 1900's that stood directly across the street from my childhood home, and a block over on South Capitol Street where the dome of the United States Capitol is in sight, Nationals Stadium now looms, and upscale apartment and condominium complexes have risen behind it. The have, have less, and have not coexisting side by side. And tonight, the wealthy and the poor dead here together on Half Street.

Overtaken by guilt once again, I slowly shook my head, lost in self-recrimination.

Snoop Dogg's *Gin and Juice* began playing somewhere…coming from one of the open apartment windows where the curious watched the spectacle on their street. And just like that, I flashed back to South Capitol Street, SW last summer…

***

Last July on a hot Friday night like this one I was working high visibility patrol in uniform, "redeployed" in the Seventh District, on the far end of South Capitol Street in the Washington Highlands, near the D.C./Maryland line where Southern Avenue, SE borders Oxon Hill. Around 0145 hours, the operator of a stolen black Crown Vic attempted to evade a Safety Compliance Checkpoint Patrol Support Team (PST) Group A that was operating in the 4500 block of South Cap. When the driver rolled up on our checkpoint, he immediately executed a frantic U turn and before Officer TD Neilson could put the Chase Car in gear, the stolen Crown Vic, tires smoking and squealing, smashed into a mighty oak tree on the southwest side of South Cap near our checkpoint. So close, my second wife, pretty young thing Officer Ursula Kane, recklessly dashed toward the smashed Crown Vic. Naturally, I followed her.

The rest of our checkpoint team looked on as we sprinted toward the Crown Vic just as its doors sprang open and four males poured out of the wreck, Snoop Dogg's *Gin and Juice* blaring from its radio. The suspects hoofed it in four different directions. Ursula and I dug in and stayed on the driver. TD Neilson followed in the Chase Car.

Our thug was agile; chasing him had been like trying to catch a hat on a windy day. Just when my fingers were about to grab hold of his clothing, he would break and cut in a different direction, juking me like a running back.

The rabbit ran behind an apartment complex up on a hill in the 4400 block of South Capitol Street, SW and then cut between the buildings and ran around front, back down a steep hill toward the street. I increased my speed…and realized too late just how steep that hill was.

My mistake was devastating. I lost my footing and rolled head over heels down what seemed to me to be a mountainside. I could hear Officer Kane laughing at the top of the hill behind me as I tumbled like clothes in a dryer.

When I finally regained my footing, I shook my head and then spotted the suspect running in the street, back toward the 4500 block of South Cap.

Disheveled and dusty, the knee of my left pant leg torn and bloody, I continued my foot pursuit. Ursula continued laughing as she followed me.

I finally got a good grip on the suspect's wife beater tee shirt and slung the little man against a parked Chevy Tahoe.

The foot chase over, Officer Kane hung back and caught her breath.

I spun the suspect around, clamped the cuffs on him, and then spun him back around to face me. I summoned my best Clint Eastwood squint and stared him down.

As I huffed and puffed, I was filled with pride. I nodded as I thought, *the old man's still got it. Yeah! I ran down a young'n! Laugh at* that, *Ursula. Yeah.*

I read him his rights, but he did not acknowledge he understood them. I looked in his eyes and nobody was home.

 The suspect heaved and threw up on my combat boots. I caught a whiff of his liquor-soaked body and finally realized that the kid was drunk. I had caught the suspect not because I had outrun him but because he simply could not run anymore.

This apprehension was *not* a victory for senior citizens everywhere.

Under a streetlamp, I looked the suspect over and wondered how old he was. He had a beginner's moustache, but he looked like he was only twelve years old. Maybe thirteen.

I went through his pockets looking for ID and found a wallet which contained a fake DC driver's license claiming that he was Denzel Middleton, age 31. Thirty-one, my ass.

A junior high school photo ID and other identification in his wallet confirmed he was fourteen years old.

As the adrenaline rush began to subside, I noticed the pain in my knee. I examined the area and saw my scraped flesh bleeding beneath the tear in my slacks.

Officer Neilson parked the Chase Car alongside us and climbed out. He walked around the car and looked me over. He then pointed down at my torn pants and said, "Need a paramedic, partner?"

I shook my head.

Ursula pointed at the rip in my pants. "Oh," she said. "You need some ointment for your boo-boo." Without missing a beat, she added, "You need a shoeshine too."

"You've got to hose them off first," Officer Neilson observed. "I'm not transporting him, Luther. He is *not* going to mess up my cruiser. Call for a paddy wagon..."

Ursula tisk-tisked Neilson. "That's politically incorrect. We don't call them paddy wagons anymore. Paddy is a racial slur..."

"Okay." Neilson conceded. "A wagon. They can hose it down."

As if on cue, the boy leaned forward and vomited again. Ursula and Officer Neilson jumped back.

"I'll call for a wagon," my wife said.

My partners and I divided the work between us. While we waited for the transport vehicle to arrive, Ursula did the paperwork on the recovered stolen auto and the accident report and arranged for the Crown Vic to be towed to the impoundment lot of the Seventh District headquarters located on Alabama Avenue SE, and contacted the owner to advise him of the status of his vehicle and where he could pick it up; and Officer Neilson and I worked on the PD 251 Incident Report, the PD 163 Prosecution Report, and PD 81 Property Receipt for personal items taken from Denzel.

We had put a good dent in the arrest paperwork by the time the transport vehicle arrived. After the transport officer loaded Denzel into the patrol wagon, we all climbed into TD's cruiser and followed the wagon to D.C. General Hospital, located on Capitol Hill in the vicinity of the Stadium/Armory Complex; D.C. Jail; the City Morgue, home of the Office of the Chief

Medical Examiner for the District of Columbia; and Congressional Cemetery.

Due to Denzel's medical condition and his status as a prisoner who had not yet been booked, we could not put him in one of the treatment holding cells in D.C. General's Strong Room where he would be guarded by MPD officers on duty there; we had to guard Denzel ourselves. It was a long night, so it was not hard for me to find a few minutes to clean and bandage my wounded knee. Too bad there isn't a treatment for wounded pride.

We finished filling out the paperwork as we took turns guarding Denzel in the triage area of the ER while he was treated for alcohol poisoning. All the while he remained handcuffed to a gurney, an IV in his left arm below his "2pac Lives" tattoo.

Denzel's doctor commended us for our good deed. He assured us that if we had not brought Denzel to the hospital when we did, he would have died. The scrawny kid's blood alcohol level was 0.49. Denzel had nearly made a fatal error, but now the teenager had been given a second chance to live and learn. Thanks to us.

Ursula, church girl that she was, looked at me and said, "God moves in mysterious ways, His wonders to perform."

I could not argue with that.

Denzel Middleton would have died. Wow. I had no idea that I was saving a life when I caught him; I was just doing my job.

Saving a life is a great feeling. My partners and I did not discuss it, but I believe they felt the same pride and self-satisfaction. They must have. We were fighting the good fight, and this was a victory.

Early that morning while my partners continued to guard our prisoner at the hospital, I responded to D.C. Superior Court to "paper" our case. I discussed the case with a prosecutor, and he decided not to prosecute, despite the fact that Denzel had a lengthy history of Unauthorized Use of a

Vehicle offenses. He argued that the prosecution could not prove that the lad was operating the stolen vehicle; he'd probably simply been a passenger, also negating the additional charges of Driving While Intoxicated and Driving Without a License. My argument that three police officers had witnessed him behind the wheel of the stolen car did not hold water. The prosecutor shook his head and said, "It would just be your word against his. I'm sorry."

We continued to guard our prisoner until he could be transported to the Youth Division and processed prior to his release. It was a tedious undertaking.

At one point early that afternoon, when Denzel was lucid, I asked the fourteen-year-old what he'd been drinking last night.

"Thug's Brew," he grunted.

"What's that?"

"A fifth of Hennessy and a bottle of Moët," he told me.

I asked, "The four of you – who were in that car – shared a fifth of cognac and a bottle of champagne? Is that all you had to drink?"

Denzel slowly shook his head. "No, man. We *each* had our *own* bottles of Hennessy and Moët."

"Each!" I said.

"Yeah," Denzel assured me. "We chugged them. First one to finish was the winner."

"Who won?" I asked.

He swelled with pride and replied, "Me."

I snickered, shook my head and said, "That Thug's Brew is expensive. In more ways than one. You are lucky to be alive, son. You know that, don't you?"

Denzel shrugged.

I said, "You keep that up and you won't live very long. And if you keep getting behind the wheel when you're drunk out of your mind, you're going to take somebody with you."

Denzel shrugged.

The doctor released Denzel at about 1600 hours. We then transported him to the Youth Division way the hell up on Rhode Island Avenue, NE for processing.

We booked Denzel and asked the desk sergeant to hold the kid until a rep from Child and Family Services took custody of him because his parents or legal guardian could not be located. God knows we tried. When we found that his mom's listed phone numbers were no longer in service, TD went the extra mile and drove by Denzel's house at 0400 hours, but no one was home.

When the work was finally done, TD, Ursula, and I barely had enough time to go home, shower, change our uniforms, and report back to the Seventh District station on Alabama Avenue, SE for roll call at 1800 hours.

Up all night, guarding a prisoner, all that paperwork, all that driving. Whew! We were tired. But it was a good kind of tired. We felt great. We had job satisfaction. We had saved a life…maybe more than one, and were fighting the good fight for truth, justice, and the American Way. And made some decent overtime to boot.

The morgue wagon pulled up and stopped in front of the yellow police line tape on my end of Half Street SW. I walked over to the utility pole where the tape was tied at one end, loosened it, and let the tape drop to the ground. The morgue wagon rolled over it into the crime scene, over to the bodies. I retied the yellow tape to the pole and watched the morgue personnel exit the van. One walked to the back of the van and opened the doors while the other walked over to the detectives and the Medical Examiner.

I fired up another Newport with my Zippo *Anarchy* lighter and slowly shook my head as I considered all the dark days ahead, I will have to cope with this bitter truth:

Denzel would have died last summer if I had not saved him, but instead, he died here tonight in this car wreck and took a family with him.

ON MY HONOR

P.S. Harman

Detective Jason Cavanaugh tried to appear cool and calm. He was sitting in his Captain's office receiving news he had been waiting to hear for weeks.

Federal Drug Task Force.

He could feel the beads of sweat forming on his upper lip and faked a slight cough to wipe it dry. "Thank you, Captain. I really appreciate the opportunity."

Detective Cavanaugh made detective two years earlier and way ahead of schedule. He was only twenty-eight years old but he was bright, good looking, well liked and used to things going his way. The Federal Drug Task Force assignment, however, had eluded him and he was starting to think it might not happen. But today changed all that.

The Feds.

He was going to be working with The Feds. The top tier of law enforcement. Maybe it would even lead to him leaving his small department for bigger things. He loved his small-town agency. Seventy-five officers and a town that was called a city but in reality, consisted of only 120,000 people. The agency was run by his mentor, Chief Charlie Deane. Chief Deane was a seasoned and principled public servant. He was leading a department of community policing officers long before the phrase or the approach was in vogue. To him, policing was about public service, not power and one was either on board with that or had to find another agency. Detective Cavanaugh revered his Chief and his approach to policing and he imagined the federal journey on which he was about to embark would be more of the same, albeit on a larger scale.

"Good luck, Jason," he said with a handshake.

"Hi," Cavanaugh said to the receptionist after entering the non-descript and unmarked federal building. "I'm Detective Jason Cavanaugh."

He confidently handed the receptionist his transfer letter. "Oh, my," the older woman said pretending to clutch invisible pearls. "Aren't you a breath of fresh air? I'm Dottie. Pleased to meet you."

"Pleased to meet you as well, Dottie." He smiled.

"Follow me," she purred.

He followed the mischievous older woman into the commander's office where she introduced Special Agent in Charge (SAIC) Don Wagner. Wagner shook his hand firmly and gave him the lay of the land, explaining that the Task Force was primarily made up of four federal agencies.

"DEA, ATF, IRS and ICE along with a smattering of local officers."

"IRS?"

"Yeah, I know, but you can't believe the information these guys have access to and they're easier to work with than the FBI, so we tolerate them." He pointed to a poster on the wall of a photo of a 1040 tax form, a gun and the words: *IRS: The only agency able to take down Al Capone.*

"They're hanging their hat on a collar from 1931?" Cavanaugh laughed.

"I know, right? But like I said, good resources. You'll see." The SAIC said as he walked him into the room of cubicles. "Here's your desk. Mary will get you set up with a case. That's Mary Mansfield, she'll be your crime analyst. One of the best in the business, even though she's IRS," Wagner said, winking.

He used the induction paperwork given to him by SAIC

Wagner to get his email set up, order his business cards and memorize his desk phone number, as the few people in the cubicles around the room generally ignored him save a few nods. Minutes later he jumped when he heard the sound of a bell being rung. A bell, that looked more at home on a ship, that hung on the wall next to the conference room. A short, loud, hobbit-looking middle-aged man was ringing the bell and yelling, "That's right, ladies and gents! One-hundred and fifty-eight thousand dollars!"

"Go away JERKin!" one of cubicle jockeys retorted.

"It's Gherkin, wise ass, not Jerkin. Hey, a newbie! Don't try to keep up with me, kid. Can't be done!"

Cavanaugh smiled and nodded and was about to get up and introduce himself when a hundred-pound wave swooped in on him. She placed her hand on his shoulder, sitting him back down and spun his chair around back toward his computer before dropping a pile of paperwork in front of him with a thud.

"You're Cavanaugh, right?"

"Right."

"Scootch over a second." She hip-checked him to the side while she pulled up a data entry screen on his computer.

"I don't…" He started to say.

"It's pretty straight forward. Take these bank statements and enter the data based on these columns."

Finding his footing he stood up, his 6'2" towering over her. He smoothed his tie before extending his hand. "Hi. I'm Detective Jason Cavanaugh and I think there's been some mistake. I'm not here for data entry."

"Oh. I see. Hey, fellas," she said addressing the three men and two women in the room including Gherkin, "He's not here for data entry." The room exploded in laughter. Mary didn't laugh or take her stare off his but slowly a smile crept over her face and her green eyes softened. "Hi, I'm Mary. Sorry about that."

"You're forgiven." He smiled back at the little spitfire

handing her back her pile of paper.

"Oh, no Detective. That part wasn't a joke. You need to enter all that."

"But, what's the case? I haven't been briefed yet."

"We'll talk about that after you get this done. I know it's probably not how you're used to doing things but I promise it will make sense later. Anyone shown you the break room yet? Want some coffee?"

He nodded and followed her down the hall. She couldn't have been more than 5'2" with short wavy blonde hair, a tight little body and mesmerizing green eyes that he clearly recalled even as he followed her from behind. They chatted as they filled their cups, both of them taking their coffee black and clicking their cups in purist unity. She told him she had been with IRS as a crime analyst for eight years. Her job was to take all the pieces of a case and put them together in a way the detectives, the bosses and the courts could process.

"So, you work the cases," he said as more of a statement than a question.

She looked at him with surprise, pleased that he understood what very few acknowledged. "I *assist* with the cases. You have a lot of work to do, Detective." She nodded toward the bull pen.

For the next two weeks Cavanaugh diligently completed his data entry assignment. Months and months of bank records. It was tedious, mind numbing and not at all what he thought this Task Force assignment was going to be. When he finished with the final bank statement, he carried the pile to Mary Mansfield, laid it on her desk and folded his arms as he stared at her. "Now what?"

"Come with me."

In the conference room was a case file laid open laid open on the table. Operation Delta. There were charts and graphs of large sums of money, travel schedules, photos and profiles.

"Drug dealers?" he asked, his excitement starting to build.

"Don't know. All we know now is that these two are moving a lot of cash. Your job is to figure out how to move the money from them to us."

"What?" he asked, sure that he had heard her wrong.

"I mean, if you can find out what they are up to that would be great but it's not critical. First you'll need to set up surveillance."

"Wait. You lost me."

"The Task Force doesn't really care about making a criminal charge. You shut down the money, you shut down the enterprise."

He thought on that for a minute. It made some sense, not a lot but some. "But if you don't know what crime they are committing, how do you know if this money is illegal money?"

Her eyes grew serious and sad. "You don't and they don't care."

"They who?"

"All of them. The agents, the bosses, the U.S. attorney's office, your department."

"My department?"

"Sure, your department gets a cut of the take. Why do you think you're here?"

He shook his head, trying to wrap his head around the objective. He moved his thought process back to what he could understand. "You said surveillance. We're a long way from that,. There's a lot more I'll need to know."

"You already know," she said with a Cheshire smile, tapping her nail on a name on the display board. "What time does he get up?"

He looked at the name and realized it was the same one as on the bank records. "I don't know. How would I know that?"

She waited patiently until his synapses started firing.

He looked up from the case file, his eyebrows rising. "I don't know when he gets up but he hits the Starbucks on

Fifteenth Avenue every morning between seven and seven thirty."

"Then what?"

"He goes to the gym on Jefferson where he gets a juice at the juice bar, probably on his way out, based on the time."

She nodded. "What else?"

"He plays golf at Denton Greens, dines often at Bridgerton's, he pays a boat slip fee to the Canton Marina, drives a BMW that he gets serviced at Phillips BMW and flies…" Cavanagh glanced back down at the file. "Delta airline exclusively."

Mary beamed.

Wow, he thought. *Bank records tell the story of your life.* He decided to ignore the statement she made that was making his gut churn—*find a way to move the money from them to us*—and chose instead to focus on the investigation.

Two weeks of surveillance yielded little in the way of results. Cavanaugh sat with Mary in the conference room reviewing his notes. "It's clear that Janet Harris, the Delta flight attendant is involved but they could just as easily be two people who are dating."

"You've spent two weeks and a lot of resources and the boss will be looking for you to move forward on this. There are other cases waiting."

"Move forward on what? I don't have anything," he objected.

"You have the SARS form from the bank reporting that the targets have been structuring their deposits. You're not getting this are you?"

He shook his head. "I mean, yes I know what a SARS form is and I know what structuring is. Multiple cash deposits over a short period of time kept to just under ten thousand dollars to side step the reporting requirement."

"Very good," Mary said, lightly teasing him.

"I pay attention. But beyond that…" He shrugged.

"In 1996," she started, "the SAR, Suspicious Activity

Reporting System was developed by FinCEN, the Financial Crimes Enforcement Network as part of the Bank Secrecy Act. These forms, also known as form FDIC 6710/06 s are completed by banking institutions and then discreetly funneled to the five primary law enforcement agencies, 52 state agencies and 25 state bank regulators. The idea was that people who deal largely in cash should be suspect, though I have to tell you that has not been my experience in the eight years I've been here."

"What do you mean?"

"I mean, federal officers and politicians decided that since drug dealers deal in cash, anyone who deals in cash should be suspect. It's never felt right. In my time here I've learned that lots of people deal in cash and they don't have a criminal bone in their body. They're just in cash businesses."

"You and my Chief would get along great." He smiled. "Please continue."

"I won't go through the whole thing because its long and dry, so let me just focus on structuring because that is the favorite target of this particular task force. We get a SARS that someone is structuring, we subpoena the bank records and confirm that there are multiple cash deposits just under $10,000, we freeze the account and then we wait. The premise is that criminals won't call to get their money back, honest people will. Again, not my experience. Then five years ago, that asshole JERKin got here and starting kissing butts at the U.S. Attorney's office. He and a new AUSA, looking to make a name for himself, put their money-grubbing heads together and figured out a way to keep the non-criminals from getting their money back as well and pretty much take criminal investigation out of the equation all together because real police work takes too much time. They didn't want the collar. They wanted the dollar."

He smiled at her use of the police term for arrest. Damn, she was smart. And the more incensed she got, the greener her eyes became.

"Hey!" she barked. "Pay attention. They used the civil statute instead of the criminal code to charge them with structuring. Now it didn't matter if they were criminals or not. If they structured, for any reason, we could freeze they account and seize the money."

"Nobody cares that there are non-criminals being caught in the net?"

"No. All they care about is the money," she said with disgust. "The money gets collected by the AUSA's office and distributed among the feds, staties, locals. Everyone gets their vig. *Capiche?*"

"Legalized extortion," he said, with bewilderment.

"Yes!" she shouted and then got up to fully close the conference room door.

"My Chief will never go for this."

"He already has. By sending you here, he already has."

"You think he knows about how it really works, though?"

"I don't know," she said honestly. "But he knows he's getting paid. Look, I'm sorry to dump all this on you, especially since there is nothing you can do about it. This is a big money-making machine for the federal government and anyone who gets in the way will get rolled over. Trust me, I've tried."

As the weeks passed, "Operation Delta" man never did call to find out why his $357K had been seized by the government. Cavanaugh tried to reason that his inaction was proof he was guilty of something but not knowing for sure left him unsettled.

"Attention everyone!" Gherkin yelled as he rang the bell. "The kids first take! Three hundred and fifty-seven thousand dollars!"

The room erupted in applause as Cavanaugh looked at the ground and tried to pull away from Gherkin's awkward buddy embrace.

***

As the months passed, Jason Cavanaugh and Mary Mansfield became closer through their mutual attraction and mutual disgust of public servants acting as bag men for the federal government. In a few cases they were able to create a criminal nexus, though the U.S. Attorney's office was only interested in *the take*. Even when there was enough probable cause for a search warrant, the first question was always, "How much in confirmed assets?" If there were no assets, the request to proceed with a search warrant was denied.

He wanted to talk to his Chief but his Chief had sent several emails commending him for his great work and touting how the money was being spent: bullet proof vests for the K-9's, additional de-escalation training, new patrol rifles. Cavanaugh realized there were some things a Chief might not want to know.

Mary helped him review SARS forms and together they came up with a point system that would be indicative of the presence of criminal behavior thus easing his conscience and bolstering his investigative posture. It added a lot of time and surreptitious snooping to the case but at least it held a better than average chance that the money seized was related to true criminal activity. The point system consisted of factors such as a prior criminal record, a lack of any legitimate employment, a life style that didn't match the bank account, etc. It also allowed them to spend more time together, something they clearly both wanted. Long days stretched into long dinners and eventually to coffee afterwards at his place. They were both falling hard even though he knew she had a strict rule about dating agents. He was falling for her too. Hard. It was a rare enough experience for him to know it was happening. The guys in the office assured him that she didn't date, hadn't dated and would never date an agent but that didn't stop him from the occasional deliberate brushing of thighs or from holding her gaze a few seconds beyond the bounds of office decorum.

That their point system had to remain a secret between them, another expression of intimacy, added to his sleepless nights. If anyone knew they were pre-investigating SARS reports before pushing them forward they would, at least, be ostracized and at worst, transferred. They both were determined to create a run of "highly probable" criminal cases they could eventually take to the boss so they could try to change the course of the Task Force.

There were occasional setbacks when Cavanaugh could not contain his convictions. "You guys are aware that you are public servants, right?" he said lecturing his colleagues in the bull pen on the Constitution and the responsibility that comes with so much power. He was often met with eye rolls and laughter and once even found a card board box under his desk marked "Soap Box."

An agent approached him quietly to try to explain. "Jason," he said quietly. "You know I was Arlington PD, right?"

Cavanaugh shook his head.

"Five years. Feds don't bond with the public like we do. They are so removed from the public they often don't grow that muscle of compassion or service like we do. They've never protected a battered spouse at midnight, or held the hand of a dying person at an auto accident."

"So, you think this okay?" he asked.

"No. Its just an observation I wanted you to consider."

One afternoon he sat his desk typing up notes when he overheard Gherkin on the phone in the next cubicle. He couldn't hear the other end of the call but it was clear what was happening.

"Mr. Arrons, the fact the you made those deposits the way you did already makes you guilty."

Pause.

"Well sir, that's a great story and it might even be true but right now this money is being seized under a civil code. There is no charge, no crime, no jail time. But I must warn you, if you insist on trying to recover this money you will be charged under the criminal code with a Class 6 felony. You okay with that?"

Pause.

"That's what I thought."

"Gherkin!" Cavanaugh yelled as he launched out his chair. "You can't do that! That's extortion! What the hell is the matter with you? Does he have a legitimate explanation? Something you can check out? You know – investigate?!"

"Here we go," sighed Gherkin as he hung up the phone. "Irrelevant. His story is irrelevant. Whether his story is true or not is irrelevant."

Mary shot a warning look at Cavanaugh and discreetly shook her head no.

"You're all okay with this?" He looked around the room at the rest of the task force members. "You're really all okay with taking this money without any investigation?" A few shrugged their shoulders and one looked at the ground. Mary interceded and led him from the bull pen to break room to calm him down.

Months later, Mary lay in Jason Cavanaugh's arms after a particularly challenging case, that they decided it was better to discuss at his apartment rather than the office. It was this night when they finally gave into their passion.

"I just don't get it," he said. "They seem to have no regard for the public they serve at all."

"I hope that isn't what you were thinking about ten minutes ago?" She purred.

Jason laughed. "No, of course not. Ten minutes? Hey lady, that was longer than ten minutes. Set the stop watch on your phone. Let's go again!"

"Not necessary," she laughed.

"By the way, I heard you never date agents," he said putting a finger under her chin and tipping her face toward his, making her blush.

"Oh, is this a date?" she answered.

He laughed. "Fair enough."

She propped up on her elbow and looked into his dark eyes. Her tone turned serious. "How did you become this man?"

"What do you mean?"

"You've got principles. Ideals about the job."

"So do a lot of cops."

"But yours don't seem… I don't know, weathered? You still believe in them."

"My Chief," he replied warmly. "I didn't have much in the way of male role models. My father left when I was five, but Chief Deane was there for me. I was in the Police Athletic League and he was always there, as a coach, a mentor and a man. His devotion to the community, including criminals, never wavered. He taught me not to cut corners, that I had as much responsibility for honest people as I did for dishonest people and if was going to put someone in jail it needed to be because there was no other way and it need to be one hundred percent solid."

"Then why don't you talk to him about this?"

"I think I'm afraid to. What if it turns out he does know and he's okay with it?"

She nodded and put her head on his check, wrapping her arms around him. She fell asleep hugging him tightly.

As he and Mary's case log slowly started to reflect a pattern of "probable" criminal behavior, they carefully noted and tracked the point system they would eventually present to SAIC Wagner. All was going as planned until Operation Pakistani Floor.

Awani Misad was a legal Pakistani immigrant. He came to the U.S. with his parents at age fifteen, finished high school, became an American citizen, learned a trade, and married.

With some help from his parents, he purchased a floor installation company and worked very hard. Eventually, Misad landed the Home Depot floor installation contract for the tri-state area. It was a windfall. He could pay his parents back and could finally afford to purchase a home for his family. His wife, however, had other ideas. When the money started to "roll in," she started spending it just as quickly. Misad, determined to save for a house and realize the American dream, stopped bringing home his paycheck. Instead, he cashed his check brought home half of the cash to his wife and put the other half in a shoebox in a closet. He spoke with his brother and business partner about the plan and his brother agreed to support the ruse that the amount he brought home to his wife was all there was. After fifteen months of scrimping on everything, Misad had saved over $60,000 in cash and met with a real estate agent. The agent advised him that his earnest money down payment couldn't be in cash and instructed him to deposit it into the bank. When he told his brother this, his brother cautioned him, "It is illegal to deposit too much cash in America. You must be careful."

Misad went to the bank and asked the teller in broken English, "How much is illegal to deposit?"

"What do you mean? You mean the cash limit before you have to declare?" she asked.

He nodded, not quite sure what she meant.

"You mean the declaration form? Ten-thousand dollars," she said.

Misad returned to the bank that same day and every day after to deposit $9,900 until his $60,000 was all safely and legally in the bank. The deposits triggered a SARS form which triggered a Task Force seizure by an agent who was abruptly reassigned, so the case and the seizure were transferred to Detective Cavanaugh. He and Mary applied their point system of investigation. It didn't look like criminal activity. The next day he received a call from Awani Misad asking why his money was taken. He agreed to come in, waive his rights and be interviewed. Following the interview, Detective Cavanaugh and Mary spent the next week confirming his story all the way down to the teller who remembered him specifically asking "How much is illegal?"

In the conference room Cavanaugh, Mary, SAIC Wagner and Gherkin discussed the case.

"He didn't know he was doing anything wrong," Cavanaugh said through gritted teeth. "He was trying to follow the law."

"It doesn't matter." Gherkin chimed in. "He *broke* the law. I didn't write the law but that's the law and he broke it. The money is ours. It's not our fault he doesn't speak English well. You have his confession. He waived his rights and the money is ours. That's it."

"That's not it!" Cavanaugh slammed his fist down on the table, looking to Don Wagner for help.

"Jason, listen," Wagner began, "It was tough on all of us when we first got here but you get used to it. This is how the game is played. That said, I don't want you working a case you're not comfortable with so I'll kick it to Gherkin. That's why I asked him to be in this meeting. He'll handle everything from here on. You'll just have to testify to the confession. Easy."

"Easy is right! Easiest sixty-K I ever made!" Gherkin cackled.

"I won't do it."

"Do what?" Wagner asked.

"I won't testify for the prosecution."

Mary's eyes widened.

"Excuse us." Wagner nodded to Mary and Gherkin. Gherkin chuckled as he was leaving the conference room. Once they were alone, Wagner turned to him. "Jason. I understand, I do, but this isn't an option. You'll be subpoenaed. You will have to testify."

Cavanaugh said nothing.

***

A week later Cavanaugh sat with Don Wagner in the U. S. Attorney's Office for the Southern District with assistant AUSA Dick Jenkins, who was assigned to the case. Jenkins was incensed and threatened to charge the young detective with obstruction of justice.

Cavanaugh glared at him and set his jaw. He had no intention of backing down.

"Detective Cavanaugh you appear to be too invested in this case." Jenkins assessed. "Who is this guy to you? He's no one and he broke the law and we're just doing our jobs."

"He didn't break the spirit of the law. This law was designed to catch criminals. He's not a criminal."

"Detective if you continue on this path you are going to make a very poor name for yourself on this Task Force. They might even send you back to your agency. Now are you on board or not?"

"Not."

"Please, don't do this, Jason," Mary begged him later at his apartment. "I told you this is big money. You can't stop them. Just testify and ask your Chief to recall you."

"Somebody has to stand up, Mary."

She nodded, knowing he was right.

"Jason," she said looking into his eyes. "You have a servant's heart and I love that about you." At the word *love*, his eyes melted into hers. "But I don't think you fully understand what is at stake here. They could ruin you. They could hurt the reputation of your department and I'm afraid it won't change anything."

"There is only one way to find out," he said resolutely.

She nodded and kissed him. If they went down, they would go down together. She was all in.

**

When the court date finally came, everyone assembled in the court room. Asim Misad, his brother, his parents and attorney, AUSA Jenkins, a worried Mary, a grinning Gherkin, SAIC Don Wagner and Detective Jason Cavanaugh. Everyone arose from their seats as the judge entered the court room. Dick Jenkins leaned over the seating partition and whispered to Cavanaugh, "Got a special guest for you, Detective."

Cavanaugh turned to see his Chief stride through the courtroom door. Chief Deane nodded to him and sat down in the back row of the court house. Mary caught his eye and mouthed to Cavanaugh, "Chief Deane?" He nodded and felt the blood creeping up his neck to his face. He turned to give Jenkins a dirty glare. But it was AUSA eyes that widened when the U. S. Attorney General himself walked in next and sat down next to Chief Deane.

The clerk began to call the case. The AUSA looked nervously at Cavanaugh and said, "Last chance. Next stop, obstruction of justice." But even as he said it, he flicked his gaze nervously toward the back of the room where the Attorney General was seated. Cavanaugh followed his gaze in time to see the AG shaking his head 'no.' Jenkin's face fell.

The judge called the AUSA for a second time.

"Is the Government ready to proceed?"

"Uh, no sir." AUSA Jenkins said quietly. "The government withdraws the case against Asim Misad, sir, and will be releasing the hold on his assets."

Mary and Jason looked at each other astonished. Gherkin slapped his hand on the hard wooden seat.

"Detective Gherkin," the judge growled. "Is there a problem?"

"No, sir."

"Another outburst like that and I'll find you in contempt."

"Yes, sir," he said sheepishly.

The judge exited the court room.

Don Wagner grabbed Cavanaugh's hand and shook it hard. "That's a good Chief you have there, Cavanaugh."

"Yes, I know," he said, still puzzled over what had just transpired.

The AUSA left without a word. Asim huddled and hugged with his family and nodded to Detective Cavanaugh.

As Chief Deane approached, Cavanaugh started to apologize, "I'm sorry about all this. I should have called you."

"Yes, you should have. Thank goodness your partner had better instincts." He nodded to Mary. "It's nice to meet you in person, Ms. Mansfield."

Mary's face reddened.

"I guess I'm off the Task Force?" Cavanaugh asked.

"Absolutely not. When Mary called me and told me what was happening, I met with SAIC Wagner and the U. S. Attorney—or as I like to call him, my friend Charles—about what was happening."

They all laughed.

"It was decided that your point system is a much better way to go. You and Mary will be laying out the program for this office and Federal Tasks Force and U.S. Attorney's Offices across the country."

Jason smiled at Mary.

"What about Gherkin and the others," Cavanaugh asked. "They—"

"Gherkin is being sent back to his agency. Anyone else who doesn't get on board will be, too." He held out his hand, and Cavanaugh took it. "You've made me very proud, Jason. You always have."

THE WEATHER OUTSIDE IS FRIGHTFUL

Jim Doherty

It was 0145 hrs, Wednesday, 23 December. I'd just gotten back onto Interstate 90, the Indiana Toll Road, after having shaken the doors on a Social Security Office in Michigan City.

My bit, supposedly, in the Global War on Terror.

For the last ten days, I'd been assigned to spend the twelve hours between 2000 and 0800 protecting all the federal government offices within the 1300-odd square miles of northwest Indiana between Gary and South Bend.

All by myself.

And I didn't even know precisely what I was supposed to be protecting all those facilities from.

We'd gotten the word on 12 December.

Not that there was all that much word. The District Director had been notified by the Regional Director, who'd undoubtedly been notified by the Commissioner, who'd been notified by God knows who, of a vague "terrorist threat" against the United States Government. A threat that was supposed to be carried out sometime during the Holiday Season.

No details. No persons to be on the lookout for. No specified target. The only thing we were notified of was a dim and indistinct "threat."

And the upshot of this vague "information" was that every member of our district, and, indeed, every officer in our agency across the length and breadth of the United States and its territories, was now working a twelve-hour day, seven days a week, until further notice.

I'm a federal cop. But the agency I work for's a lot lower on the Government's law enforcement food chain than the glamour outfits like the FBI, the DEA, the Secret Service, or the US Marshals.

My employer is called the Federal Patrol Service (FPS), which is the police arm of the Public Building Section (PBS, not to be confused with the viewer-supported TV network), which is, in turn, the real estate management division of the Government Services Agency (GSA). The GSA is the outfit that provides all the other federal agencies——with workspace, furniture, office equipment, paper, pens, and all the other lubricating materials the US Government's two million plus employees need to keep operating.

The way I usually explain FPS to people who've never heard of it (which is most people) is that, if you shoved the thousands of government office buildings and property together so that they formed one big city (which would be the fifth biggest city in the country if they did that), we're that city's local police force.

The problem for us beat cops in the FPS (and there are less than a thousand of us nationwide) is that they're *not* all shoved together. So we spend an awful lot of time sailing on a sea of murky jurisdictional waters as we travel from one little island of federal authority to another. The GSA doesn't like it when we get involved in police activity "off-property," but it's often unavoidable. We can't simply drive by a violent or dangerous offense and pretend we don't see it just because it's not happening on federal property. Not when we're in uniform, driving a marked squad car that says "POLICE."

I'd been working this shift without a day off since the word, sparse as that word was, had come down. I still hadn't adjusted to working nights. There are only twelve uniformed officers in the Chicago District, including one lieutenant and two sergeants, and we cover the entire state of Illinois, the southern half of Wisconsin, and those 1300 square miles in the northwest corner of Indiana that I mentioned. Ten consecutive nights of twelve-hour shifts. One hundred twenty hours without a day off, and we'd be working Christmas Day, New Years, and, if things kept going like they were, probably Valentine's Day and Ash Wednesday on the same schedule, on the lookout for the trouble we'd been warned of but about which we'd been given no specific information.

I was exhausted. I hadn't adjusted to sleeping days, and couldn't get the quality rest I needed to prepare me for the arduous night duty. I felt like I needed to prop my eyelids open with a pair of matchsticks. I'm not a coffee drinker, but I was drinking gallons of the stuff during this detail just to try to keep me awake with some semblance of alertness. Cherry Dr. Pepper, my usual caffeine delivery system, just wasn't up to the job. But I was paying for it by not being able to sleep deeply when I finally hit the sheets after going off-duty.

And to add to my travails, I'd suddenly found myself driving through a blizzard.

It's called "lake effect snow." It's what happens when frigid arctic winds blow across a large expanse of water, like Lake Michigan, a few miles north of where I was driving. The warm water vapor floating above the lake is drawn into the wind where it freezes, forming snow clouds. Once the wind hits the leeward shore, the snow starts falling, and, if the wind's blowing strong enough, the result is instant blizzard.

Maybe people who grew up with this kind of weather can handle it better than me, but I was raised in the San Francisco Bay Area. Where I lived, snow was a tourist attraction you had drive hundreds of miles into the Sierra Nevadas to see. I never learned how to drive in a sudden snowstorm.

I slowed down to about 40, and moved over to the right lane.

A few minutes later I was passed on my left by an SUV going about 70.

Damn fool!

He (or perhaps she—I couldn't really see in the darkness and snow) had Kansas plates. He was weaving back and forth, apparently unable to keep the car straight, and, for about a half mile, he straddled two lanes, though the lane dividers were still visible despite the sudden snowstorm. He was continuously making what seemed to be deliberate lane changes, though to no real purpose that I could see, since there was no one he had to get around. These lane changes were made without signaling.

And he was doing all this in front of a marked police car.

Taking into account that it was the holiday season, when people tend to celebrate, this was a collection of driving patterns that would lead an experienced law enforcement officer, such as myself, to believe the driver was impaired by some sort of recreational chemical.

Of course, here's where we get into those murky jurisdictional waters I mentioned. Drunk driving is a state offense, and I'm a federal cop. Now, in the State of Illinois, where I usually work, federal cops are designated as "state peace officers" in the Illinois Combined Statutes, which allows us to take action in a breaking situation. Our bosses at FPS aren't happy about that, and had even gone so far as to issue memos stating that FPS is not covered by that statute, but case law and an opinion issued by the State Attorney General's office, backed up by a memo from the local US Attorney, said otherwise, so those memos, with some grumbling, had to be rescinded.

Thing is, while many states have such a statute, there are some that don't, and I wasn't sure which one Indiana was. In any case, with no other cars on the road, the danger wasn't that immediate. I tried to reach my dispatcher back in Chicago, but between the snow and the distance, I couldn't get through on the radio. I pulled my government-issued cell phone from my belt, dialed 911, and asked for the State Police when I got an emergency operator.

"Indiana State Police," came a professional sounding voice a few seconds later.

"Yeah, hi," I said. "This is Officer Dan Sullivan, Federal Patrol Service. I'm heading east on the Toll Road, just passing mile marker 62. I'm following a Mazda CX-5, Kansas plate 1456 George Sam Yellow. He's speeding, straddling lanes, unable to keep straight, and giving every indication of driving under the influence. But I'm federal. Do you have a trooper in the area who's available to make the stop?"

"We'll send someone. I'll call you when he's getting near."

"Thanks," I said, and ended the call.

Five minutes later the cell buzzed, and I answered.

"Federal Patrol Service. Officer Sullivan."

"Indiana State Police. We've got a trooper coming up behind you right now," said the caller.

I looked in the rear-view mirror and saw a pair of headlights.

"I see him," I said. "I'll move over so he can get behind the Mazda. I'll cover when he makes the stop."

"10-4. Thanks," said the dispatcher.

I moved over to the left lane, and let the trooper's squad pull ahead of mine and behind the apparent DUI, then pulled back to the right lane as the trooper lit him up.

The Mazda immediately accelerated, but started to fishtail, and the driver, apparently thinking better of flight, slowed down, regained control of the car, and pulled over to the shoulder.

The trooper got out and went over to the passenger side. I got out and took a standing position on the passenger side of the trooper's squad. The trooper knocked on the passenger side window.

That window suddenly exploded as the inside of the car lit up with gun flashes. The trooper, driven backwards, fell into a supine position on the highway's shoulder.

I drew my pistol and started walking forward, firing what I later learned was eight rounds at the driver's silhouette through the rear and passenger side windows of the Mazda as I advanced. I saw the silhouette slump forward.

I approached slowly, opened the passenger side door, and looked in, ready to fire at the slightest movement.

The driver was slumped over the steering wheel, his eyes open and unblinking, his right hand still gripping his weapon, a nine-millimeter semi-automatic. Specifically a Beretta 92. What the military calls an "M9." I'd carried one myself for several years, during a period when I was working my first federal cop job, as a civilian officer in the Department of Defense Police. Didn't really care for it much, but that was less because of the weapon itself, than it was that I associated it with a job I'd never really enjoyed.

The pistol was tightly gripped. Perhaps in a cadaveric spasm, although I couldn't really say for sure that the guy was dead. He wasn't moving, and I was reasonably sure I wouldn't find a pulse, but it was too soon for there to be "positive signs of death." Without those positive signs, it wasn't my place to make that call.

I left the gun in his hand for the moment, not yet up to trying to pry it loose. Instead, I hit the magazine release, and slid it out of the bottom of the pistol grip, and pulled back the slide to remove the round under the hammer, then locked the slide back.

I pocketed the mag and the loose round and turned to the trooper.

"How you doing, pal?" I asked.

"Took one in my right arm, and one in the belly, right side, just below the vest. The rest of the rounds the vest stopped. But it still hurts like hell where they hit."

"Hurts is better'n dead. What's that hospital in South Bend, about a mile or so from the freeway exit?"

"*Free*way? It's a *toll* road. Nothing free about it."

"You can take the boy out of California, but you can't take the California out of the boy. To me, any road with no intersections and a speed limit that's 55 or more is a freeway.

Now what's the hospital?"

"Memorial on North Michigan."

"Anyplace closer?"

"Not that I know of. Anyway, Memorial probably has the best E/R."

"OK. I don't know how long it's going to take to get an ambulance here in this weather. Think the best thing is just to drive you there myself."

"Yeah. I agree."

"I think the gunman's dead, but just so I don't get accused of being inhumane, I'm going to pile him into the back seat, and take him with us."

The trooper grimaced and moved his hand to his wounds. "Yeah. Okay."

I helped him into the passenger side of the front seat of my squad, then went back to the Mazda. I dragged the body (and I was all but sure that's what it was, a dead body) out to the side of the road, pried the pistol loose, stuck it in a pocket of my jacket, and patted him down for any other weapons. Finding none, I handcuffed him, hands behind, dragged him back to my squad, put him into the back seat, which was a very awkward business, and seat-belted him in.

Then I got back on the cell, called 911, got transferred to the State Police, and told them I had a wounded officer I was taking to Memorial Emergency, along with the wounded suspect.

It was still colder than the proverbial mammary gland of an evil sorceress, but the wind had died down and the snow was abating, and I was able to make pretty decent time to Exit 77, the South Bend exit nearest the hospital. It took me about ten minutes, sirens blaring and lights rotating, to get from the scene of the shooting to the Emergency Care Center at South Bend's Memorial Hospital. The trooper, whose name was Bart Feeney, was removed from my squad with dispatch, and his treatment started immediately. The suspect, still unidentified, was, unsurprisingly, pronounced dead on arrival and moved to the hospital's morgue.

I got out my cell phone and tried to call my dispatcher in Chicago, but the weather was affecting enough of the cell towers between South Bend and Chi-Town that I wasn't able to get through.

I asked one of the nurses if I could use a hard line, and finally managed to make contact. I talked to Sergeant William Fredericks, perhaps the single most useless supervisor I've ever served under in my nearly ten years of law enforcement service, state, city, and federal. And I've served under some real incompetents, so that's saying something.

To say that he received the news that I'd been involved in a gun battle, and not just in a gun battle but one that had occurred "off-property," would be wildly understating the case. And, since he was the ranking officer on duty, he was afraid he'd be held responsible.

"Willy, I couldn't ignore a possible drunk driver plowing down the road in the middle of a blizzard. But it's not like I was the one who made the stop. I called the State Police to do that, precisely because it's *their* jurisdiction."

"But why'd you have to stay and cover him, Danny?"

"'Cause I'm a cop. And 'cause there wasn't anyone else. Besides, if it turned out the driver was drunk, I was the trooper's PC. He'd need my name and contact info for his report. Anyway, if I hadn't've covered him, he'd've been *killed*. You understand that, don't you? If I'd just driven off and let him make the stop himself, he'd be dead right now. What kind of bad publicity do you think *that* would've generated for FPS? So you're just going to have to excuse me if I regard saving a brother cop's life as just a tiny bit more important than worrying about making a bunch of bureaucrats at the Public Building Section uncomfortable."

"But, Dan-*nee*," he whined. "This is your *third* shooting! They're not going to like this."

"Well, it's nothing *you've* got to worry about, Willy. *You* were back in the office. And it wasn't *your* decision to make all of northwest Indiana *my* beat during this whole undefined 'crisis.' Just make the God damned notifications and stop worrying. None of it'll bounce back on *you*."

The ISP investigators got to the hospital first, and, after questioning me at great length, we went back to the site of the shooting. I rode in their car. Once I was able to relax after getting Feeney and his still-unidentified assailant to the hospital, I'd started shaking badly. The enormity of having taken a life had gotten to me once I'd accomplished all the immediate tasks.

I've been in more shootings than the average cop, but, even at that, it wasn't something that happened every day. And killing someone's not easy to process emotionally, even if you're completely justified.

I didn't want to drive 'til I got control of the shakes, so I left my squad at the hospital.

There was a forensics team going over the suspect's vehicle and Feeney's squad. I'd already handed the Beretta, the magazine, and the round that'd been under the hammer over to the ISP dicks. They handed it to the one of the forensics guys. The forensics guys asked me for my weapon.

"Can you get me another one? Just as a loan. Eventually I'm going to have to drive a marked squad back to Chicago, and I don't fancy doing it unarmed."

One of the ISP dicks handed me his duty weapon, a SIG-Sauer P227 in .45 calibre. I handed my S&W M&P to the forensics guy, and holstered the SIG.

"What'll you carry?" I asked.

"I always carry a SIG P365 as a back-up. Just get it back to me when you can."

With that he handed me a business card, so I'd know where to get the gun back to him.

After another hour or so in the frigid, but no longer snowing, outdoors, we started back to the hospital.

The ISP guys cut me loose, but Special Agent Bradford Klopus, one of the two 1811 criminal investigators assigned to the Chicago FPS district (beat cops like me have the Federal Job Classification "0083," uniformed police officers), was waiting for me. He was a big, burly shaven-headed guy whose main investigative technique was intimidation. He and I had never really clashed, but had never really hit it off, either. I'd been hoping that the assigned investigator would be Joe Rudolfo, with whom I had more of a rapport. No such luck.

He questioned me for another hour or so. By this time it was past 0500 hrs. The sun was starting to rise, but my eyelids were starting to droop.

"Sullivan, you better not try to drive back now."

"I've still got three hours of my shift to go."

"Never mind about that. You find yourself a motel and get a few hours of shuteye, then head back and turn in the vehicle. After that, consider yourself on administrative leave, with pay, until further notice. I don't see that you had any choice here, Sullivan, but the suits aren't going to like this, so be prepared to go through some hell before you come out the other side."

I nodded.

I did as Klopus suggested. Once I was in my room, I tried to call home to let my wife, Katie, know where I was and why I wouldn't be home for a while. The call went through, but Katie didn't answer, it being still some hours before she was due to wake up, so I left a message to keep her from worrying.

Some ten hours later, which included seven hours of sack time, two hours driving back to the FPS Office at 536 South Clark (the snow had stopped, and the Toll Road was less slippery, the wind having blown most of the snow off), and an hour changing out of my uniform and into my civvies, placing the gun the trooper'd loaned me in my gun locker and retrieving my own personal weapon, then answering some questions from the day watch sergeant (completely superfluous questions, since he wasn't in any way involved in the post-shooting investigation), I went officially off-duty. After another hour, consisting of riding an el train from the Loop to the Brown Line stop on Western Avenue, a bus ride north on Western to the intersection nearest our house in the Bowmanville neighborhood, and a walk for the last few blocks, I was finally home. It was 1700 hrs by this time.

Well, hell, I was off-duty. It was 5PM.

Katie was waiting for me, looking worried.

"Get my message?" I asked.

She nodded, then said, "What happened?'

"I don't want to go into details right now, Sweetie. I'm just too damned tired to go over it again. Short version's that I got into a shootout covering a state trooper making a car stop on the Indiana Toll Road."

"You're not hurt, are you?"

"No. The other cop took a couple of rounds, but I'm fine."

"Will this mean trouble for you?"

"Most likely. It happened 'off-property,' and you know how GSA is about their cops getting involved in stuff 'off-property.' And that's on top of its being my third shooting since getting hired by the FPS. Right now, though, I'm so wrung out, I don't even care anymore. Just point me toward a bed."

Being on administrative leave with pay turned out, at least in the short term, to be a blessing. Since I was barred from field duty, or even office duty, I no longer had to work the twelve-hour shifts. The next day was Christmas Eve, so Katie and I drove downstate to her home town, Bloomington, and spent a few days with her folks. We all opened presents together on Christmas morning, went to Mass together later that morning, had a huge Christmas dinner at mid-day, napped for awhile, and spent the late afternoon and evening eating sandwiches made from the dinner leftovers, while we watched *It's a Wonderful Life*, the Alastair Sim version of *A Christmas Carol*, and the original *Miracle on 34th Street* on the tube. Later, after the folks had turned in, Katie and I watched a more recent Christmas movie, *The Nativity Story*, just to remind us what we were actually celebrating that day.

The paid time off continued through New Years, and for some time beyond.

On 8 January, I was called into the office to answer some questions put to me by some PBS suits. In the preceding days, I'd driven down to South Bend, stopped at the District 11 ISP station, and exchanged the SIG I'd been loaned for my issued S&W, then stopped at the office to place the S&W in my gun locker. So, equipment-wise, everything was returned to normal.

The PBS guys were, typically, tone-deaf about the realities of law enforcement at the street level.

"A drunk driver has nothing to do with protecting our buildings. Why'd you have to get involved?"

"Because a drunk driver is a clear and present danger, particularly in that kind of weather. If I'd ignored him, and it came out that an FPS officer saw him and did nothing, we'd probably be liable for any damage he caused. Do you have any idea how many people are killed every year by drunk drivers?"

"No. Do you?"

"I know it's in the thousands. If you want I'll Google it for you. And I know that the only reason it isn't more is 'cause cops arrest so many of 'em."

"We'll put that aside for the moment. Why'd you have to stay and back up that highway patrol officer once he arrived?"

"State Police," I said.

"Come again?" said the clueless bureaucrat.

"In Indiana, it's the State Police, not the Highway Patrol. It's the State Police here in Illinois, too. Where are you from, anyway?"

I know what you're thinking. That was a silly nit to be picking under the circumstances. But the cluelessness these guys had about law enforcement was annoying the hell out of me. Was it too much to expect them to know the correct title for the organization?

"That's hardly the point! The question I asked is why you took it upon yourself to cover the other officer once he was there to make the stop."

"Because making car stops, particularly at that time of night, is one of the most dangerous things a cop can do. Close to a third of all cops murdered in the line of duty were making traffic stops. The odds of survival go way up if there's a backup officer standing by. In any case, he'd need my name and contact info for his report and I'd need his for mine. And let's not forget the most salient point of all. Trooper Feeney was actually shot! If I hadn't've been covering him, he almost certainly would've died! Do you really rate a cop's life as being less important than not getting involved in police matters 'off-property?' 'Cause if that's what you're saying, gentleman, I've got to tell you that's too ruthless a form of calculus for me."

"We're liable for anything one of our officers does. It's easier to defend the actions of an officer if he's actually in our jurisdiction."

"Think so? How would it have looked if I'd driven off once Trooper Feeney arrived, and he wound up getting murdered? A murder I could've prevented if I'd just stayed. A murder I *did* prevent, 'cause I *did* stay. If I hadn't've been there to prevent that murder, what kind of bad publicity would *that* have generated for GSA? If you're going to slam me, then slam me, but, know this. If the same thing happens again in the same way, I'll take the same actions. And I'm willing to bet that if there *is* any bad publicity that's generated over this, it'll be over you disciplining me for saving another cop's life. You know it and I know it. So go ahead and do whatever you're going to do. I'm past the point of even caring. If you don't have any further questions, I'm leaving."

"We're not done here!"

"Fine. Then ask whatever questions you still have, so we can get this little Inquisition over with."

They sat their gnashing their teeth. They wanted to slam me down hard. And, maybe, in the end, that's just what they'd do. They didn't think in terms of "right and wrong." Words like "duty" and "honor" didn't register with them. Their decision would be based on nothing more or less than what was best for the bureaucracy.

In a way, though, it wasn't really their fault. When GSA was set up a few years after WW2 ended, police work wasn't part of the package. They were founded and organized to be the government's property manager and storekeeper. Period. There was a uniformed security detail within the GSA called the US Guard Service. Employees of the USGS were designated as "security guards" (currently classified as "0085"), not "police officer" ("0083"), but all they did was entry control and static posts. They had no arrest authority, and no training as cops.

But then came the 1970's, an era of civil disobedience run rampant. Demonstrations on GSA-operated properties, protesting the Vietnam War, racism, sexism, and any other societal ill that the demonstrators thought the Government should immediately fix, made it necessary for the GSA to depend on local cops to protect them when such demonstrations got out of hand.

This didn't sit well with the guy who occupied the Oval Office at the time. He wanted *federal* cops dealing with those demonstrators. Cops he, as the chief executive of the Federal Government controlled. Not local cops he had to go hat in hand to a local mayor to get help from. So he ordered that the Guard Service be redesignated as the Federal Patrol Service, that its employees be upgraded to "0083," sent to the Federal Law Enforcement Training Center, and given the power and authority to deal with the demonstrators themselves.

I often describe FPS as the Church of England of law enforcement. Which is to say, it was founded by a discredited leader for an ignoble purpose. For Henry VIII, it was so he could put aside his lawful wife and marry the woman he was hot for, with the appearance of Church approval. For Nixon, it was so he had his own personal police force to give leftist demonstrators exercising their First Amendment rights a thumping whenever it suited him.

But after the Vietnam era passed, and Nixon left office in disgrace, the GSA was still left with a full-fledged police force they wanted nothing to do with. And, what was worse, as the former guards left, they were replaced by applicants who were interested in being professional cops, not static watchmen.

And the tension between GSA employees who were hired expecting to do police work, and administrators who wanted nothing to with a profession that was rife with possibilities for civil liability, has continued ever since.

The two of them stared at me silently for a few more moments. When that failed to intimidate me, they finally dismissed me.

Two things got me off the hook.

The first was that the Governor of Indiana, and the Superintendent of the Indiana State Police, notified the FPS Commissioner that they wanted to give me an award for saving Trooper Feeney's life.

That might not have been enough, all by itself. After all, the GSA doesn't answer to state officials.

But the second was a confidential word that was passed from Assistant Director of the FBI for Counterterrorism to the

Director of the FBI, and then from the Director of the FBI to the US Attorney General, and finally from the US Attorney General to the Chief Administrator of the Government Services Agency.

I never got all the details—I don't have that kind of clearance—but apparently, the guy I shot was part of whatever the nebulous movement was that had been planning whatever it was they were planning against whatever federal property they were targeting. In other words, out of all the FPS officers they had working twelve-hour days, seven days a week, in what pretty much amounted to a "Hail Mary" play against the forces of evil, I'd been the one to actually encounter one of the bad guys we were out there trying to interdict.

Inadvertently, I'd actually done precisely what they had me out there to do.

Now, suddenly there was talk of my getting a US Office of Justice Assistance Public Safety Officer Medal of Valor, perhaps even getting it handed to me from the President himself, as well as an FPS William L. Lumberloch Outstanding Service Award (William Lumberloch being an FPS officer who'd died bravely in a shootout in the lobby of a government office building in Orlando, Florida). There were even rumors that the FPS Commissioner was going to put me up for in the Police Officer of the Year Award given by the International Association of Chiefs of Police.

None of those things happened. The higher-ups at GSA talked the OJA out of giving me the Public Safety Medal, and absolutely refused to consider me for a Lumberloch Award, or to allow me to be nominated for IACP Cop of the Year. Maybe they couldn't discipline me, but they could force me to eat some humble pie.

What they could not do was control the decisions of the Governor and the ISP Superintendent. When I was notified that I would be given an award from the State of Indiana, I knew I was off GSA's hook.

Some months later, I received a certificate, signed by both

the governor and the superintendent, along with a medal and a pin, for valorously saving the life of Trooper Feeney. No pomp and circumstance. But I did get a decoration I could wear on my uniform.

And it was a hell of lot more recognition than my own agency had given me.

Author's Note: It should be noted that there is no federal law enforcement agency called the Federal Patrol Service, no Public Building Section for such an agency to be a subsidiary of, nor is there a Government Services Agency that is the parent organization for either the PBS or the FPS.

There are *actual agencies that, in real life, perform the same functions that, in my story, the Federal Patrol Service, the Public Building Section, and the Government Services Agency fill in fiction. But, for various reasons, among them the way federal law enforcement so frequently gets rearranged at the drop of a hat, or the whim of a bureaucrat, thus automatically making any story about them seem dated, it was convenient for me to create fictional counterparts for the real-life agencies.*

Though the names have been changed, the bureaucratic attitudes displayed in this story reflect those of the real-life counterparts.

CLEAN, GREEN, AND OBSCENE
A.B. Patterson

- 1 -

"But that's not ethical," bleated our squad's new probationary detective, seemingly out of nowhere.

Both Jimmy Morse and I turned as one unit, leaving the conversation we'd been having, a conversation between two detective sergeants.

Neither of us uttered a word initially, such was the shock of the impudence and complete lack of deference. What the hell were they teaching at the Academy these days?

Detective Constable Caleb Breeze looked like his last shave had been his first. And if he kept preaching about ethics as if he knew what he was talking about, then his next shave might be his last.

Back in the day, you had to do five years in uniform before you could apply for the detectives. Five years of violent domestics; sudden deaths and suicides; thieves, muggers, and housebreakers; hopped-up car thieves; psycho meth-heads; and vicious pub brawls. Basically five years of learning that society was one big shit-fight.

Now, the "new-direction" police hierarchy were avoiding all that reality. As long as the new coppers had their university degrees, they could apply for the detectives after their twelve months as a probationary constable ended.

Young Caleb had a double honours degree in criminology and social studies (he'd reminded the squad several times) and he'd done his twelve uniformed months in the Policy Review Unit at Headquarters.

So, just about ready to run the squad.

And his facial expression was a carbon copy of the ovine stare of self-righteousness that all the religious zealots have perfected. He was like a televangelist with a Glock.

I wanted to smack him.

I thought Jimmy was going to.

"Who the fuck asked your opinion, probationer?!" he roared instead. "The conversation was between myself and Detective Sergeant Harrington."

The squad room went quieter than a morgue.

The young detective flinched at the boss's bellowing baritone. He said nothing.

"That was a question, idiot. Answer it."

"I … I thought…"

"You're not here to think, yet. You're here to do as you're told and hopefully fucking learn something about being a cop. And I'm not even happy about that. When you've dealt with angry men who want to rip your nuts off and feed them to you, and you've locked up a bevy of real crooks, then you get to think. Understand, you academic retard?"

"You … you can't speak to me like that. It's disrespectful and hurtful. Our sensitivity training covered this."

Jimmy went a shade of beetroot and exploded. "You wouldn't understand what respect is, you useless bastard!"

He reached in his pocket and pulled out a set of car keys. They hit the probationer in the chest.

"There you go, son. My squad car. Take it down the road to the car wash and get it cleaned. Bet they didn't cover that in your double-woopity-doo fucking degree, did they? Oh, and make sure it's fucking spotless: dirty cars are one of *my* sensitive spots."

There were some sniggers in the background.

"Now get out of my fucking sight."

Caleb nodded, "Yes, Sarge."

As he walked towards the door, Jimmy called after him, making him turn.

"And son, remember this lesson from today: I'm a detective senior sergeant and the boss. And as the boss, when I want to hear an arsehole, then I'll fart."

The room dissolved in laughter as Caleb left, looking like a beaten puppy.

Jimmy beckoned me into his office and indicated to close the door behind me. "You think I was too hard on him?"

"Nope. If he'd already proved himself, then yeah. But he knows shit. And he needs to learn his place. A squad can't function otherwise."

"Yes. That's another part of the Academy curriculum that seems to have died."

"Probably got replaced by Wokeness One-O-One."

Jimmy laughed. "And don't forget Feelings Two-Two-O. I think this police force is heading to hell in a hand-basket, mate."

I chuckled. "Yeah, well they probably have units on basket weaving at the Academy, too. Wish I was as close to retirement as you, Jimmy."

"We need a drink."

I nodded. "Yep. And we need to do something about that probationer. An honest politician in Parliament would be a better fit than he is in the squad."

"Can't disagree there."

"Mate, he's been here less than a fortnight and that's the third time I've personally heard him use the E word in here. Plus a couple of the lads have mentioned it, too. That probationer is becoming a massive problem."

"Yes, we need a plan. Some old-school thinking." He looked pensive, then at me. "You free after work?"

"Are the Kennedys gun-shy?"

"Good. Meet you at your local, nice and away from here."

"Cool, see you when you get there. I'll be in the main bar."

"Excellent. Now I need to get back to this strategic fucking plan for next year."

I grinned at him. "That's why you're the boss and get paid the big bucks."

"Piss off, Bruce, you're now buying this arvo." He winked at me.

"Fair cop. See you later."

I went back to my desk.

"Not ethical" my arse. It was just the usual discussion about letting the squad take Friday afternoon off for a long pissy lunch, to make up for all the hours of unpaid overtime in the last month. The give-and-take of the job. And even with occasional long lunches, we still gave the job far more than we took.

- 2 -

I finished the shift off tidying up the exhibits for an upcoming trial and waved at Jimmy as I headed out. His grimace in return indicated he was still trying to be strategic.

I dumped the squad car at my apartment block, and headed straight for my local, the Flat Out Lizard, a couple of blocks away. I didn't bother stopping into my one-bedroom hovel that was all I could afford to rent after the divorce years back. No, the hovel was only good for sleeping and screwing.

I did, however, love my local pub. I was the closest thing to a shareholder they had. And it was old school. I had my own dedicated place at the bar, well-earned in more ways than just patronage, and all the locals knew and respected it.

I stepped into the dim interior, which I always found relaxing, and strode to the bar. Zed, one of the two guys who owned the joint, was polishing glasses. There were very few patrons.

Zed grinned as he looked up and saw me.

"G'day, Bruce. Good to see you, mate."

"Yeah, Zed, it's been ages."

He laughed and looked at his watch. "Mate, it's been at

least sixteen hours."

"Yeah, I'm slipping. Old age, mate."

"The usual?"

"Absolutely, thanks."

However, something was not right. There was a young bloke sitting on my stool.

My stool! Outrageous!

I slapped my hand on the woodwork.

He stopped playing on his phone and looked at me and Zed, an inane stare like a stunned mullet.

I sauntered towards him. "You're in my spot."

"Sit somewhere else, there's plenty of space."

Zed put my beer on the mahogany bar.

The young punk's cheek deserved a smack in the mouth. I took a gulp of beer instead. "Can you read, mate?"

He looked at me and sneered. He was failing the attitude exam, dismally.

I pointed at a brass plaque on the edge of the bar. "Read it."

The sneer took over his whole face. "Why the fuck should I?"

"Because, arsewipe, I fucking said so." I pulled back my jacket to show my Smith and Wesson .38 Special. I'd stuck with the old six-shooter: hated the plastic feel of the new Glocks all the younger detectives were carrying. The gunmetal cameo got a sudden change in expression from dickweed.

He read the plaque, looked at me, then Zed, then back to me. He swallowed hard. The moving Adam's apple was a tempting target to punch.

"Umm … about this spot being reserved for a detective who stopped a robbery."

I nodded as he grew nervous. The attitude of entitled arrogance had disappeared, replaced with the uncertain anxiety that better reflected his callowness.

Zed pointed at me. "This detective walked in on an armed robbery five years ago."

Zed leaned over the bar, grinning and enjoying the sport. "If you look closely at the wall there, you can still see the stains from where this detective blew the cunt's brains out."

The lad's voice box rose and fell again, like a fleshy yo-yo.

Zed leaned even closer. "It was beautiful, mate. A poetic symphony of good versus evil. 'Kaboom!', then 'Splat!', as the brains sprayed over the wall, like a smashed watermelon." Zed made an exploding gesture with his hands. "And ever since, this has been his spot."

The punk went even paler, and slid off the stool. "Sorry, detective."

I nodded, deciding against correcting him with "detective sergeant". One lesson was enough for him today. "Thanks, son."

I turned to Zed. "His next one's on me."

The young buck hauled his deflated ego over to a table and sat down. He resumed playing on his phone.

I occupied my rightful stool and guzzled the ice-cold beer.

Zed lined up a second. Good man.

Zed, or Gianni Zappa on his paperwork, was one of those salt-of-the-earth types: hard as nails but with a heart of gold, for the right people. His Italian parents had emigrated to Australia just after the war ended in Europe. Zed had been born here and was well into his sixties now, but he looked as fit as a Mallee bull.

At age twenty, Zed won the only lottery he would ever win – the birthday ballot draw for young Aussie men to be conscripted to go and fight in Vietnam. He did two years over there, returning home when the last of the Australian infantry battalions were pulled out in '72.

Zed poured himself a beer and we chinked glasses.

"How's the squad going?"

"Good, mate. The boss is great. He'll be joining me shortly. You'll like him. We have a little work dilemma to discuss, and we figured there was no better place than my favourite bar."

"Cool. I'm just going to pop down to the cellar, so can you

keep an eye on the bar for a few minutes? The evening barmaid will be here any time now."

"No worries, I'll try not to drink it dry."

Zed laughed. "Yeah, and try to keep your hands off young Donna when she arrives." He disappeared into the stairwell.

"Won't make any promises there," I called after him.

He emerged from the cellar a few minutes later, just as Donna was taking station behind the bar. I grinned at her and she smiled back.

Before I could start any flirting, Jimmy walked in off the street. I waved him over.

"Bruce, this is where you capped that armed robber, isn't it?"

"Exactly the spot." I pointed at the brass plaque.

Jimmy read it with an admiring nod. "Beautiful."

Zed plonked a beer in front of him. "Yes, Bruce saved my life that day, I reckon."

Jimmy took a long swig. "Yeah, and he saved the taxpayers the cost of a trial, too."

"Zed, meet my boss, Jimmy Morse."

"Always pleased to meet the detectives, and welcome to my humble bar."

They shook hands.

"Likewise to meet you, Zed. Bruce has told me about his favourite watering hole. I've been keen to get down here."

Jimmy sat himself on the stool next to me, and Zed lined up two more beers.

"Cheers," said Jimmy, swallowing the remainder of his first. He pointed at a framed black-and-white photo of a platoon of soldiers. "Bruce tells me you were in 'Nam?"

"Yep. That fucking birthday ballot. Never forget that day. Happy twentieth, Gianni. Now here's your jungle greens, a seven-point-six-two SLR, and an air ticket to Saigon. Then two years of becoming a man, the hard way, and learning that no one really gives a shit."

"I missed that possibility, thankfully," said Jimmy. I didn't turn twenty until it'd all been over for a couple of years. But all credit to you and the boys who went."

Zed poured himself another beer and raised his glass. "To all the lads who never made it back here. Lest we forget."

Jimmy and I stood momentarily and said, "Lest we forget," in unison.

Jimmy pointed at another photo frame, this one of Zed, still in army greens, with a stunning Vietnamese girl next to him. They were standing in front of a typical Australian suburban bungalow.

"Your wife?"

"She was. Her name was Huong. It means pink rose in their language. I met her in Saigon when I was on R and R. Fell head over heels in love. Asked her to marry me and come back here. Her family had been killed in the war, so she jumped at the chance."

"Something good came of the war for you then," said Jimmy.

"Yeah, for a while. It wasn't easy for her back here. Especially since my old man wouldn't have a bar of her. When I took her to the folks' place to introduce my new wife, the old man told me to get the 'gook whore' out of his house."

"Ouch," said Jimmy.

"Yep. So I told him to apologise and never call her that again. Stubborn old Italian bastard stepped up to me and told me I was dead to him and I could fuck off with my prostitute wife."

"So what did you do?"

"I belted him so hard that his jaw broke in four places."

"Fair enough," said Jimmy.

I'd heard the story before, of course.

Zed continued, "Yeah, it was ironic, them being immigrants about twenty years earlier. And they'd had to put up with some racism themselves, like all the Italians and Greeks coming out after the war. So I wasn't expecting how he treated Huong. Anyway, then I belted the prick a whole load more, until he passed out."

Jimmy raised his eyebrows.

Zed smiled slightly. "Told him the rest was for all the times he'd hit Mum. Then Huong and I left. Never saw him again. Used to catch up with Mum occasionally for lunch."

"And she got on okay with Huong?"

"Yeah, like a house on fire. When we found out Huong couldn't have kids, that broke Mum's heart. I was their only child, so it hurt all the more I guess."

Jimmy pointed at another photo with three young adults standing together, smiling. They were obviously Vietnamese. "So…"

Zed grinned. "Yep, my little tribe, but all adopted."

Jimmy nodded. "Yeah, didn't think they looked half you, mate."

"No, we adopted three orphans from the wave of refugees that came as boat people after the war. They're all great kids and have done well here." Zed pointed at them one at a time. "Engineer, nurse, and architect. I love 'em to bits, as did Huong."

Jimmy raised an eyebrow. "She passed away?"

"Cancer. Ten years ago. She never made it out of surgery. Still, at least she didn't suffer for long."

"Small mercies," I said.

"Tell me," said Jimmy, "did your old man report you to the coppers for flogging him?"

"Not exactly. The hospital called them due to the serious injuries. I'd done a thorough job on him. But he didn't want to press charges. Too humiliating, I reckon, getting beaten up by his son."

"So did they ever speak to you?"

"Yeah, a couple of detectives came around. I was still on base back then. I told them the whole story straight up, didn't leave anything out. Then the detective sergeant shook my hand, said well done for sticking up for the ladies, and told me that as far as they were concerned it was justice done. I can't remember the exact phrase he used, it wasn't one I was familiar with. Anyway, that was the end of it."

I laughed. "'Summary jurisdiction' I'd bet."

"Yes! That was it!" said Zed.

"Ah, the good old summary jurisdiction." Jimmy looked positively wistful. "Wouldn't bloody happen now, mind you. You'd get the book thrown at you."

"Probably," said Zed. "But enough of me, Bruce says you guys have got a problem you need to sort out."

He poured more beers.

"Yep," said Jimmy. He proceeded to explain all about our ethical probationary detective.

When Jimmy had finished, Zed nodded knowingly. "Yes, we had a couple of similar problems when I was in the army. We called them 'the clean, green, and obscene brigade'. I'll tell you how the platoon sergeants fixed those problems. Might give you some old-school inspiration."

Several beers and large plates of steak and chips later, Jimmy and I had hatched our plan.

Donna asked for my card as I left. Sweet. You wouldn't be dead for quids.

- 3 -

So it was down to me to work Caleb into the gutter that all good detectives thrived in, ripping him out of any shred of his comfort zone, and generally making his life a misery. But it all had to be the detective experience, not simply overt bullying. Jimmy's words hung in my mind: "Be as hard as nails, but not an arsehole. He's still one of us, sort of. With your deft touch, Bruce, I give him three weeks, tops."

Monday morning, the crew arrived gradually before eight.

Our most senior detective, Steve Dart, came up to my desk with two coffees, one for me.

"Cheers, Steve, you must have read my mind."

"Always," he smiled. Then he lowered his voice. "What the fuck are we going to do with Mister Ethics? He's only been here a fortnight and the crew have had a gutful."

"We're onto it. When Caleb arrives this morning, he's going to get the news that he is partnered with me full-time until further notice, for special duties. The plan is to ride him out of here."

"Shit, rather you than me. I'd shoot him before the first week was up."

I chuckled. "Yeah, so might I yet. And just quietly let the team know that we've got this in hand. We don't want morale dropping. They just need to hang in there for a bit."

"No worries, will do."

Ten minutes later, Caleb walked in.

"Detective Breeze," I pointed at him.

"Yes, Sarge?" He sauntered over, looking nervous.

"Looks like you drew a winning lottery ticket last night."

"What do you mean, Sarge?"

"You're coming off Team Two and working full-time with me, special duties, until further notice." I tried not to grin.

Some snorts of stifled laughter rippled through the squad room.

"Why?" whined Caleb.

I saw a smiling Jimmy appear behind him. "Because I fucking said so, probationer. Got a problem with that?"

Caleb turned to face the booming voice.

"No, Sarge."

Now I was grinning, and a dejected Caleb turned back to look at me.

"Okay, probationer, get tooled up and grab some car keys. We're off out to schmooze with some informants."

He said nothing, looking dumbfounded, and went over to the key rack.

First stop was Fat Luigi's espresso bar and gelateria. That was the front of the premises anyway.

I directed Caleb to park in the private bay next to Luigi's black Series 7 BMW. The number plate read "FLUIGI". The story went that he applied for "FATLUIGI" as his personal plate, but that the Motor Registry refused to allow the word "fat" on a plate: politically incorrect, apparently. So he settled for "F" instead. The story also went that a competitor, not in the gelato side of the business, had cheekily suggested that the new number plate stood for "Fuck Luigi". Said competitor turned up in a dumpster with his throat cut.

I knocked once on the metal-plated back door.

It was opened by a colossus in slate-grey Armani with a bulging armpit.

He nodded at me. "Detective Sergeant Harrington."

"Hello, Fred. The boss is expecting me."

A slight grin cracked the armour of Fred's face. "Yes, he told me."

I winked at him.

He looked at Caleb. "New detective. Well, you must do the initiation."

"What?" gasped Caleb, as we stepped inside.

Fred grabbed a shot glass from a counter and filled it from an unmarked bottle of clear liquid.

"Ah, Luigi's finest grappa," I said. "Get it down you, probationer."

"But…"

"No buts. You can't come in here unless you do Luigi the respect of sampling his grappa. And if you don't come in here, you're no bloody use as a detective."

He glared miserably at me and took the glass from Fred.

"Down in one, detective," said Fred. "It's the easiest way."

Caleb took a sniff and screwed up his face.

"Come on, probationer, we don't have all bloody day.

Grow some balls. Preferably of the hairy variety."

He closed his eyes and tossed the rocket fuel down his throat. No sooner had he placed the glass on the counter than he leant over a rubbish bin and puked.

I looked at the smiling Fred. "Mate, they just don't make them the same these days."

"Lightweights, I agree. Still, easier for our business." He grinned.

Caleb stood back up, looking green.

"Follow me, son, we have work to do."

Fred gave three knocks unevenly spaced, opened the door, and we went in.

Fat Luigi and four other middle-aged Mediterranean men were sat around a card table, cards and cash all over the green baize. The air was so thick with smoke it resembled a vichyssoise.

"Be with you after this hand, Detective Sergeant." Luigi's voice sounded like concrete coming down the chute of the cement truck. No doubt a sound he was intimately familiar with. The formality was for the benefit of his audience: they needed to know his connections.

I leant against the wall and lit a smoke.

Caleb stood there looking as uncomfortable as a virgin at a bikies' barbecue.

He whispered to me, gesturing at the card game, "Isn't that illegal?"

"Shut up."

The hand finished and Luigi instructed a pause in proceedings. He hauled his 150kg up from his seat and waddled over. We shook hands.

"Always a pleasure, Bruce. Who's this?"

"A new probationary detective. We're trying to train him."

"Poor student," said Fred. "He threw up your finest grappa, boss."

"Fuck!" said Luigi. He waved his finger at Caleb. "You need to harden up, son."

"Exactly," I added.

Luigi pulled a folded piece of paper out of his shirt pocket and passed it to me. "My ears out there tell me the Chinese pricks have a shipment coming in hidden in refrigerators. All the details are here."

"Thanks, Luigi. We'll work our magic."

Caleb couldn't help himself. "But, Sarge, this card game?"

I winked at Luigi, then turned to Caleb. "And what's wrong with it, son?"

"It's illegal gambling."

"That's an offensive comment to make in Mister Rinaldi's premises, probationer. And there's nothing illegal about a card game using pretend money. Isn't that right, Mister Rinaldi?"

He grinned. "Quite correct, Detective Sergeant Harrington. It's just pretend money. We make it look as realistic as possible to give us more enjoyment."

I looked over at the table. There had to be at least forty grand in the various piles.

"Let's go," I said to Caleb.

I shook hands with Luigi and Fred, and tipped my forehead to the other Mafiosi. They all waved in return.

As I pushed Caleb out the doorway, Luigi put his hand on my shoulder, pointing at Caleb's disappearing back with his free hand. "I can always let you know the next time we're doing a foundation pour, Bruce."

I laughed. "Shit, I hope it doesn't come to that."

Caleb had another puke behind the car.

"Give me the keys, I'll drive. You nurse your tender little head."

"Okay, Sarge," he said, wiping his mouth with his handkerchief.

"Let's go get a coffee."

Fifteen minutes later, we were sipping cappuccinos in the car. Caleb was glum and silent, but a couple of times he looked like he was about to utter something. More gems of ethical wisdom, no doubt.

"Come on, son, spit it out, whatever it is."

"Well, that money in the card game looked real to me. And that makes it illegal gambling. We can't turn a blind eye to that."

"Son, it's pretend money. Leave it alone."

"But they were obviously mafia. Why are we being nice to them?"

"Fuck me, you really need to tune in. Firstly, even if it was gambling, there's a whole lot of worse shit that the Establishment turns a blind eye to on a daily basis. Secondly, Fat Luigi gives me some real juicy drum that leads to great arrests and busts. This tip off today will be A-grade, mark my words."

"But what about *his* criminal activity? How is that any better?"

"Caleb, your study and books have taught you that ethics in policing is black and white. Suits the comfortable woke agenda, these days. But it's bullshit. This is reality, and ninety percent of reality is shades of grey. And some them are grey with brown stains. Can you get your head around that?"

"I don't know. It just seems wrong to me. Commit a crime and get arrested. And anyway, Luigi is probably just using us to take out competition."

I laughed hard. "Of course he bloody is. But you are going to have to learn that we can never sort out all crime, and it's better to have the criminals we can deal with operating, rather than the scum we can't reason with."

"Still think it's wrong." Sounded more like a petulant ten-year-old sitting next to me. The thin blue line was on a woke diet into oblivion.

"Son, you and I are going to be seeing a lot of this reality this week, so you best start thinking about whether you can deal with it. No shame in deciding that a headquarters desk is more your cup of tea. Okay?"

"Yes, Sarge."

Tea was certainly more his beverage than grappa, that was for sure.

I let him recover for the rest of the morning as we checked out a few addresses for vehicle regos. He wasn't the talkative type, unless he found some aspect of ethics to rant about. It was going to be a very long week, and then some.

I'd made two calls before heading out with Caleb that morning. One had been to Fat Luigi to get Fred organized. The other call had been to Miss Felicia, the madam at an up-market brothel. Another case of some mutual favours.

After Caleb had wolfed down a burger for lunch into his thoroughly emptied guts, I broke the news to him.

"Right, another informant to go and see. You're driving again." I threw him the keys.

In the car, I gave him directions and we arrived at Felicia's establishment, Kiss the Kitty.

"What's this place?"

"Son, what do think it is? Shuttered windows in the middle of the afternoon, three CCTV cameras along the front wall, and a front door that looks solid enough to withstand a charging elephant."

He shook his head.

Well, I didn't seriously think he'd ever been in a brothel, but I thought the dumbest detective in the world could have figured it out. That's the trouble with too much academic education, when it replaces street smarts. Or what we old-school blokes call "common dog fuck".

"Caleb, this is a brothel. You know what one of them is?"

"I've never been in one. Why would I know what it was?"

Yeah, he probably didn't even wank. Probably unethical as well.

"I'm friends with the madam, and she gives me great drum, too. So let's go."

Truth be told, Felicia gave me a whole lot more than drum.

I rang the doorbell and smiled up at the nearest camera. The heavy door clicked and I pushed it open.

Felicia was standing in the floral-scented reception area, classical piano playing softly over the sound system. She was wearing a cobalt-blue Emma Peel jump suit, the front zipper half way down her abdomen revealing the deep cleavage between her firm, prominent breasts. Sensational.

"Detective Sergeant Bruce Harrington, welcome you sexy beast! So glad to see you, darling."

She wrapped her arms around my neck and planted her luscious lips on mine. She didn't spare the tongue. Yeah, she always stirred my loins.

Two of her girls, in translucent lingerie that left them as good as naked, were looking on with come-fuck-me grins.

Felicia disengaged from my face and took hold of my hand. "Let's go to my office, darling, and talk business. Mona and Siren here will entertain your new boy. Look after him, girls."

She led me to the office. She closed the door behind us.

"We're not open yet, so they can play with your problem boy all they like."

She flicked a switch on her desk and the wall-mounted flat screen fired up, showing the reception area.

"Let's watch the fun, handsome. Drink?"

"Yes, baby." I cupped my hand over her butt cheek in the skin-tight jump suit as she leant over to open the bar fridge.

"Oh, big boy, I think you need to come visit me when you knock off work today."

"I'll be here."

"Good." She poured two glasses of bubbles, her standard fare, and passed me one as she gently pushed me onto the red leather couch. Then she parked her delightful posterior in my lap. That got some movement starting.

"Let's watch the show."

We chinked glasses and she wiggled her bum on top of me. I groaned.

"Later, Bruce, we're trying to sort out your problem child here."

"Can't wait."

"Ooh, look! It's on."

I dragged my gaze from Felicia's bulging bosom and looked up at the screen.

Caleb was pinned on a couch in the reception, with Mona and Siren either side of him, half on him and gyrating their breasts in his face.

Felicia picked up a remote and turned the sound on.

"No, no, stop…" came Caleb's piss weak protest.

"Oh, baby, I just *love* detectives," said Siren, running her tongue up Caleb's cheek.

"Yeah, baby, you can do *both* of us," added Mona, running a finger along his crotch.

His erection was evident, even on camera. Well, at least he was partly human, then.

"You have to get off me!"

"Oh no, baby, we're only just starting," said Siren, winking up at the camera.

"Felicia, it's perfect. I owe you for this."

The viewing was priceless. Poor bloody Caleb was at a complete loss.

We let it go on for a little longer as we finished our drinks. We swapped a bit more spit, and then it was time to go.

I walked back into the reception area. Mona and Siren were still smothering Caleb in teasing lust.

"Okay, son, time to go. Work to be done. I hope you paid for that treatment. These girls have to earn a living, you know."

Felicia giggled. "If more men were like him, we'd be bankrupt. See you this evening, handsome."

She kissed me and the two girls dismounted from the distraught Caleb.

He jumped up and almost ran for the door.

Felicia frowned. "Hell, Bruce, what is the Academy

producing these days?"

"Don't ask."

Back in the car, Caleb's shaking hands fumbled with the car keys.

"You right to drive, son?"

"Yes, Sarge."

"Don't tell me you want to whinge about that sensational visit, as well."

"They're filthy tarts. And prostitution is just wrong, unethical."

"Says who, son? Not the law, if it's a regulated brothel. And that one certainly is."

"But it's just wrong," he whined.

"No, that's just your opinion. You are entitled to it, but that's all it is. Those girls in there are doing sex work of their own free will, their choice. You don't have some moral right to decide what they do with their bodies. Anyway, didn't you like a bit of attention?"

"No, it was disgusting."

"You still cracked a fat, son. I saw."

He went scarlet. "But…"

"But nothing. That was a perk of the job that most detectives would have loved. This really isn't for you, is it?"

He stared at his lap.

"Okay, let's head for the office. Sort out some paperwork."

"Yes, Sarge."

- 4 -

For the next three days, I dragged Caleb around the whole pastiche of the seedy, sinful, and criminal. Always a phone call first. I had a wide range of contacts and had a lot of respect around the traps with a reputation for only dishing out the full detective treatment to those real arseholes who desperately needed it. It's about us old-school Ds and discretion. It's about being a human as a cop, and not a robot.

By the Thursday afternoon, I had hauled Caleb through a panoply of organized crime hangouts, titty bars, more brothels, the wank-tanks, and the city's finest gay sauna. That last one was gold: Caleb ran for the door after the owner, Mike, had rubbed his butt cheek.

Yeah, by Thursday I had him on the ropes, reconsidering his future. I have to say, for someone of the supposedly young woke brigade, he didn't handle diversity too well. I guess woke is usually selectively so. When it suits.

On Friday morning, everything changed. I didn't know it then, but it would end up rupturing my world as well.

Jimmy grabbed me as soon as I got to the office.

"Mate, there's a task force started yesterday for that rape and murder on Tuesday in Summervale."

"Yeah, nasty one. Wealthy woman who owned a boutique."

"Yes. A lot of political pressure coming down."

"Typical. If she was a murdered hooker no one upstairs would give a fuck. We're sending staff?"

"Yep, including you. Upstairs specifically used your name: they need experienced sergeants as well as troops."

"Shit. What about our little project with idiot boy? It's going bloody well so far."

"Mate, just think about all the overtime you can rake in. I hear there's no budget limitation on this one. And idiot boy is going with you. Along with Jenny and Wallis."

"Okay, I'll gather them up as they come in and we'll head for the operations annex. See you on the other side."

"Good man."

Whilst I was still able to work Caleb hard for the days that followed, it was all routine detective work, chasing down serials for the task force. The gutter wasn't available to me. He worked hard enough, but was as sullen as a jilted teenager.

On day eleven of the task force, there was a major breakthrough and a suspect was dragged in. The guys from Homicide, running the task force, did the interview, but there was no actual confession, although he ranted at length about women getting what they deserved. The villain, George Sneddon, was a three-time rapist, so he knew the ropes: all direct questions got a "no comment". The sexual assault was bang on his MO and there was a heap of useful circumstantial evidence, from what I heard in the debriefing afterwards. No DNA, as Sneddon had learnt his lesson there, too. The hypothesis was that he escalated to murder this time to prevent the victim from talking. Perfectly plausible. We'd all seen case studies of escalating behaviour in our training, and I'd seen a couple of perfect examples along the way.

So that was it, case closed. Backslapping galore, a call from the Minister to the task force head, a media feeding frenzy, and a few cases of cold beer sent down from the Detective Commander.

The next day was wrap-up day for the task force, readying everything to move it back to Homicide. All the laborious collation and evidence-logging work was being done by the juniors, under supervision. That meant my privilege of rank made for a slack day. After a casual lunch, I stayed on in the café to read the papers for a while.

"Working hard there, Bruce?" Jenny Richards, smiling, sat down opposite me.

"Jen, you'll be a sergeant one day. And then you won't get stuck with all the tedious paperwork on a task force. Are you guys done, or just taking a break?"

"I needed to chat to you."

"Mister Ethics giving you the shits again?"

She didn't smile, however. That took me by surprise. I put my newspaper down.

"It is him, but it's complicated."

"Okay, spit it out. Don't keep me in suspense."

"Well, you know Caleb is working with the other probies on the evidence logging team?"

"Yeah."

"He came to see me at lunch. Said he thought something shonky was going on, or 'unethical' as he put it."

"Look, Caleb would think farting in church was unethical. What's he latched onto this time?"

"He says some evidence has been deleted and not included in the brief of evidence for the prosecutor when Sneddon fronted court this morning."

"So why hasn't he spoken to me?"

She looked hesitant. "He's scared of you. Plus he thinks you might be part of it because you're old school like the guys running the task force. And…" She lowered her eyes. "…he mentioned the old Jarvis case that you were on."

That pissed me off. "Jenny, get on your phone and tell that little shit to get down here, now!"

Fifteen minutes later, Caleb appeared. He stood three metres away, looking like an infatuated adolescent too shy to knock on a girl's door.

"Sit!" I pointed at a chair.

He obeyed.

"Too scared to speak to me? Fucking hell, I'm your sergeant, son. I should be the first person you speak to if there's a problem. And what's this shit about the Jarvis case?"

Both of them looked at the table. He looked ready to vomit. "Well…"

"I'm about to lose my temper, Caleb."

Jenny put a hand on his shoulder. "It's okay, go on."

"I'm sorry, Sarge. They used the Jarvis case at the

Academy when we studied miscarriages of justice. And I know you were on that case."

Yes, I certainly had been. Every one of us who had been on that task force five years earlier wished we hadn't been. We'd celebrated long and hard after Sid Jarvis, a known paedophile, went down for the abduction and rape of a twelve-year-old girl. Problem was, he hadn't done it. Couldn't have, as it turned out. But we weren't to know that until much later.

"Yes, Caleb, I was. And it was done in good faith."

"But there was evidence that proved he couldn't have committed the crime."

"Again, correct. Evidence that only emerged two years after his conviction. So, we got the wrong guy, but at the time on all the evidence, he looked good for it. It was all circumstantial, but the prosecutors were happy with it. And, as it went, so was the jury."

"But it's still a miscarriage of justice and that's unethical."

"Shit, Caleb. Okay, a miscarriage of justice, fine. But one that happened in good faith. And that is not unethical. Had we had that later piece of evidence, then things would have been different. We didn't fabricate anything, and we didn't hide anything. Son, sometimes mistakes happen. That's fucking life."

He pondered that. "Okay, but what I've seen this morning is unethical."

I sighed. "Okay. Go on."

"There was a witness statement and photograph that have been completely removed from the evidence logs and the brief. And the references have been removed from the case management system. I found it in the discard box I was assigned to sort out."

I stared at him.

"He's right," said Jenny. "I checked over it after Caleb told me."

"Why would anyone do that? We'd want every bit of evidence we can get for this prick. Did you read this statement,

Caleb? Maybe it's been deleted because it's an irrelevant detail."

He passed me some folded pages.

I read them. And then twice more.

Oh, fuck!

If this witness was telling the truth, as the appended photo with its time and date stamp seemed to corroborate, then George Sneddon was twenty kilometres away from Summervale at the moment Margot Baden-Sewell was being raped and bludgeoned to death in the back room of her store.

"Caleb, you've done the right thing. And for once, finally, I agree with you on something being unethical."

He looked stunned. "But the Jarvis case…"

"Was different. We got it wrong, but it wasn't our fault. This … this is deliberately removing evidence in order to ensure the wrong piece of shit goes to prison. It's called perverting the course of justice."

"I can't believe they'd do it," said Jenny.

"Unfortunately, Jen, this case is the perfect storm. Politically sensitive high-profile case that everyone wants solved in a hurry, combined with some overly ambitious detective sergeants who can sniff rapid promotions coming their way."

They looked at me in stunned silence.

"But that's not the worst bit. I don't actually care if Sneddon does time for something he didn't do, because scum like him have always got away with a whole lot of stuff they should have done time for. No, the real problem here is that the barbaric animal who butchered Margot Baden-Sewell is still out there. Fuck!"

No one spoke.

Caleb sniffed and looked at me. "Sarge, I've been doing lots of thinking. This really isn't for me. I want to go back to the Policy Unit. Please?"

"Son, I think that's the right decision. Leave it with me. Meanwhile, take tomorrow off and then it's the weekend.

We'll have you starting back at headquarters on Monday."

"Thanks, Sarge." He gave me a sad smile and walked off.

"Fuck, what are you going to do?" asked Jenny.

"I'm going to go and get thoroughly pissed as I contemplate my career suicide. I am, as they say, boxed in and buggered."

I lit a smoke.

"Option A, I let one animal, albeit the wrong one, go to prison, whilst the right animal stays free, to no doubt do it again. Option B, I go to Internal Affairs, thus breaking one of the only two inviolable rules in the detective brotherhood."

She frowned. "What's the other rule?"

"Never screw another detective's woman. Or man, in your case."

"Oh, I see. Why don't you get Caleb to go to Internals. He's going to go back to uniform anyway."

"Yeah, some blokes would do that. And I can see the appeal, even the logic. But that's not me. As much as I don't like Caleb, making him do this would be unfair and gutless on my part. And for all my flaws, those two are not on the list. I'm the sergeant here. I need to do this."

"Is there anything I can do to help?"

I chuckled. "The last female copper who asked me that ended up naked in my bed."

"I can think of worse ways to spend a night."

"As delicious as your offer is, I'm going to be shit company tonight, even for the Jameson bottle. But…"

She smiled and stared at me.

"But, I'd like to take a raincheck if the offer is open."

"Sweet, call me."

- 5 -

I called Jimmy first thing the next morning, struggling out of my Jameson haze. Out of respect, I wanted him to hear it from me first.

"I don't envy you, Bruce. I don't have any time for those show-pony blokes at Homicide. That sort leech off the benefits of our brotherhood code, but they'd throw you or me under a bus if it would advance their careers. So don't ever think they've got the loyalty for you that you've always shown. Mate, you've been solid as long as I've known you. You do what you need to. Take a few days off. I'll cover for you."

"Thanks, Jimmy."

I showered, put on my best court suit, and got a taxi to Internal Affairs.

By the middle of the next week, the Director of Public Prosecutions had no-billed Sneddon and he was released.

The media went feral. I smiled bitterly at the irony of the Jarvis case being trotted out again in every news story.

Two days after that, I certainly wasn't smiling as I watched a bulletin of another rape and attempted murder, in the back of a shop with the same MO.

However, Lady Fate was smiling on the police that day, not that we deserved it. A patrol unit had been just two blocks away when a caring citizen had called in a man in a balaclava going in the back door of a shop. The uniformed crew were there in minutes, heard screaming and kicked the door in. They got to the scumbag as he was beating the naked, violated woman with a tyre iron. As it transpired, this was the right offender. He ended up getting charged with nine attacks over the last two years.

A fortnight had gone by since I took leave and I decided it was time to surface. I thought I'd stop in to the Captain's Corner bar in the city, the Friday afternoon watering hole for a lot of the detectives. Jimmy had texted me back to say he'd be there.

I walked in and got a beer, then found Jimmy further along

the bar. We shook hands.

I'd noticed some of the guys conspicuously ignoring me, but others it seemed were up for a comment or three.

Another sergeant at the bar started it.

"Fuck me, Bruce, I never thought I'd see the day that you'd rat out any of the boys."

That was the trigger for others: the bravery of the mob.

"Yeah, you're a dog, Bruce."

"Woof, woof!"

"You got a bloody nerve showing your dog face in here."

"Piss off back to your new mates at Internals."

"Woof, woof."

I swallowed my beer. Time to go. In more ways than one.

"Oi, Jimmy, you got a leash for that dog of yours there?"

Laughter.

"Woof, woof."

Jimmy turned. "Listen you wankers, Bruce is one of the most solid blokes here. If those two arseholes at Homicide had done their job properly, instead of thinking about their next promotion, then another woman wouldn't have been raped and beaten into a coma. And while you pause to think about that, given we are supposed to protect people before thinking about our own interests, I'm going to drink elsewhere. Fuck you!"

There was a tense silence. Jimmy was the longest serving detective in the bar, and none of the others, not even the other senior sergeants, would take him on. At least not directly.

We walked out.

The Flat Out Lizard felt like an oasis, as usual.

I'd already told Zed everything, but gave him a summary of the other bar.

He smiled. "First, you've done the right thing, no matter what they throw at you. Second, you should've been drinking here, not in another bar."

We laughed.

"Thanks, Zed. You're more of a brother to me than a lot of the brotherhood, it seems. There sure as hell is no reward for being a whistle-blower."

"No, there is not," said Jimmy. "But I'll always drink with you, mate."

"Thanks, Jimmy. I'm not looking forward to next week back at the office."

"About that … I won't be there."

"What?"

"I'm putting in my papers a bit earlier than planned. This episode has been the last straw."

I nodded. "Lucky bastard. I wish I could. It's never going to be the same, is it?"

"No, mate, it's not. Officially, you'll be commended and held up as a shining example of great police ethics."

I choked on my beer. "If only Caleb could hear that."

"Look, he didn't fit in, regardless, so we did do him a favour."

"Yeah. Don't know what I'll do, though."

"Take some more leave, think it over. But don't rush back. No matter how officially praised you are, out of the public eye the old guard will treat you as a leper. You need to find a new direction."

Zed finished writing on a piece of white card. He passed it to me. "From my favourite philosopher."

I looked at it and read aloud.

"I have tried as best I could to be a man of ethics and that is what has cost me the most."
– Albert Camus

"Whoa, Zed, that's deep right now."

"True, though."

Jimmy nodded. "Yep."

"I think I'm going to rename this pub, Zed: The Ironic

Lizard."

They laughed.

"Oh, Jimmy, I meant to say earlier, but things went south. I spoke to young Caleb yesterday."

"Really?"

"Yeah, wanted to see how the young bloke was settling back into his desk job. He was loving it."

"No surprise. Some guys belong behind desks."

"And you know what? He thanked me for not throwing him to the wolves. Said he respected me for that."

"Well, bugger me," said Jimmy.

"And," said Zed, "perhaps something from his ethics rants rubbed off on you Bruce, even subconsciously." He grinned as he poured more drinks.

I raised my glass to him. "Well, Zed, since I'm facing the cost of my ethics, how about free drinks?"

He laughed. "I'll be closing up in a few minutes. Then we can get seriously hammered."

"As long as we do it ethically," I said.

We all laughed.

Yeah, despite everything, I still wouldn't be dead for quids.

BLOODY IRONY
Erik Djernaes

Sven sat down in the expensive Danish designer chair that he knew cost at least as much as his monthly pay as a cop. Then he looked up at the sign in front of him, Bank of Denmark, and was reminded how much he hated being here. In a few minutes some other bank guy would show up, and he would have to pour his heart out again to get the money he needed. A "bling" sounded from his front pocket, and he took out his cell phone. In surprise, he looked and smiled at the text from his American colleague, Bill.

> HI, BUDDY. WHAT'S UP IN GOOD, OLD COMMUNISTIC DENMARK? LIFE IS FINE HERE IN GEORGIA, AND I JUST WANTED TO LET YOU KNOW THAT NEITHER YOU NOR YOUR STUPID POINTS OF VIEW ARE FORGOTTEN, LOL. TAKE CARE, MY FRIEND, AND NEVER FORGET TO LOCK AND LOAD. BILL.

Many years ago, he and Bill had been part of the UN peace-keeping force in Kosovo. Police officers came from all over the world to assist in building up Kosovo as an independent state after the war with Serbia. Both were on the same patrol team and gradually became good friends. Sven recalled with joy the many hours they spent on patrol, discussing and laughing about whether Denmark with its high taxes and government interference in public life was really a communistic Chinese province, or if real football was played with a round, and not an oval, ball.

Sven took a closer look at the attached photo in the message and smiled even more. With his curly black hair and mustache, Bill still looked like Tom Selleck in the 80s, and he still fitted the t-shirt that Sven had made especially for him as a farewell present when they left Kosovo. On the front was the American flag, but instead of fifty stars, it had fifty .44 Magnums. Above the flag it said: "Magnum-Spangled Banner" and below, "In Gun We Trust." Bill had loved the T-shirt, and even though they agreed on most things, it had become a symbol of the issue that mostly separated their opinions. The right to carry a gun anywhere and at any time was just as fundamental to Bill as the freedom of speech and having a beer after work. "It's part of the American culture," Bill usually argued when they discussed the two countries very different gun laws. "And I would never allow for some asshole to decide my destiny just because I didn't have my gun to defend myself or my family."

Sven could see Bill's point. But then again, he didn't see the need to be armed in his spare time, and he didn't mind that in Denmark it was only police officers on duty who were allowed to carry a gun.

Dumb foreigner, was all Sven got to write in return to Bill before a voice interrupted him. He looked up, and beside him stood a man with slick, blond hair and a dark blue suit. With his pimples and boyish face, the guy looked like he had just graduated from High School, Sven thought.

"Sorry to keep you waiting, Mr. Madsen," the guy said with a light voice that matched the teenage-look. "My name is Dennis Jacobsen, and I'm the manager of the bank's loan division," he said and sat down in a matching designer chair on the other side of the wooden desk.

"That's all right, and you can call me Sven," Sven said in his nicest tone and put the phone away. He was going to let Bill know later that he was more than just a "dumb foreigner."

"Okay, Sven. I've looked at your loan application, and just like my colleague that you've talked to earlier, I'm also sorry to inform you that the bank can't provide you with the loan you're asking for," Dennis said with a fake understanding smile that he had probably once been taught at a banking course should make it easier for the customer to accept a negative answer.

Sven clenched his fists under the desk and breathed heavily through his nose. He couldn't believe this and was about to say something when Dennis continued.

"As you can see on this chart," Dennis said and leaned over the desk to show Sven a graph full of numbers, "you need another one thousand kroner in your monthly income to qualify for a loan of the desired four hundred thousand kroner. I'm sorry, but that's the policy of the bank. And if you have followed the news the last few years, you will know that all banks are under a lot of pressure and that we can't afford to lose more money."

Sven felt like grabbing that fucking self-important pimple head by his collar and telling him a thing or two about life. For ten years, he had been a loyal customer in the bank and never missed a payment. And now that he desperately needed a loan, he had to listen to some dumbass in a suit talking to him like he was an irresponsible kid.

"Yes, I understand that, but I had hoped that you could see that I've always been a trustworthy customer and that you could make an exception. Please, I need the money for saving the life of my daughter," Sven said and hated himself for having to sound like a beggar. But his 18-year-old daughter, Eileen, had cancer, and to improve her chances of surviving significantly, they had to go for four treatments at a private hospital in Germany. The only problem was that each treatment cost 100.000 kroner, and he didn't have the money.

"I understand your situation, Mr. Madsen, but bank policy is bank policy." Dennis Jacobsen once again tried his appreciative smile, and this time backed it up by solemnly folding his hands. "And as you surely understand, we have to be very careful about taking risks. Not only in our interest but more important, in the interest of all our customers."

"But, it's only one thousand kroner per month. I can do extra work," Sven burst out, before a woman's scream from behind interrupted him.

Dennis Jacobsen immediately jumped up from his seat, and with big eyes, he pointed eagerly in the direction of the scream.

"It's a... it's a bank robbery," Dennis Jacobsen stuttered before turning his panicked stare to Sven. "You're a policeman. You must do something." Without another word, he squatted down and hid behind his chair.

As Sven turned around, he saw the back of a tall, skinny person wearing a black hoodie, black sweat pants, white sneakers, and a black ski mask running towards the bank's exit. In one hand, the robber had a yellow plastic bag and in the other a large, gray butcher knife.

"Help, he robbed me!" the woman by the counter screamed before her voice devolved into a terrified cry.

The sight immediately triggered Sven's instinct, and even though he passed his 45th birthday last year, he still felt like a hunting dog, trained to hunt down and capture the fleeing fox. With all muscles alert, he kicked his chair aside and took on the pursuit.

Outside, the robber had gotten a good lead, but Sven's weekly soccer practice now paid off, and he slowly reduced the gap between them.

"Stop! Stop, it's the police!" Sven yelled. He tried to control his heavy breathing from the sudden cold-start-sprint.

Shortly after, the robber skidded to a sudden stop and turned around to face Sven.

"Stay, uh, uh," the robber started before having to pause to catch his breath through the ski mask's small and narrow mouth crack. "Stay away, uh, or I'll stab you," he yelled and swung the knife in Sven's direction 30 feet away.

"Now, put down the knife and don't make it worse," Sven replied with an effort to sound as calm as possible. With his pulse lowered, he took a step back and recalled an important lesson from the use-of-force training at the police academy - distance is your best friend against a knife-armed attacker.

"You fucking leave me alone, or I will kill you with this!" the robber yelled, and as if to underline the size of the big knife, he demonstratively held the knife out in front of him. Then he turned around and continued sprinting down the road. Sven followed, and after a short distance, houses began to appear on both sides.

Suddenly, the robber made a right turn into a garage. Sven's jaw tightened as he lost visual contact. Still going on the hunting instinct, he turned the corner to the garage at full speed before he realized his mistake. The garage was only about 30 feet long and closed on all sides, so before he managed to stop, he had himself cornered by the end. With the robber standing right in front of him with his knife raised, ready to stab him in the stomach.

"Fuck!" Sven's curse burst out and instinctively, he wished that he had subscribed to Bill's point regarding dealing with a situation like this. If he only had his gun right now. Instead, he got his hands up to cover his body and be as ready for a fight as possible.

"Didn't I tell you to fucking leave me alone?" the robber yelled in Sven's face while restless moving his feet and swinging the knife in front of him. "Didn't I?"

"Easy, easy now," Sven said as calmly as the fear of suddenly having a butcher's knife possibly stabbed in his gut allowed him to speak. The robber seemed like he could panic any time, and there was no need to make the situation even more tense by yelling at him.

Like an angry, desperate predator deciding whether to attack or not, the robber kept moving his feet from side to side while breathing heavily and mumbling to himself behind the mask. Sven thought that this might be his only chance, and just as he was about to launch a surprise attack, the robber threw the knife hard to the ground.

"Fuck!" he yelled and ran out of the garage.

Still in shock, Sven stood back and tried to slow down his racing heart. He leaned back, closed his eyes, inhaled deep, and felt as grateful to be alive as he had ever felt before. Then he opened his eyes and set the hunting dog inside him free again.

In no time, Sven was up alongside the robber, and with a swift move, he grabbed him by his shoulder and took him down.

"Do you know how fucked I am now?" the robber yelled in desperation as they fought on the asphalt.

During the struggle, the robber's ski mask rolled up on the left side, and just as Sven had the robber pinned to the ground with an arm lock, he noticed the brown, heart-shaped mark under the robber's left ear. A mark he hadn't seen for at least ten years.

"Justin," Sven burst out in surprise without thinking.

"How the fuck do you know my name?" the robber asked in surprise. Aggressively, he tried to get out of the lock and turn his head against Sven.

"Lay still," Sven commanded and tightened the lock. He didn't want Justin to recognize him now, even though he probably wouldn't. At least he hadn't so far, which was likely because the last time they'd met, Justin was only eight years old, and Sven had a full beard.

Back then Justin had started in Eileen's class when he and his nineteen-year-old mom moved from Sweden to Denmark. Half a year before, Justin had watched as a rival Hell's Angel member killed his biker dad, and his mom quite reasonably didn't feel safe in Sweden anymore.

For some reason that Sven had never figured out, Justin and Eileen became best friends. Justin never wanted them to spend time at his apartment, so almost every day after school they came home to Eileen's and played. Often, Justin also ended up staying for dinner and even spending the night. Sven remembered how Justin and Eileen used to sleep under the same blanket and how Justin, one morning at breakfast, asked if he could be Eileen's brother.

Justin's mom had been sweet and nice but in no way capable of taking care of an eight- year-old boy. Often she didn't come home at night, or she showed up drunk or under the influence of drugs at the kids' school. Sven had tried his best to help Justin, but suddenly one year later, Justin didn't come to school. The story that circulated was that he had moved to another part of the country, but Sven didn't know for certain. He recalled how sad Eileen had been that Justin moved without saying goodbye. Sven later found out that Justin's mom had gone to prison for dealing drugs, and Justin was moved, against his will, to live in a foster home.

Sven's thoughts were interrupted by Justin's trembling body and his crying from under the ski mask.

"I'm, I'm going to be blind now," Justin cried, and all his former resistance was now replaced by sulking.

"Blind. What do you mean?" Sven asked, unsure that he had heard the boy right.

"What do you care?"

"Tell me."

"I got some heroin without paying up front, and when it came time to pay the thousand kroner I didn't have the money. Then yesterday they told me that I now owed them one hundred thousand kroner, and if I didn't pay them today at two o'clock, they would take me and blind me with acid. That was the only reason why I robbed the bank," Justin said with a low emotionless voice. Just like he would have answered any other question. Then he started sulking as if he was once again reminded of the consequence of his answer. "Now I wish I stabbed you in that garage so they could get the money and leave me alone."

Sven stared at the shaking body beneath him. It wasn't the first time that he had heard such a story, but for the first time, it hit him right in the heart.

Sirens of patrol cars sounded around them, and Sven figured that it was only a matter of time before his colleagues would find them. So if he was going to do something about the most fucked up idea that he had ever come up with, he had to do it now.

"Now, listen up kid. And listen carefully, because if you make me repeat myself, I'm probably gonna end up regretting what I'm about to say. Do you hear me?" Sven asked, and to be sure that he got Justin's attention, he squeezed his arm a little further up his back.

"Ouch, yes, I hear you," Justin sobbed and lay completely still.

Moments later, Justin did as ordered. He swung his now free left arm back and hit Sven in the face with his elbow. Then he got up, grabbed the yellow plastic bag, and ran like hell.

Sven sat down on the asphalt and felt his sore right eye. It would probably swell up and get all kinds of colors, but it would be fine again. A patrol car with lights and sirens approached and stopped right in front of him. As the colleagues got out of the vehicle, Sven looked at his watch; ten till two. "All right," he mumbled and ran the story over in his head one last time—after a short struggle, the robber managed to escape with the money, and Sven had no idea who he was or where he was running.

Like it was yesterday, he saw the two little kids in front of him—sleeping peacefully together, and Justin asking at the breakfast table if he could be Eileen's brother and live with her forever. Yes, no matter how wrong his decision was, he couldn't have made any other choice. He took a deep breath and was now thankful that he didn't have his gun when he rounded that corner into the garage.

Back in the bank, Sven briefly talked to the detective in charge of the investigation and was then introduced to another bank employee.

"Hello, Mr. Madsen. My name is Jonas Smith, and I'm the bank's regional manager. And I just want..." Smith trailed off as he looked at Sven's eye. He pointed. "I'm sorry, but your right eye really looks bad."

"Oh, yeah, I got that just before the robber got away. Don't worry about it." Sven wondered why the bank's regional manager wanted to talk to him.

"Okay. Well, first of all, and on behalf of the bank, I want to let you know how much we appreciate your effort to try and catch that guy. And secondly, I would also like to apologize for my colleague's misunderstanding regarding your loan application. I have looked at the papers and personally made sure that you will get the loan of four hundred thousand kroner. And even at an interest rate one percent less than normal." Jonas Smith put his right hand out for Sven to shake.

"Well, thank you very much," Sven said. As he shook Jonas Smith's hand, he felt a blend of mixed emotions. Of course, he was happy about the loan, but he wasn't sure that Jonas Smith would have done him the same favor if he knew the real story.

"Oh, and if it's not too much to ask, could you please call my daughter and give her the news?" Sven asked. "That would make her so happy."

"Sure, no problem," Jonas Smith answered and smiled as he wrote down Eileen's phone number.

On his way out of the bank, Sven was stopped by a uniformed colleague.

"Hey, have you seen this?" the colleague asked and showed Sven his cell phone. "04-901 spotted the bank robber up at the train station, just as he was about to hand over the money to two well-known Albanian criminals. Some guy caught it all on his phone, and now it's gone viral." The colleague pressed play.

Sven now watched a male and a female police officer standing next to each other, filmed from behind. The male officer had his gun pointed at three young men, who all stood about forty feet away, with their sides to the patrol officers. All were dressed in black, and it looked like the guy on the left in white sneakers was handing over a yellow plastic bag to one of the two other guys.

"It's the police!" the male uniformed police officer yelled. "All of you, get down on the ground. Now!"

Apparently, the criminals hadn't noticed the police before then. As if shocked by the sudden yelling, the guy on the left jerked his body and dropped the bag to the ground. The two men on the right turned their heads towards the camera and then started running. Quickly the female officer grabbed the microphone by her shoulder.

"Two male suspects from the bank robbery, all dressed in black, are running east from the train station along the railroad tracks. 04-901 over," the officer called before putting the microphone back.

The guy on the left didn't move an inch but just kept his gaze straight ahead. Then he put his left hand into his pocket and turned his front to the officers.

Sven felt his heart seem to stop beating when facing the guy on the camera. Ten years ago, Justin's face had been warm and alive, but now his wild hair, and desperate staring eyes mostly reminded Sven of a stressed stray dog pushed too far.

"Stay there and show me both of your hands," the male officer ordered.

Justin took a deep breath. Then, still, with his left hand hidden in his pocket, walked resolutely towards the officers.

"I've got a knife, and I'm going to fucking stab you," Justin said coldly while continuously walking and staring directly at the male officer.

"Stop, or I'll shoot!" the officer yelled back.

Justin kept walking.

"Now, please stop," a nervous male voice suddenly shouted. It came from the guy filming, and his voice made the female officer turn her head toward the camera.

"What are you doing? Get away from here," she directed him, before a louder and more aggressive voice took over.

"I'm going to fucking *kill you*!" Justin screamed and accelerated at the officers with his left hand still hidden.

On the screen, Sven watched the male officer's gun move slightly up and down twice, as the burst of two gunshots sounded. Like in a movie, Justin reacted by stopping, looking down at his chest, and then collapsing backward to the ground. Shaped like a cross, he laid completely still on his back with both arms out from the body.

"Suspect shot at the train station," the female officer called down her microphone as her partner quickly moved towards Justin. "We need an ambulance."

"Fuck, there's no knife," the male officer said after searching Justin's pockets.

"What?" his partner asked.

"Why did you say that you had a knife when you didn't?" the first officer cried out, holstering his gun.

"Oh shit," the man filming muttered from off-camera.

The male officer knelt beside Justin and started doing CPR with hard pushes down on the man's motionless chest. "Why, why?"

Then the filming stopped.

"Some crazy shit, huh?" the colleague said and looked at Sven.

"Yeah," Sven answered and turned away. He felt like shit. All this fucking mess was his fault.

A "bling" sounded from his pocket, and Sven took out his cell phone to check the text.

HI, DAD. GUESS WHAT? SOME GUY FROM THE BANK HAS JUST CALLED AND TOLD ME THAT YOU WERE ABLE TO GET THE MONEY FOR MY TREATMENT. I'M JUST SO HAPPY, AND I KNOW THAT I'LL MAKE IT. I LOVE YOU. EILEEN.

Sven closed his eyes, took a deep breath, and now only felt sorry about one thing - that he would never get to thank Justin for being Eileen's perfect brother.

FULL SERVICE

Scott Kikkawa

"Sixty dollar."

"Sixty bucks? I thought the house fee was fifty."

"Now Sixty. Sixty dollar."

"When did that happen? Last time it was fifty."

"Last month. One month already sixty dollar."

What the hell. What was I going to do, turn around and walk out over ten bucks?

I fished three twenties out of my pocket and handed them over to the woman sitting behind the Formica-topped counter. She was mid-fifties trying to look thirty and doing a good enough job for a compromise at forty. By the accent, she was Mainland Chinese, but her English was good enough to suggest she'd been around for a couple of decades, immigration status courtesy of some love-struck G.I. or cash-deficient barfly in need of a quick ten grand. Whoever the lucky guy was, he was long gone, the divorce decree probably coming just after the marriage hit the two-year mark to ensure a ten-year green card. I'd bet that her driver's license—California, New York, Texas, Virginia or Washington State—had a name on it like Yu Ting Reilly or Hong Rui Rodriguez or something other than Chinese, a last, lingering ghost of a two-year marriage haunting all her official paperwork.

The name she used at the counter was "Jackie" and she collected the house fee for Jasmine Relaxation on South King Street in Honolulu, in that no-man's land outside of Waikiki crammed with sorry low-rise apartment buildings and seventy-year-old commercial edifices filled with dental offices and travel agencies and shady pyramid schemes masquerading as "investments". In this neighborhood, dug in like ticks on a stray dog's ass, were the massage parlors like the one I was standing in. These weren't places where hands that had seen a hundred hours of clinical practice worked all the kinks and knots out of the sore victims of auto accidents or work-related injuries. The hands here—and mouths and other wet orifices—worked the tension out of "patients" whose only ailment was a libido that needed scratching every payday.

Jackie took my cash and smoothed the bills out with her crimson-nailed fingers. Her hands were where her true age showed—gnarled and weathered by a lifetime of doing things mine were spared from by a middle-class upbringing and a college education. Success-story self-made millionaires had nothing on these women. No fried chicken chain founding father ever gave his body in pursuit of a better life. When the bills were ironed out to her satisfaction, she folded them in half and stood up and stuck them in her jeans pocket. She wore a tight-fitting dark tank top that contoured her surgically-enhanced self and lots of make up under the pink neon to complete the smoke-and-mirrors.

She reached for a pair of glasses on the counter and put them on and gave me a long look.

"You new. Not see you before."

"Yeah, I wanted to check it out here. I heard the girls are better."

"Where you go before?"

"Sakura Garden."

She smiled. No crow's feet by the eyes. Good surgeon. "Our girls better than Sakura. Good thing you come here. Good choice."

"Good choice," I said. I smiled back, but with a tinge of nervousness.

Jackie laughed. "You nice, handsome. Nice and clean. I get

you good girl."

I laughed along with her, still with some lingering nervousness. "Good," I said. "Thank you."

Nice and clean. This was massage parlor shorthand for "Local Japanese-American customer, lots of money, mild-mannered, married so he'll keep quiet." In other words, big tipper, no diseases, doesn't do drugs, won't hit the girls or ask for anything too wild.

I smirked when I thought about this. Didn't they know it was usually the quiet ones who became serial killers and active shooters? All that pent-up rage and resentment and nowhere to vent it except among people who didn't know him, and a massage parlor was full of people that didn't know him.

She stepped out from behind the counter and waved me over to follow. "Come," she said. "I give you the big room."

I nodded and jammed my hands in my pocket and followed her across the fake-pine laminate floor down a hallway with several whitewashed interior doors, all numbered with index cards with broadly-drawn numbers in felt tip marker. The cards were scotch-taped to the doors at about eye level. At the end of the hallway was the door marked "5".

"For you," said Jackie, stopping in front of the door. "Big room. Take your time."

"Do I just go in and wait?"

"Yeah. Go inside. Take off your clothes. Put on the towel. Wait for the girl. I send you a new one. Clean girl. Nice, pretty. You like. Nice girl for nice guy like you. You'll see. Nice girl."

"Okay. Thanks," I said, and opened the door.

The room was about ten feet by ten feet, not my idea of "big", but the other rooms were probably nothing more than closets with better ventilation. I went in and shut the door behind me. The room was illuminated by a pseudo-Japanese lamp with shoji door-like wood-frame-and-paper panels around a naked bulb. The bulb was pink, and it threw off a weird, Christmas-like glow, like the window display in a closed drugstore or the neon of a Chinatown porn shop. On the floor was a twin sized mattress, no frame, no box spring, just a mattress on the floor. The lamp sat on the floor next to the head of the mattress, and next to the lamp was a box of tissues. There was a large, white folded towel on the mattress at its foot. There was nothing else in the room.

I knelt next to the mattress and gave it a sniff. The sheets smelled like fabric softener and looked like they had been recently changed. The towel similarly had that fresh-out-of-the-dryer scent. This was always a plus, because establishments like this never got a visit from the Department of Health. That the manager of the place kept the sheets fresh was a sign of a competitive individual. Honolulu was a small place, and word traveled quickly, even among a subcommunity like brothel customers. These so-called "mongers" even had their own Facebook group, where they'd compare notes on everything from the blowjob quality to the brand of tissue on hand for post-coital clean up (pickier mongers insisted on Kleenex and not the generic big box brand, citing "sensitive foreskin").

This establishment was definitely savvy to the chatter. Clean sheets. Kleenex. Laminate flooring mopped and swept regularly. Fingers crossed that the shampoo tables here were just as clean.

I looked back at the closed door and noticed the hook and a single drycleaner wire hanger dangling from it. I removed my penny loafers, then my socks and tucked my socks into the shoes and placed them next to the wall near the door. I got undressed, and hung my clothes up on the hanger, my chinos and dress belt and reverse-print aloha shirt, the so-called "Brooks Brothers Suit of Hawaii". Nobody here wore an actual coat and tie to the office. Are you kidding? It rarely dropped below eighty degrees out, even in the dead of winter, if you could call it that. Only three guys wore a suit in Honolulu: attorneys going to court, the guy walking you to your table at that French restaurant in the Halekulani, and the gorilla who held the door open for you at Tiffany's who knew how to say, "Thank you, come again" in both English and Japanese.

I folded my boxer shorts and stuffed it inside the neck of my shirt on the hanger and tucked my tortoiseshell framed glasses in to the shirt's pocket. I looked at my clothes hanging from the hanger on the peg. Jesus, I dressed just like the swarm of Japanese office dweebs on Bishop Street in downtown Honolulu. Nice and Clean. At least my folks were proud of my clothes, though they'd surely disapprove if they knew they currently hung from a wire hanger in a brothel. But the outfit did make these women eager to please, even if no discount came with the service.

No discount was the point when it came to guys like me. Good Japanese boys from Kaimuki or Manoa or Hawaii Kai could afford to tip the girls lavishly. This is why I always got the VIP treatment whenever I walked into a place like this. Girls fought for my attention in a way they never did in high school. What a difference twenty years and a paycheck makes.

I picked the white, fuzzy towel up off the mattress and wrapped it around my waist. It was nice and warm and felt like it wouldn't give me a rash. I paced back and forth in front of the mattress for a couple of minutes when I heard a gentle, little knock on the door and a husky feminine voice say "Hello? Can I come in?"

"Yeah," I said, my voice raised a little to make sure it traveled through the wood. "Come in."

The door opened slowly, letting in some of the scant light of the hallway into the room. I could see her silhouette traced by the glow from the neon-framed clock that hung on the wall outside the room. Her hair was bleached light reddish-brown, which was all the rage with Asian women under seventy years old. Her hair was shoulder length and fell nicely, like it might have been professionally done. I thought if she shook her head, her hair would swirl in slow motion about her neck like a shampoo commercial. Her neck was long and graceful and her figure was curved attractively with a tiny waist. She wore a sheer lace robe over a black bra and panty and six-inch heels. In other words, she looked like a lot of women I had come to visit in a room like the one I stood in.

She stepped into the room and shut the door behind her. I could see her face now in the pink glow of the paper-shaded floor lamp. It was a pleasant face that reminded me of a bank teller or an elementary school health room aide. She smiled and I could see a slight gap in her teeth. She had character and had a real person aspect about her that set her apart from the flesh-for-cash monsters I was used to seeing. By her accent, I placed her origin as Mainland China, like Jackie out front.

"My name Jessica," she said. "What's your name?"

"Steve," I said.

"Steep?"

"Steve. With a 'V'."

"Steef," she said, smiling and showing me the gap in her teeth again. Close enough. "Hi, Steef. Nice to meet you." She moved toward me and threw her arms around me, holding her form up against mine with a gentle pressure. I put my arms around her.

"Nice to meet you," I said into her hair. It smelled like strawberry pancake syrup.

She gave me a light, gentle kiss and said, "Come. Let's get you wash up."

"Okay," I said.

She took my hand and led me toward the door. I looked up at my clothes hanging on the wire hanger with some concern. She caught me looking.

"It's okay. Your stuff okay here. Nobody touch."

"Are you sure?"

"Yeah. Nobody touch." She broke out in a low laugh. "You worry too much. Come, we get you wash up, wash away stress. Then no worries."

"All right. If you say so."

Jessica grabbed my hand and led me out of the "big" room

back into the hallway. She pulled me to the left, down a corridor that ended in a door. On the door was another index card scotch taped at eye level inscribed with "SHOWER" in black marker. She opened the door and the scent of drugstore body wash and warm, wet tile hit me in the face with the moist air. She peeled the index card off the door and turned it around before sticking it back on the door. The opposite side of the card read "OCUPIED". It was missing a "C", but I admired the effort when they could have settled for "IN USE." What the hell. Everyone in the place knew what it meant: naked man on a wet vinyl table getting scrubbed by a woman in fancy underwear. So, I wasn't going to worry that someone would barge in on my "body shampoo".

She closed the door after we entered and told me to wait by the door. The room was lit up by a hideously bright fluorescent fixture. The whole room was tiled from floor to ceiling. The only thing in it was a homemade wooden table with heavy legs topped by a green vinyl pad. Jessica grabbed a garden hose coiled up in the corner, turned the faucet on and wet the vinyl, then took a sponge and scrubbed it with soap before rinsing it off. It was a show to show me that I wouldn't be lying on the bodily fluids and shorthairs of the guy before me.

She removed my towel and hung it on a hook on the door.

"You lie down," she said.

"Which way?"

"I wash your back first."

I got on the table on my stomach somewhat tentatively. The pad was wet but warm as the water out of the hose was heated. I felt the bath-temperature water cover my back as she wet me with the hose. It felt comfortable. Then I felt the Japanese nylon washcloth scrub me from neck to heels with blue body wash from a tall container in the corner. Then I was rinsed again.

"Turn over," she said.

I did as I was told and got on my back. I was hosed down once again and lathered up and scrubbed. She made a conscious effort to avoid my crotch, passing around it and washing my thighs down to my feet, even passing the washcloth between my toes. She handed me the soapy cloth.

"You wash yourself," she said. She pointed between my legs.

"Okay," I said. This was a common practice to avoid any contact with the customer's genitals prior to negotiating a price for sex services to follow the bath and massage. I obliged and gave myself a good cleaning while she watched. She had a vested interest in making sure I was as clean as I could be down there. I got a better look at her in the brightly lit shower room. Jessica was a well-preserved specimen in her mid-forties. The heavy makeup made her age indeterminate in the dimly lit mattress room, but under better light the illusion faded. It was difficult to tell if she had been in Hawaii for a while, because her skin was nearly as pale as the tiles in the shower room. This wasn't surprising—these women rarely set foot outdoors. They ate in the kitchen in the establishment and slept on the very mattresses they serviced the customers on.

Jasmine Relaxation, like all of its counterparts in the area, was open 24/7. Jessica probably got her sleep between five in the morning and noon, when business was slow. The occasional early-riser weirdo might come calling, and one of those poor women would be roused into action, forced to do her hair and makeup in ten minutes or less while the geezer in his sweatshirt and P.E. shorts would lounge on the faux-leather sofa next to the reception counter. The "lucky" girl would do what Jessica was doing to me, but while half asleep. Massage parlor life. After having been in a few of these establishments, I developed a strange appreciation for the effort these women put into their craft. In a weird way, it reminded me of bakers who wake up at two in the morning or novelists who hammer away at the keyboard until the sun comes up. Maybe it had something to do with the fact that these women made more per hour than bakers or novelists.

I chose not to torture them by showing up at the crack of

dawn. I came at the comfortable "business" hour of seven in the evening, when it just got dark. In Honolulu, it always gets dark around the same time.

Jessica rinsed me off and shut off the faucet and coiled the hose up neatly. She fetched the towel off the hook on the door.

"Stand up," she said.

I stood up.

She dried me off with the towel and wrapped it around my waist with an expert touch.

"Massage time," she said.

I nodded. We exited the shower room. She flipped the index card on the door back to indicate the shower room was once again vacant. We headed back to the Room Number Five. She shut the door behind me.

"Lie down," she said, taking the towel from around my waist and folding it and placing it in a corner on the floor. "I do your back first."

I did as I was commanded, getting prone on the mattress and lying still. The washing with the warm water had relaxed me enough to put me on the edge of drowsy. Out of the corner of my eye, I could see Jessica shed her flimsy short robe leaving her in her lingerie. She didn't bother removing her heels. She disappeared from my field of vision and I felt the mattress gently give as she stepped onto it, then lowered herself to straddle my back. She was light and warm and feminine. She placed her small hands on my shoulders and started kneading lightly, with barely any pressure at all. As far as massages went, it was bullshit. A light backrub that said *this is not what you're really here for, so let's cut to the chase.*

Sure enough, after just a few seconds of pressing my neck and back, she stopped and lay down next to me. I could smell the cheap, floral shampoo in her hair and the powder on her face.

"You handsome guy. You Japanese?" she asked.

"Yeah."

"I like Japanese guy. Nice and clean. *Daisuki.*"

"English. I don't speak Japanese."

"You local boy."

I nodded.

"What you like tonight?" she asked.

"What do you have?"

"You like suck?"

"How about something more?"

"You like Full Service?"

"Uh, yeah. Full Service. How much?"

"Two hundred dollar."

"Two hundred? That's a lot. It's One fifty at Sakura."

"You like. Stay long time. I promise, you like."

Full Service. That was massage parlor parlance for oral and vaginal penetration. It was the standard fare on the menus of all these places. Full Service was ostensibly an hour, but usually lasted much less than that. Once the customer actually finished, all he wanted to do was get dressed and get the hell out of there.

"Okay," I said. I stood up and fished a wad of twenties and my phone out of my pants hanging on the door.

"Why phone?" she asked.

"I need to call home and say I'm going to be late," I said. Then I added sheepishly: "I'm married."

"Okay," she said. She handed me my phone. "You call. I wait."

I made my call.

"Hi honey. I'm sorry. I'm finishing up a report. I'll leave soon. Just eat without me. Sorry."

I hit "record" after I terminated the call and extended my hand with the cash to her. She made a grab for the bills and I quickly withdrew my hand, holding the cash back over my shoulder.

"That's two hundred dollars, right?" I asked.

"Yes," she said.

"And for that I get full service?"

"Yes."

"You sure?"

"Yes," she said, now impatient. I let her have the cash and I stopped recording. I got up, put my phone back in my pants and returned to the mattress.

. Jessica counted the bills in the dim light of the lamp. She nodded, and tucked them in her short robe on the floor and pulled out a small, shiny two-inch square. A condom.

She returned to the mattress and showed me the condom package.

"Okay?" she asked. "I put on for you."

"Wait. Can I just lie down and hold you for a little bit? Just for a couple of minutes before we start? I don't want to rush this."

She smiled broadly and positioned herself next to me on the mattress. "Okay," she said. "I make nice, like girlfriend."

"Yeah," I said. "Like girlfriend."

Girlfriend. For hire. Some guys liked that, and arguably it wasn't really the sex they paid for. It was knowing they had something intimate with a woman, even if it was fleeting. I'd also guess that a lot of those women took care of the customers with some trace of genuine affection as those men were providers in a way, a real means of support and financial security. Maybe it really was a relationship, even if it had a shelf life of an hour.

We lay there for what seemed like an interminable amount of time. I let myself take in her scent and held her against me with my eyes closed. The near-drowsy sensation was just about to take complete hold of me when I was jarred out of the peaceful embraced by thunder at the door: loud, violent knocks that threatened to splinter the cheap wood.

"POLICE! COMING IN!"

The door flew open and I stared up at the muzzle of a nine-millimeter handgun attached to a big body in a dark blue raid shirt.

"Shit," I said. "Shit."

"You two," the big body commanded, "move apart."

"Can I put my clothes on, at least?" I asked.

"Where are they at?"

"On the door."

The cop came in. He commanded me to face away from him, which I did. I could hear him remove my clothes from the hook and shake them, and when he was convinced there wasn't anything in there that could hurt him, he threw them on the bed."

"Put 'em on," he said.

I hastily got dressed.

"You," he said to Jessica. "You sit there on the bed and don't move." She nodded and moved to the end of the mattress.

"Hey," I said to the cop. "We didn't do anything wrong. I just got a massage, that's all."

"Shut up," he said.

"I mean it. We didn't do anything. I just got a massage from her, that's all."

"Shut the fuck up. I didn't ask you to tell me what happened here yet."

"Well, that's what happened."

The big cop rolled his eyes. "Annie!" he bellowed out in the hallway.

A female officer in a raid shirt turned up at the door of Room Number Five.

"Stay with the girl," said the big cop. "I'm gonna take Mr. CPA—who-didn't-do-nothing outside and have a talk with him. He won't fucking shut up."

"Attitude adjustment," the cop called Annie said to me. "This isn't going to be fun for you."

"I'm not a CPA," I protested. "I sell insurance."

"Shut the fuck up, CPA. I hear one more thing outta you, I slap your fucking head. Understand?"

"Yeah, I'm just saying…"

I was shoved out into the hallway by his big, meaty hand.

"Move," he said.

I moved.

The hallway and the reception area out front were a sea of navy-blue raid shirts emblazoned with bright golden yellow: HPD POLICE. Two cops as big as my escort were standing over Jackie, asking her where the money was kept.

I was given another shove out the door and pulled out to a big black Chevy Suburban with tinted windows and pushed to the other side of the vehicle, out of view of the occupants of the raided massage parlor.

"I think you look more like a CPA than an insurance agent," said the big cop.

"Same shit," I said. We both laughed.

"Good job tonight, Steve. Half hour. That's gotta be a record. You sure you got the violation?"

"Have we met? What do you think, Paul? Full Service, two hundred bucks. She said it. I got it on my phone. It'll stand up in court."

"Just fucking with you. I know you always get them to say it. Your shit's in the back," Paul said, opening the door to the Suburban. I leaned in and dragged a duffel bag out. I pulled a raid shirt out and changed into it. I got out of my khakis and pulled a pair of BDUs on and traded my loafers for tactical boots. I fished in the bag and found my badge and hung it around my neck, then put my gun belt on.

"All set," I said.

"Almost," said Paul. He tossed me a ski mask. I pulled it on over my head. This was so the women inside wouldn't recognize me as a cop in case we had to raid the place again. Undercovers like me were in short supply. I'm small and Japanese and I don't look like a cop. I look like… well, I look like a CPA.

I pulled the ski mask over my head and adjusted it so I could see out of the eye holes.

"Much better," said Paul, nodding. "An improvement."

"Don't hate me because I'm beautiful. Hate me because you're not."

Paul laughed and clapped his big hand on my shoulder. "And what's this 'honey, I got reports to do' shit?"

"I had to change it up. 'I won't be home for dinner' and no explanation was getting old."

"You're an artist. Come on, Steverino," he said. "Let's get in there and bag all those condoms and lube." He handed me a few evidence bags and a black Sharpie.

"After you."

We went back in for what felt like the hundredth time. We were going to book women who were raising the cash they needed to put their kids through college or smuggle other family out of abject misery. Full Service was the only way most of them could do it.

I hated that I was so good at standing in their way.

ONE FINE DAY

Frank Zafiro

They watched the video of it on the news. As the anchor described the event, Bowen tuned him out. Instead, he stared intently at the uniformed figure on the screen. He wanted to urge the officer to stop, to change tactics. The threat seemed controlled, so the next move was to transition away from pinning the man to the ground.

He said nothing, though. The video was a recording. The officer's actions had already been taken a day ago. The fate over everyone in the video was already sealed.

"My God," Kristen said. She sat next to him on the couch. Her hand had been resting on his forearm. Now her fingers clutched at his skin.

Bowen still said nothing. More time passed on the screen. Bystanders urged and demanded action. The man on the ground begged, his pleas coming in shorter and shorter breathless bursts. The officer did not move. As Bowen watched, the seconds were torturous.

When the newscast finally cut away, Kristen let out a whispered curse. "Can you believe that?"

"No," Bowen said. "It looked bad."

"*Looked* bad? Sean, they *killed* him."

"Yeah, that's what the news said."

He could sense her shock. She withdrew her hand from his forearm. "You want me to switch over to the *other* network to see if they even *mention* it?"

"No." He didn't want to fight with her. Not about politics,

where they differed. And not about this, either. He had a sinking feeling that they'd never be able to fully understand each other. His world and hers were too far apart. Somehow they managed to stay together for almost two years in spite of that.

Kristen wouldn't be put off so easily. "You're not going to defend that, are you?" Her incredulous tone had other elements lurking within. Anger, and disappointment.

"No," Bowen said again. "I only just saw it. I'm processing."

"What's to process? That cop held that poor man down, a leg across his neck, until he died. And even then, he didn't let him up." She motioned toward the television. "We just watched the same video, right?"

"It looks like that's what happened," he conceded.

"It *is* what happened."

"Okay. But here's the thing: we don't know what else happened, before this. Or what was happening around him."

Kristen leaned away from Sean, her expression twisted in disbelief. "What could possibly have happened to deserve what that cop did?"

"That cop?" The contempt in her voice irritated him.

"Yeah, that cop. He murdered that man, and you won't even say it after seeing it happen with your own eyes."

"Now it's murder?" Bowen shook his head. "You're making a pretty fast jump to that conclusion, aren't you?"

"We just watched it!" she flared.

"And we only saw –"

"I think you should leave."

Bowen could hear in her resolute, curt tone that there was no room for discussion.

He left.

That night, as he pulled the bullet-resistant vest over his head, he replayed the conversation in his head. With the luxury of having more time to process what he'd seen, he realized how the exchange must have seemed to Kristen. He likely sounded like he was defending the deadly actions of the officer in the video. He wasn't. In his mind, he was withholding final judgment until he knew all the facts. His reaction to what he saw was overwhelmingly negative, but it was in his nature, and his job, to want to know the entire context. Kristen's context was constructed from a different experience, one more rooted in society, whereas his was heavily influenced by his profession. Therefore, she had all the context she needed from the video itself. She saw what she saw and knew her truth.

Bowen strapped the vest into place and reached for his uniform shirt.

It's not that easy, he thought. *It's not that simple.*

But as he dressed, the images from the video haunted him.

After a rote roll call with no mention of the event, he found himself on the street in his patrol car. Dispatch sent him on the same kinds of calls as always. Burglary reports. Suspicious circumstances. Domestic violence. Even a neighborhood dispute call over a tree with errant branches, something he didn't see often on graveyard shift. Most of those types of arguments happened in the day time.

The radio was hopping until after one, then tapered off. After clearing a stolen vehicle report call, he drifted toward the high school, expecting a message at any moment. True to form, the mobile data computer (MDC) dinged. He glanced at the screen.

Lunch.

Right on time.

Even though he'd been headed in that direction, he still wasn't first to the field. Gant beat him there. He sat in his car typing, so Bowen waited. Lily and Mark showed up a couple of minutes later. The pair rode double most nights, and always seemed to cash in on some good arrests. Bowen imagined it made having to endure the innuendos that always came with a male and female cop in the same car worth it to them.

He used the MDC to check out for a meal break, grabbed his lunch box, and exited the patrol car. Out of habit, he turned on his portable radio as soon as he swung the door closed. Lily and Mark sauntered over. Both carried bags from home as well. Bowen didn't know what Lily brought, but he could guess that Mark's fare included a protein shake.

Gant joined them. The smell from his McDonald's bag made Bowen's stomach rumble.

"How can you eat that crap?" Mark asked him.

"This is fine American cuisine," Gant argued.

"It's garbage."

"So you don't want the extra fries I bought?"

"No," Mark answered automatically. Then, after a moment, he said, "Wait. You've got extra fries?"

"Nope."

Mark scowled at him. Bowen smiled slightly and caught Lily doing the same. It felt good. He'd alternated most of the shift from focusing on whatever call he was on to being alone in his car, thinking about what happened with that cop on TV, in that city halfway across the country.

The foursome settled onto the bleacher seats. Before them, the high school track laced around the football field. Bowen had gone to a different school, but he knew the others graduated from this one.

There was some conversation while they ate, mostly rehashing calls they'd been on earlier in the shift, but the group seemed subdued to Bowen. Then again, he realized he might be projecting.

"You see that shit on the news?" Gant asked, finally bringing it up.

All three nodded.

Gant shook his head. "Mark my words, that is bad mojo for us, too. It's going to be like Ferguson all over again."

"You don't know that," Lily said.

"Sure, I do. You watch. We're going to be answering for what that dumb fuck did."

Mark had been raising his protein shake to his lips. He stopped suddenly. "Dumb fuck? Are you talking about the cop?"

"Who else?"

"How about the suspect?"

Gant cocked his head. "You mean the guy pinned on the ground, who couldn't breathe?"

"First off, if you can say that you can't breathe, you're breathing." Mark took a swallow of his shake. "And we don't know jack shit about what was happening on that scene. So condemning a brother —"

"We kinda do, though," Lily put in.

Mark turned his face toward her. "What, you, too?"

"I'm just saying, we all saw the video."

"Well, good for you. You saw part of an event from one angle for a limited period of time with incomplete details. By all means, let's be like the general public and judge away."

"Why are you being so defensive about it?" Gant asked. "You saw it, too. It looks *bad*."

"I'm not being defensive," Mark asserted. "I'm being reasonable. I'm not jumping on board the emotion train. I'm waiting for all the facts, and I'm giving a professional police officer the benefit of the doubt. Which is what you should be doing."

Gant shook his head. "Sorry, man. I agree with what you're saying most of the time, but not here."

"What's different about this?"

"Come on. You *saw* the video. How long did he have that guy pinned? He should have transitioned to something else. Sat him up, transported him, or something. Not pinned him there until he died."

"Maybe you're right."

"*Maybe?*"

"Yeah," Mark said. "And maybe they already tried to put

him in a car. Maybe he fought with them. Maybe the crowd around them made any transition completely unsafe."

"You don't know that."

"Neither do you. That's my point. You're trying to sit in judgment but you weren't there."

"I wasn't," Gant admitted. "But the video –"

"Fuck the video!" Mark snarled. "You should know better than that." He stood up and tromped down the bleacher stairs toward the parked car without looking back.

Bowen watched him go. "He's not completely wrong," he said quietly.

"He's not completely right, either," Gant replied. He popped a fry into his mouth and chewed. Behind him, the patrol car door opened and slammed shut. Gant glanced up at Lily. "Sorry I got him riled up."

She shrugged. "He was already a little raw over it. You know why."

Bowen did. Mark had been raked over the coals a little over a year ago by a cell phone video of an arrest he'd made. The suspect fought ferociously for over a minute, but the video only caught the very end of the struggle, in which Mark landed three hard punches to the suspect's mid-section while the two of them grappled on the ground. Without the moments leading up, the action appeared brutal and unwarranted. The media played the video relentlessly and there were calls for Mark's firing.

Eventually, the department released the video from his body worn camera. Although jerky and difficult to follow due to all of the grappling during the arrest, the video was enough to convince all but the most ardent detractors that there was more to the situation than they'd previously thought. But by then, the damage was already done. Public officials had made statements that they didn't want to back away from. Media coverage of this new development paled in comparison to the original furor over the cell phone video. The resolution—and Mark's exoneration—wasn't what the public remembered.

And *that* was what Mark remembered.

"He'll be fine," Lily said. "He's still sore on the subject. Besides, he bleeds blue."

As if in answer, Mark hit the horn of the patrol car.

Lily sighed and wrapped up the remaining half of her sandwich. She muttered a "see you" to Gant and Bowen before ambling to the marked unit. As soon as she got into the passenger seat, the engine rumbled to life. The car zipped from the lot.

The two of them ate in silence a while longer. Then, wordlessly, they left the bleachers and returned to patrol.

He didn't call Kristen after shift that morning, or when he woke up in the afternoon. He thought it best to give both of them some space. When he turned on the news, he realized it had been a good choice.

Protests were everywhere. The list of cities included major metropolitan areas all across the country. When he switched to the local news, he saw protestors gathering near the courthouse and downtown. That surprised him a little. This little corner of the Pacific Northwest wasn't nearly as politically active as Portland or Seattle. For people to gather here in River City in significant numbers, the reason had to be something that resonated deeply.

He spent the rest of the afternoon seeing and hearing about those reasons.

Unlike the previous night, roll call was anything but rote. The shift lieutenant briefed everyone on all of the precautions command was taking. The Crowd Management Team (CMT) was on standby, ready to respond if any of the gatherings became too large or unruly. Bowen didn't understand why they didn't just deploy now, while things were still relatively peaceful but he long ago stopped trying to figure out the logic that the white shirts operated under. In his experience, they caused as many problems as they solved.

"Third Shift will remain in the field to handle high priority calls-for-service," the lieutenant said at the front of the room. "Second shift is being held over to answer calls as well. You all will be deployed to relieve first shift at the courthouse. They've been there since late afternoon monitoring the protestors."

"They're still protesting?" Mark asked. The disgust in his voice was plain.

The lieutenant eyes narrowed. "Apparently so, or I wouldn't be dispatching assets to address the situation, would I?"

On a normal day, Mark might have popped off with something good, something that was just disrespectful enough to amuse the troops but not enough to warrant a reprimand from even this tight-ass lieutenant. But tonight, the veteran officer only pressed his lips together in a frown and said nothing.

The lieutenant let the silence sit a few moments in what Bowen assumed was a bit of a flex. Then he said, "Everyone carries pepper spray and batons on this assignment. No exceptions. The sergeants have your deployment orders." Then he turned and strode from the room.

Their sergeant rattled off the locations and who each officer was relieving. Bowen made a note, even though he doubted he would forget in the short walk from the roll call room to the courthouse square. The Public Safety Building sat on one edge of that square. The only reason he hadn't seen the protestors on his way in was because the employee parking and entrance was all on the west side of the building and the square was to the south.

Bowen geared up and made his way out the west doors of the building to trudge around the corner. As he rounded the building, the size of the crowd surprised him. There were hundreds of people spread across the large courtyard, spilling around the east side of the courthouse and into the Mallon Street cul-de-sac that dead-ended right at the middle of the square. Several news vans were parked in the cul-de-sac itself.

There were an array of signs, from the benign pleas for peace to "Black Lives Matter" to ardent calls to disband the police. A light hum of conversation came from the assembly, along with the occasional slogan being shouted. A lone beachball bounced and hopped across the top of the crowd.

"Beautiful," Mark muttered next to him. "It's a goddamn party now."

"Come on," said the sergeant. "Let's relieve first shift. It'll be dark soon and they're already late for their bedtime and haven't had their cocoa yet."

No one laughed.

The sergeant led them toward the crowd. A rumble of concern, even anger, went up as they approached. Someone shouted, "They're coming to beat us now! You watch!" That elicited an even louder reaction. But as each officer took up a position and the officer relieved stepped away, the crowd seemed to realize the only thing happening was a mundane shift change.

Bowen's assigned position landed him front and center, about twenty yards from the front doors to the Public Safety Building. The crowd seemed thickest at this point. He stepped into the spot vacated by an older cop whose name he couldn't remember. The veteran officer didn't bother looking at him or murmuring any thanks for being relieved. He only turned and strode purposefully away.

"He was grumpy," said a woman a few feet in front of Bowen and to his right.

At first, he thought about not answering. His training said not to engage with the crowd. To avoid being part of the situation as much as possible, because engagement almost universally devolved into something negative, and only served to fuel the fire. But Bowen could sense the mood of people in the square. It wasn't happy by any means but the vibe was far from violent.

So he engaged.

He shrugged noncommittally. "Hot day in uniform. Tired feet, I guess."

She smiled at him. The lines at the corner of her eyes crinkled when she did. She looked to be around forty. She wore a pair of faded jeans and baseball-style T-shirt with a peace symbol on it. Her dishwater blond hair hung just past her shoulders. Next to her, a woman of about twenty wore the same shirt, only the bottom had been cut off to expose her belly. Her jeans were also cut off into shorts with white strands dangling at her thighs. In between the two pieces of fashion-damaged pieces of clothing, a glimmer of metal winked up at him from her navel. The younger woman had the same color hair, though hers was pulled back into a ponytail.

"I offered him water earlier," the younger woman said. "But he wouldn't take it."

Probably worried that it was poisoned, Bowen thought. He didn't say it, though. He was sure that both women, who he had decided were likely mother and daughter, would have been appalled at the thought. And insulted. They might have considered the officer to be paranoid, but Bowen knew better. People did horrible things, and it wasn't paranoid to be safe.

"That was nice of you," he said instead.

"Hey, we're here," the mother said, waving her hand at the assembled crowd, "because of what one cop did. Not because of all cops."

"Thank you," said Bowen.

He stood his post. Over the course of about forty minutes, he learned that the two were actually aunt and niece rather than mother and daughter—Karen and Mindy. What started as a comment or a brief exchange slowly worked its way into on ongoing conversation with the pair.

Karen joked about her name becoming a meme in popular culture, saying that she'd consider making the switch to her middle name if it wasn't Beatrice. Mindy steadfastly refused to share her own middle name, and her aunt kept her confidence. The conversation drifted to them asking him about his career—how long had he been a cop, how did he like his job, all of the standard questions.

He could feel it leading up to something, though he didn't think either woman was being purposefully manipulative. What was happening in front of them was just too big to ignore.

"It's a hard time to be a cop, I bet," Mindy said.

"I think it's always been a hard time."

"But now, with everything happening…"

"Yeah," Bowen admitted. "It's getting tough."

"You saw the video, right?" Mindy shook her head sadly. "It was horrible. Cops like that…"

"They shouldn't be cops," Bowen found himself saying.

"Exactly!"

"African-Americans have been getting treated badly by police for a long time," Karen said somberly. "Maybe it isn't as bad here but that's only because we live in such a homogenous city."

Bowen thought about that. She was right about the make-up the city. His city was, what—eighty-five percent White? Higher? Race relations was thought experiment for most people here rather than a daily event. Outside of work, he only knew only a very few Black people. One was his mechanic, who owned his own shop near where Bowen grew up. He'd been taking his vehicles there his whole life, having inherited the habit from his father. The other association was an accident of geography—his next-door neighbors. Andy and Tisha had moved in about three years ago. He and Andy talked occasionally. Less frequently, they shared a beer over the back fence. He kept meaning to invite them over for a barbecue or something but never got around to it. The most intimate thing they'd done is exchange house keys for emergencies and house-watching when one or the other of them traveled.

Was that a friendship? Bowen thought so. But did he really

know Andy, beyond the superficial? Probably not any more than his neighbor knew him.

He was friendly with several cops who were Black, too. But he realized that it was a work friendship, like many that he had with other cops. They had the blue in common, and the work, not necessarily anything else.

"It's time." The loud, tinny voice barked through a bullhorn. A news camera slid through several crowd members to get a shot of the organizer.

Bowen tensed. He could feel the other cops on the line do the same. But no one made any sudden moves, other than dig into bags and pockets. He watched cautiously until he saw what they were pulling out.

Candles.

Karen held hers close to her heart, and so did Mindy. Bowen watched as one of the candles was lit near the center of the crowd. That candle lit another, then two, then four. The flickering candles spread throughout the square.

"It's 9:25," Karen explained to him. "It's when he died."

Bowen didn't have to ask who she meant. He kept his thoughts to himself, and didn't point out the obvious-to-him time-zone difference. Instead, he kept a respectful silence. Nothing he could say would be good in this moment but almost anything could turn bad.

But Karen wasn't finished. "When all of the candles are lit, we're all going to take a knee."

"All right."

"You should, too," she suggested.

Bowen blinked at her, cocking his head slightly. "Me?"

"You said that guy shouldn't be a cop. So that means you believe what he did was wrong. That's what we're here for, too. Too say it was wrong and things need to change."

He didn't answer. The idea seemed ludicrous to him at first. But as the flames danced from candle to candle, filling the square, he wondered about that. The way Karen put it made sense. Maybe, as corny as it sounded, the way forward was together. And if most of the protestors were like her and Mindy, that gave him some hope.

Karen received a light for her candle and tipped it to Mindy's. Her wick was tipped in flame. Then both women knelt. Bowen heard Karen's knees pop as she did so.

He hesitated a moment. His training told him to remain standing. Don't become part of the situation. But that advice was for violent protests, for riots. Those might be happening elsewhere in the country but not here. Here, maybe they could forge a different way.

Bowen lowered himself to one knee. The leather of his duty belt creaked as he knelt. He met Karen's eyes, and then Mindy's. Karen reached out a hand toward him. With his left hand, still keeping his gun hand free, he took her hand. Karen squeezed. Mindy clapped her hand on top of theirs and squeezed again.

A murmur began somewhere in the crowd. It slowly morphed into singing. Bowen recognized the verses of "We Shall Overcome." Karen and Mindy joined in hesitantly. Bowen remained silent.

There was only so far he could go.

After the crowd sang several songs, including "Amazing Grace," the organizer called for silence through the bullhorn. The people accommodated, becoming silent and still. The organizer said, "Eight minutes and forty-six seconds." Even through the loudspeaker, the words were spoken in a hushed, reverent tone.

Once again, Bowen didn't need to ask what the significance was. He'd seen the video.

The time passed achingly slow. The occasional cough or shuffle of feet were the only sounds that came from the crowd. Traffic from nearby Monroe Avenue suddenly seemed louder than before as it washed over them.

Bowen remained kneeling. He kept his hand clasped to Karen's and Mindy's. He listened for any disturbances. He scanned the crowd as best he could from one knee. At some point, he saw one of the news reporters catch sight of him and hurriedly direct the camera operator to point the camera toward him. Bowen ignored them.

During the silence, he let his thoughts range. At first, he thought about all the rage out there in the world. But after a few minutes, he realized that there was no way he could understand it. Not because he was a cop. Because he was White. He'd lived a sheltered life in a sheltered pocket of the country. It wasn't that racism didn't exist here. He just hadn't experienced it or seen it because there were so few people that lived here who might be the targets.

Finally, as the moments dragged on, he wondered how terrifying it would be to fight for breath for this long, finally succumbing to darkness…

His reverie was finally broken by the organizer's voice. "Thank you. And thank you for making this a peaceful protest. That is how we will effect change. Good night, everyone."

Slowly, people in the crowd rose to their feet, Bowen among them. He released Karen's hand.

"Thanks," she said. "You've given me some hope."

Bowen nodded to her. "Me, too."

Like the ending of a concert, the protestors slowly made their way out of the courtyard, drifting off in several directions. The news cameras finished getting shots of the departing protestors and the line of cops that remained standing in the near-empty square.

The sergeant waited until most of the protestors were gone before he ordered, "Stand by, I'm calling the shift commander."

The cops relaxed and the disciplined line of blue blurred and mingled in anticipation of dismissal. Bowen brushed the dirt from the knee of his uniform.

"What the fuck was that?" came a sharp voice from behind him.

Bowen turned to see Officer Randy Cartwright. The lanky veteran wore a bushy mustache that drooped well past the corner of his mouth, no doubt beyond regulation. The dark scowl on his face was directed at Bowen.

"What was what?" he asked, even though he knew.

"That kneeling bullshit."

Bowen shrugged. "I was making a connection."

"Trying to connect with that little spinner, you mean."

"That wasn't it."

"Doing a little NFL role-play, then?"

"What's your problem?"

"My problem?" Cartwright snarled. "I'll tell you my problem. You're a fucking idiot, that's my problem."

Lily and Gant appeared at his side. "Easy, now," Gant said.

"Easy, my ass." He pointed a finger at Bowen. "That's just the kind of stunt that can set off a crowd. That's why you don't do shit like that, why you don't engage. You just stand there."

"Times change," Bowen answered. "Maybe—"

"Times change?" Cartwright cut him off in disbelief. "Are you some kind of rookie? Nothing changes but the labels people use. Figure it out."

"I was—"

"Were you on for the WSU riot?" Cartwright demanded. "When we sent a team down to help with that?"

"No," Bowen admitted. "That was before my time."

Cartwright jerked a thumb to his chest. "*I* was there. And it was a goddamn war zone. You had beautiful co-eds offering you flowers while people behind them in the dark threw bottles and chunks of concrete. I couldn't count how many times I was hit. The state trooper next to me got his leg broken. And the whole time, everyone called it a peaceful protest. Even afterward, no one told the truth about how violent things were. It was like being at the goddamn Alamo for us."

"I'm sorry, but—"

"Fuck your sorry." Cartwright waved his hand in disgust. "I hope you had a nice little moment there. Maybe even got a phone number out of it. I'm sure it will be on TV and everything. But don't think it meant jack shit. Because it didn't. All you did was put the rest of us at risk."

Bowen opened his mouth to reply.

"All right, listen up!" the sergeant announced. "We are Delta Hotel."

Bowen smirked. *Why can't he just say 'Done Here'?*

"Reassemble in the sally port," the sergeant ordered. "Second shift will be securing. Back to regular patrol."

The order seemed to cut through Cartwright's ire. He stalked away. Bowen watched him go, then made his own way down into the basement sally port to wait for a car.

The first hour on patrol seemed normal enough. Dispatch reported that there was a crowd gathering downtown at the federal courthouse. CMT remained on standby. Downtown units monitored the gathering. Meanwhile, Bowen and his platoon mates answered calls, working through the higher priority ones first. Most of the non-emergency calls had been holding for six hours or more, and he wondered if they'd ever get to them before the end of shift.

A call from dispatch broke through his maudlin thoughts. *"I need several units to respond downtown to assist David units with a civil disturbance."*

Bowen answered up, along with everyone else in the squad who were available.

"Copy," The dispatcher replied to them en masse. *"All assigned units switch to the David sector channel for further."*

When he clicked over to channel three, he was greeted with chaotic transmissions. Several officers were attempting to transmit at the same time, resulting in harsh buzz and squelch.

"Units covering," the channel three dispatcher said. Bowen could hear a slight edge of tension in the man's voice. *"David-435?"*

"Thirty-five," a woman's voice immediately replied. *"We're at the Nike store. Main and Wall. Suspects are throwing rocks at the windows and refusing orders to*

disperse."

Bowen didn't hesitate. He floored the accelerator and shot down Monroe, the quickest route to downtown. In less than a minute, he rolled down to a stop on Main, a half block from the gathering crowd. He grabbed his baton and hurried up the street.

A harried sergeant was organizing officers at the intersection while several of them stood sentry to protect the huddle. Just twenty yards away, a crowd of forty or more clustered around the shoe store on Wall Street, a narrow pedestrian only block. Bowen could see the glass doors rocking as several people jerked on it, trying to force it open.

The sergeant acknowledged his arrival with a terse nod, not bothering to interrupt his instructions or start over. "I'll give one last dispersal order and then we wade in. Slow and steady. Keep the skirmish line straight. We drive them north so they can disperse in any direction once we hit Riverfront Boulevard. Questions?"

Nobody had any. While the sergeant was speaking, Mark and Lily appeared next to Bowen.

"Form up," ordered the sergeant.

Bowen fell into line, helping to form a line of officers nearly shoulder-to-shoulder. He wished they had helmets and protective gear. Shields would have been nice, too. *Where the hell was CMT?*

"Behind us, Sarge," someone called out.

Bowen glanced over his shoulder. A dozen or so civilians were straggling along toward them. He couldn't tell what their intent was.

The sergeant ordered the officer on the two ends of the skirmish line to break off and watch the rear. Then he bellowed out a dispersal order at the crowd still determined to get through the doors to shoe store. His words were torn and fragmented by all the noise. Several bottles were hurled back toward them, along with cries of "fuck you!" One bottle skittered past Bowen's feet, filled with a noxious yellow substance that he hoped was only urine.

Before the sergeant even finished his official pronouncement, there was a loud shattering of glass and the crowd surged into the Nike store through a broken doorway.

"Forward!" the sergeant ordered them.

Methodically, the line of officers moved forward, stomping with the lead foot and dragging the rear foot behind, just as they'd been trained. The progress was maddeningly slow. Bowen's hands were slick. Sweat stream downed his temples.

As they neared the storefront, people began streaming out, arms laden with boxes of shoes. Some scurried away from the police but others loped away almost casually. Some crowd members ignored the lure of the open store entirely, focusing on the police instead. They hurled insults and small items. A coin bit into Bowen's cheek and he jerked his head involuntarily.

"Steadeeeeee!" called the sergeant.

The bulk of the crowd didn't flee but gave way to their slow advance, keeping just outside of striking distance. That was okay with Bowen. Despite the flare of anger when the coin struck him, he knew it was best if no officer had to use a baton. Doubts as to whether that was possible or not were creeping in, however.

"Sarge!" The officer's voice was high-pitched and full of warning.

Bowen didn't dare take his eyes off the crowd in front of him. He heard a couple of sharp curses from other officers. A few moments later he felt a tap on his shoulder from the sergeant.

"Form a skirmish line facing south," came the clipped command.

Bowen took a backward step. In the moment before he spun around, he saw the officers who had been to his left and right pull closer together to fill some of the gap he left behind. Then he wheeled to see what the new threat was.

The crowd of a dozen had somehow morphed into fifty,

perhaps more. The faces in the crowd were agitated and angry. Bottles sailed toward him, forcing him to duck to one side.

Swiftly, Bowen stepped forward to form a new skirmish line. He'd barely taken up his position when three men charged directly toward him. He steeled himself. When the closest one was in range, he delivered a power jab with his baton directly into the attacker's midsection.

The man's body seemed to wrap around Bowen's baton and he crumpled. One of the other attackers saw this and veered away. The other pulled up short and reached out for the man Bowen had struck. Mark shuffled forward and whipped his baton in three rapid slashes, striking the would-be rescuer in the thighs and calf. He howled in pain and lunged away, limping to the safety of the crowd.

Bowen held his ground. The man at his feet slowly crawled away. Once he was well out of striking range, several people from the crowd lifted him up. He disappeared, swallowed up by the mass of people.

Bottles and rocks flew. Bowen heard scuffles and shouts behind him as well. The sergeant called out orders almost constantly, pausing only to advise radio of their situation.

There was no advancing. Trapped along the narrow pedestrian street, all they could do was maintain their position. Assaulted by constant missiles and frequent but uncoordinated charges, Bowen focused on holding the skirmish line. His whole world became that small patch of ground. The protective vest hung heavily on his body. Beneath his vest, sweat soaked his undershirt tight to his skin. His breath came in ragged gasps as his eyes darted left and right, trying to find the next danger before it found him first.

"CMT is one mike out!" hollered the sergeant. "Hold the line!"

One minute. He could do that.

A bottle full of liquid struck his left shoulder. The spray of liquid splashed against his neck and face. He pressed his eyes closed instinctively. The bottle must have broken, he thought, or the cap was barely affixed on purpose so that—

Gasoline.

He smelt gasoline.

"Holy shit," he muttered.

They're going to set me on fire.

He scanned the crowd for any kind of flame. A lighter, a Molotov, anything. If he caught fire, the closest fire extinguisher was in the trunk of his patrol vehicle, which was now on the other side of the surging crowd. If it hadn't been already turned over, that was.

He didn't see any telltale signs of fire but his heart still didn't stop beating like a triphammer. The extended tip of his baton shifted in concert with his eyes, scanning the crowd for the next threat.

The yelling from behind him was intense. He resisted the urge to look over his shoulder to see what was happening. He had to trust that those officers would do their part. His life depended on it.

A chunk of asphalt flew through the air, striking the officer next to him. Lily let out a cry of pain. In his peripheral view, he saw her slip to her knees. He wanted to reach out and help her to her feet but felt frozen in place. He couldn't look away from the threat in front of him. Couldn't let go of his baton, even for a second. How was he supposed to help her?

The point became moot as he caught a flash of movement in his peripheral vision. Lily was on her feet again. The tip of her baton extended out toward the crowd.

Where was CMT?

Another flash of movement, this one to his left. Before he had a chance to register what it was, the brick struck his brow. He staggered back a step and collapsed. His vision rippled and went dark for a moment, then snapped back into a blurry half-light. He blinked, trying to focus. Sound was fuzzy and distant. He felt someone grab onto him under the arms and reflexively struggled, wondering if the skirmish line had collapsed.

"I got you," Mark shouted near his ear. "I got you, buddy."

Bowen sagged backward against him. He felt the thick vest beneath Mark's uniformed chest. Warm sticky blood flowed down his face.

"CMT's here," Mark said. "Hold on, and I'll get you to medics."

Bowen shook his head to clear it but the motion made him nauseous. He twisted away and retched.

Time slowed and sped up in strange intervals. He heard the crowd's yelling grow louder. Then came the unmistakable tramp of the advancing CMT, followed by the sharp crack of gunfire. He started at the sound.

"It's okay," Mark said, helping him to his feet. "Bean bag rounds and skip-fired knee knockers."

He nodded dumbly, though it took him several seconds to process the words. Less lethal weaponry. Dispersal tactics.

And suddenly the crowd was all but gone. He and the officers stood nearly alone in the narrow street. The shattered door and plate glass windows of the Nike store was the only other testament to what had just happened.

"Come on," Mark said. "Let's get you to the ER."

With effort, Bowen shook his head. "There's… in my trunk… the thing."

Mark stared at him questioningly, then glanced at Lily.

"First aid kit?" she guessed.

"Yeah," Bowen said. "Just patch me up."

Mark shook his head sternly. "No way. You're going to the ER. Don't worry about the rest. CMT will handle these assholes."

Bowen didn't have the strength to argue. Mark and Lily walked him back to his patrol car, Lily noticeably limping. She opened the passenger door, removed his duty bag and stowed it in the trunk while Mark spilled Bowen into passenger seat. The partners spoke briefly outside, then Mark got into the patrol car and fired up the engine. Glancing around quickly, he whipped the car into the roadway and headed toward the nearest hospital.

The familiar businesses of downtown flitted by the window. Bowen noticed a few had broken windows. Looters darted in and out of some of them.

He turned his head languidly to face Mark while he drove. "No I-told-you-so?" he asked.

"What?" Mark glanced over at him.

"You told me," Bowen said. "Last night, at lunch. And at the courthouse earlier."

Mark squinted. "The courthouse? You mean that kneeling shit? Dude, that was Cartwright who bitched you off about that."

Bowen blinked, then realized Mark was right. "Oh."

"Besides, there's no place for I-told-you-so," Mark said. "It's a fucking war zone. I-told-you-so is for politicians and white shirts."

"Same thing," Bowen said automatically.

Mark grinned ruefully. "Maybe your brains aren't as scrambled as I thought."

"I'm good," he said. He wasn't entirely but his thoughts were becoming clearer. His head pounded still but he wasn't dizzy or nauseous any longer.

At the Emergency Room, the charge nurse got him into a room almost immediately. Another nurse cleaned his wound and pressed gauze to the gash.

"Stitches?" he asked her.

She nodded without hesitation. "A few."

They stripped his uniform shirt and vest from him. The nurse looked at the shirt askance, holding it at an arm's length.

"Gas?" she asked.

Bowen nodded.

She shook her head in dismay, pushing the shirt and the vest into a large plastic bag.

Mark waited with him for a while, stepping out occasionally to talk on his cell phone. Finally, he stepped back into the room with an urgent expression. "I gotta go, Sean.

They need bodies to close this thing out. You'll be okay?"

Bowen nodded.

"I talked to the shift commander," Mark said. "He says you need to go home after they release you. Fill out an injury report with the sergeant in the morning. And don't worry about your car—I'll take care of it."

"All right."

"No problem. You need a ride home after they're finished with you, give me a buzz."

"Thanks."

Mark squeezed his shoulder and hustled from the hospital room.

Bowen sat in the strange quiet of the treatment room, surrounded by antiseptic smells and the distant bustle of the ER beyond the closed door. His mind flashed through the intense moments on the skirmish line. He saw the angry faces—most of them White—of the crowd. At the time, all he'd seen was a threat. Now, he wondered more about the anger. Where it came from. What drove it.

The doctor arrived. Brisk and businesslike, she ran through a series of cognitive tests with him. Then she set about stitching up his wound, assisted by the same nurse who had cleaned it. Bowen wondered if her curtness had anything to do with her being Black, then told himself it was something he imagined. She was busy. She was being professional. That was all.

When the metal instrument she used to work the needle and thread clattered into the metal pan next to the examination table, Bowen said, "Thanks."

The doctor gave him a terse nod and hurried wordlessly out of the room.

The nurse finished treating him. Then he sat for another long period of time before another nurse returned with discharge instructions. Bowen only half-listened once she finished with the headline. He had a slight concussion and received six stitches. She pressed the discharge paperwork and prescription for meds into his hands.

"Have you got someone to pick you up?"

Bowen nodded. He rose, grabbed the bag containing his uniform shirt and vest, and shuffled out of the treatment room. On the way through the ER, he spotted the same doctor who had treated him bustling from one curtained area to another, glancing down at a clipboard while she moved.

The automatic doors swung open to lead to the ambulance entrance. It wasn't a public exit but it was the fastest way out and his status afforded him the perk of its use. The spring air washed over him. Even under the large awning of the ambulance bay, it smelled clean to him.

Bowen walked a short distance so he wasn't in danger of getting in the way, then pulled out his phone. He considered calling Mark, then decided against it. His squad mates were either still dealing with the riot or would be exhausted from having done so. They didn't need another task. Besides, he didn't feel like answering questions or commiserating. Mostly, he just wanted to go home.

He started scrolling to Kristin's number but stopped. Now wasn't the time. This wasn't how they were going to work out whatever they needed to work out.

Briefly, he considered an Uber but rejected the idea. Then a thought occurred to him. He found the contact easily and hit dial.

After five rings, his neighbor's muffled, sleepy voice came on. "Hello?"

"Hey, Andy."

"Sean? What time is it?"

"About three-thirty. Sorry to wake you."

There was a rustle of movement and an exhale. "No, it's all good. Is everything okay?"

"It's fine. I mean, it's not exactly fine. I'm up at the ER, and I need a ride home."

Andy paused. Bowen imagined the sleepy man working through the information. Then he said, "The ER? Are you all right?"

"Banged up a little, but yeah. I just need a ride home."

Another pause, this one shorter. "Yeah, okay. Which hospital?"

"The Heart."

"Got it. I'll be there in twenty minutes."

It took more like thirty, but Bowen didn't mind. He considered finding a corner of the waiting room inside but knew it was likely full of people from the riot. The last thing he wanted was to go a second round with anyone still mad about what happened, whether that meant earlier tonight or something else.

The May night air was cool and bracing. It was hard for him to believe how hot he'd been while standing on the skirmish line. Now, he fought a shiver while he waited.

Andy pulled up in his Subaru Forester. He started to get out but Bowen waved him off. He opened the door and put his bag on the floor. Then he slowly clambered into the seat. His neighbor stared at him the whole time.

"What the hell happened?" Andy's voice still had a gravelly sound to it.

"You didn't see the news?"

"I saw peaceful protests before I went to bed, but…"

"Things got violent downtown later on."

Andy grunted. He put the car into gear and started to drive. The two men remained quiet for several minutes. About halfway home, Bowen said, "Thanks for coming to get me."

"No problem. I'm glad you're all right." He flicked his gaze over at Bowen. "Well, mostly all right."

Bowen reached up to touch the bandage at his brow.

They were silent again for several minutes. As they neared the neighborhood they both lived in, Bowen said, "The thing that got me was how angry everyone was."

Andy murmured a vague assent.

"How angry people are at the police," Bowen said. "I never understood that. Maybe I still don't. But I've been thinking about it tonight, and I know it's something I *want* to understand."

"Sounds like a good idea," Andy said, not looking away from the road.

"Maybe you can help me with that?" Bowen asked.

Andy didn't answer. He continued to drive until they reached their block. Then he pulled the Forester into Bowen's driveway and stopped. He turned toward Bowen. His expression wasn't angry but flat and matter of fact.

"Because I'm Black," he said.

Wordlessly, Bowen nodded.

Andy let out a small sigh. Then he said, "Sean, I like you. You're a good neighbor. And I respect what you do. But it's not my job to educate you. If you really want to understand, you're going to have to educate your own damn self."

He spoke without rancor but Bowen could hear the frustration riding underneath like an untapped current.

"Okay," he said. "I'm sorry."

"No need to be sorry," Andy said.

"I just—"

Andy held up a hand. "Don't be sorry," he said. "Just be better."

Bowen met his gaze and nodded. "Thanks again for the ride."

"Any time, neighbor."

He opened the door and slid out of the passenger seat, grabbing his plastic bag from the floor. When he shut the door, Andy gave him a short wave and backed out of the driveway. Bowen watched him guide the Forester into his garage next door. Then he turned toward his own front door.

He paused at the porch, his house key in the lock. Light seeped over the mountains to the east, a harbinger of the impending dawn. For him, the end of another long day. For others, the beginning of one.

A new day or an old day, he wondered? Bowen wasn't sure, but he knew what he hoped for. What he'd work for.

He twisted the knob to the door and went inside.

Did You Like the Book?

Thank you for reading *The Tattered Blue Line: Short Stories of Contemporary Policing!* If you enjoyed this anthology, we'd deeply appreciate it if you told your friends and family or left a review at where you got the book. And if you'd leave a review—even a short one—that would help out a lot!

All writers need feedback on their work—not only to help other readers discover them, but so they know they're delivering the goods.

Also, if there was a particular story you enjoyed in this anthology, take some time to learn about the author behind it and perhaps read more of their work. They are listed on the following pages.

ABOUT THE AUTHORS

Mark Bergin

Mark Bergin retired from the Alexandria, Virginia Police Department as a Lieutenant in 2014 after 28 years and, in the end, two heart attacks. He was twice named Police Officer of the year for drug and robbery investigations. Prior to police service he was a newspaper reporter in suburban Philadelphia, Pennsylvania, and in Northern Virginia where he earned the Virginia Press Association Award for General News Reporting. A graduate of Boston University, he splits his time between Alexandria and Kitty Hawk, North Carolina with his wife, family, and not-so-new dog. His debut mystery novel *Apprehension* was published in 2019 by Quill. Find more at markberginwriter.com.

Colin Conway

Colin Conway is the creator of the 509 Crime Stories, the Cozy Up series, and the co-creator of the Charlie-316 series (written with Frank Zafiro). He served in the U.S. Army and later was an officer for the Spokane Police Department. He lives in Eastern Washington with his girlfriend and a codependent Vizsla that rules their world. Follow his journey at colinconway.com.

Erik Djernaes

Erik Djernaes Hansen is a Danish police officer. For more than 25 years he has worked in Copenhagen with regular patrol work, investigation, and drug crimes. He is currently teaching at the Danish Police Academy in the use of force training. Last year his novel, *Brutalization*, was translated into English. The story was inspired by the movie, *Training Day*, and is about the young, male police officer, Allan, whose inner moral compass gets challenged in his pursuit to become the perfect cop.
https://books2read.com/u/mYGVxx
To contact Erik: djernaeserik@gmail.com

James Doherty

In a career spanning more than two decades, JIM DOHERTY has served American law enforcement at the local, state, and federal levels, policing everything from college campuses to military bases, from inner city streets to rural dirt roads, from suburban parks to urban railroad yards. His true-crime collection, *Just the Facts – True Tales of Cops and Criminals*, included the article "Blood for Oil," which won the WWA Spur for Best Short Non-Fiction. His first novel, *An Obscure Grave*, featuring his series character Dan Sullivan, was a finalist for a CWA Dagger Award. His Sherlock Holmes pastiche, "The Adventure of the Manhunting Marshal," was a finalist for an SFWA Derringer Award. His short story collection, *The Big Game and Other Crime Stories*, also features Dan. Lately, he's been developing a second series character, itinerant Texas peace officer Gus Hachette, modeled on real-life Lone Star lawman Frank Hamer. He was also the police advisor on the classic *Dick Tracy* comic strip, and was guest writer for a short sequence that ran in 2019.

Scott Kikkawa

A product of Hawai'i Kai in East Honolulu, Scott Kikkawa writes noir detective stories set in postwar Honolulu, featuring 442nd veteran Nisei Detective Sergeant Francis "Sheik" Yoshikawa. His critically acclaimed début murder mystery, Kona Winds, was released at the end of 2019 and spent six months on the Small Press Distribution Fiction Bestsellers List. He serves as a columnist and an Associate Editor for The Hawai'i Review of Books. Red Dirt is his second full-length novel and a third is scheduled for release in 2023. Winner of an Elliot Cades Award for Literature, the New York University alumnus is currently a federal law enforcement officer and lives with his family in Honolulu.

James L'Etoile

James L'Etoile uses his twenty-nine years behind bars as an influence in his novels, short stories, and screenplays. He is a former associate warden in a maximum-security prison, a hostage negotiator, facility captain, and director of California's state parole system. He is a nationally recognized expert witness on prison and jail operations. He has been nominated for the Silver Falchion for Best Procedural Mystery, and The Bill Crider Award for short fiction. His published novels include: *At What Cost*, *Bury the Past*, and *Little River—The Other Side of Paradise*. Look for *Black Label* in the summer of 2021 from Level Best Books. You can find out more at jamesletoile.com.

P.S. Harman

P. S. Harman served in Law Enforcement for 39 years. She retired from a large Northern Va. agency as a Master Detective and then served as Police Chief to a small agency before retiring to Fredericksburg, Va. She has published non-fiction (The Danger Zone), fiction (The Hooker, The Handyman and What the Parrot Saw) and a children's book on policing under the name Patricia Harman and continues to write thrillers in her retirement. Her son now also serves as a law enforcement officer in Virginia.

J.J. Hensley

J.J. HENSLEY is a former police officer and former Special Agent with the U.S. Secret Service. He is the author of the novels Resolve, Measure Twice, Chalk's Outline, Bolt Action Remedy, Record Scratch, Forgiveness Dies, and The Better of the Bad. He resides near Savannah, Georgia. Mr. Hensley's first novel RESOLVE was named one of the BEST BOOKS OF 2013 by Suspense Magazine and was named a Thriller Award finalist for Best First Novel. He is a member of the International Thriller Writers. He can be found at www.hensley-books.com,www.facebook.com/hensleybooks, and on Twitter at JJHensleyauthor. He blogs at Yinz to Y'all.

Elizabeth Nguyen

Elizabeth Nguyen is the Executive Director of Corporate Services at the Regina Police Service in Regina, Saskatchewan, Canada. Prior to her role as Executive Director, she spent 8 enjoyable years as the 9-1-1 Communications Manager. Elizabeth resides in Regina, Saskatchewan with her husband Erik (who is a police officer and SWAT member) and their two young daughters, Ella and Evie. She is a book nerd, amateur home chef, and reluctant runner. "9 Minutes" is her first published short story.

Pearson O'Meara

Pearson O'Meara is a former law enforcement professional with extensive experience in complex missing, abducted, and exploited children investigations. In 2019, after a distinguished 20-year career, she retired as a sergeant from the Louisiana State Police, where she managed the Louisiana Clearinghouse for Missing and Exploited Children and the Louisiana AMBER Alert Program. She also served as a Special Victims Unit supervisor responsible for investigating multi-jurisdictional crimes against children, including Catholic clergy abuse cases. In 2017, she was nominated by the National Center for Missing & Exploited Children for a law enforcement "Hero" award for her role in recovering four children abducted from California by their non-custodial mother and a registered sex offender. Pearson retired to continue her education and is currently pursuing her doctorate in law and policy at Northeastern University in Boston. She also lends her expertise and technical advice to authors, novelists, and television and film producers. A lifetime avid reader, she tired of academic and technical writing, so she decided to try her hand at crime fiction. *Routine Traffic Stop* is only the third short story she has ever written. She lives a quiet life, dividing her time between Boston and Baton Rouge. You can follow her on Twitter @pearsonomeara.

A.B. Patterson

A.B. Patterson is an Australian writer who knows first-hand about corruption, power, crime and sex. He was a Detective Sergeant in the Western Australia Police, working in paedophilia and vice, and later a Chief Investigator with the Independent Commission Against Corruption in Sydney. His fiction writing includes the PI Harry Kenmare novels and short stories, as well as crime short stories published in various anthologies and magazines. His hard-boiled, gritty, and noir writing style has been likened to that of Raymond Chandler and Ken Bruen. He's a massive fan of both of them. You can find him at: www.abpatterson.com.au

Quintin Peterson

Native Washingtonian Quintin Peterson is a retired D.C. police officer who served the public for some three decades. He is an artist, a playwright, and critically acclaimed author who has penned four DC-based crime novels, a book of poetry, and has contributed to magazines and ten anthologies, including *DC Noir*, edited by George Pelecanos. Mr. Peterson is also an Active Member of Mystery Writers of America, and the Public Safety Writers Association (PSWA).

Stacy Woodson

Stacy Woodson is a U.S. Army veteran and memories of her time in the military are often a source of inspiration for her stories. She made her crime fiction debut in *Ellery Queen Mystery Magazine's* Department of First Stories and won the 2018 Readers Award. Since her debut, she placed stories in several anthologies and publications. In 2021, she won the Derringer award. You can visit her at https://stacywoodson.com/.

Frank Zafiro

Frank Zafiro was a police officer in Spokane, Washington, from 1993 to 2013, retiring as a captain. Frank is the author of over thirty novels, most of them gritty crime fiction from both sides of the badge. These include the River City police procedural series, hard boiled SpoCompton series, and Stefan Kopriva PI mysteries. He co-authored the Charlie-316 procedural series with Colin Conway and the Bricks & Cam Jobs with Eric Beetner. In addition to writing, Frank hosts the crime fiction podcast *Wrong Place, Write Crime*. He is an avid hockey fan and a tortured guitarist. He currently lives in Redmond, Oregon. You can keep up with him at frankzafiro.com.

Made in the USA
Middletown, DE
19 April 2022

64476002R00146